SANTA'S
Baby

USA Today Bestselling Author

JADE WEST

Santa's Baby copyright © 2024 Jade West

The moral rights of the author have been asserted.

All rights reserved. No part of this publication may be reproduced, distributed, or transmitted in any form or by any means, including photocopying, recording, or other electronic or mechanical methods, without the prior written permission of the publisher, except in the case of brief quotations embodied in critical reviews and certain other non-commercial uses permitted by copyright law. For permission requests, write to the publisher, addressed "Attention: Permissions Coordinator," at the email address below.

Edited by John Hudspith http://www.johnhudspith.co.uk
Interior formatting by Sammi Bee Designs
All enquiries to pa@jadewestauthor.co.uk

First published 2024

To Nicole.

Thank you for being such a naughty elf when it came to Santa's Baby this year. You are a superstar.

Everyone who enjoyed The Naughtier List also owes you a round of applause... since The Naughtier List would have been a considerably shorter list without you.

Oh, and for Kitty Daddy. He owes you one, too.

For a full list of TWs please check out my website, but please note – this book has a pregnancy theme, and includes some past trauma regarding this.

PROLOGUE
Tiffany

I swear Christmas parties come earlier and earlier every year. Just a shame the guys booking me for them don't.

These three have been going at me for nearly an hour, and they still haven't found my clit yet. I'd relieve the torment myself if I wasn't trussed up with a tie around my wrists. I'm glad I'm getting paid over seven grand for this session. If I wasn't, I'd show them a Wikipedia map of female anatomy and get the fuck out of here.

Once upon a time, this would have been my dream – the filth itself enough to drive me crazy – but after approaching four years as a high-class hooker for the high-class 'Agency', I'm losing interest. I never thought I'd say that, but it's true.

Maybe it's time playing out its course, or maybe it's the news that hit me in the gut with a sucker punch earlier.

My best friend's younger sister is having a baby. Josh told me himself this afternoon.

Caroline – the jealous little cow who has always emulated, irritated and tried her best to outdo me – is pregnant. Loved up, happy, and due to give birth next March.

Guess she got one up on me, for once…

Fuck this. I ban my mind from playing bullshit and funnel my

1

focus back to the scene around me. It isn't my clients' fault I'm feeling like a sack of shit tonight.

The naked guy in front of me holds out a bottle of champagne for me to glug on. He's cute, with mousy brown hair and a decent length dick. Nice enough. Just boring.

His two friends are doing a bit better. They're hard at work, grunting curses as they use me like a dirty bitch from behind.

That's it, slut, one of them says, *take it like a good girl.* He starts working his hand into my pussy while his sidekick fucks my ass, and it's so much better than a token three fingers. His knuckles feel good as they grate, so I beg him to go deeper, deeper, fucking deeper.

Gentle has no place in my life. It's go hard or go home.

If only I had someone waiting for me to go home to.

The guy in front of me takes the champagne away and offers his cock as a replacement. I'll glug on it, sure enough. I stare up at him like he's the man of my dreams, fluttering my lashes as I smile. I stick out my tongue and take the slap of his cock head, giving him the moans of a dirty bitch who really wants it.

I'll always suck dick like a tasty lollipop.

My butt cheeks bounce against the dick pounding my ass, and it adds volume to the momentum of the squelching knuckles, still trying to push their way in. I wish the guy wouldn't be such a pussy when it comes to my pussy. I can take it.

I can always take it.

I frog my legs as wide as I can on the office desk, my thick thighs slippery from his efforts. I love being such a big girl. I love the deep sound of the slap my flesh makes when I'm being banged.

I moan around the dick in my mouth, concentrating on just how good I'm going to be for these guys. The performer of a lifetime. I feel at my best when I have a filthy mind and a horny body, being used by strangers who don't give a shit about me.

Being a whore is my hometown – being an entertainer is my life.

The guy with his fist half inside me squirts on a load more lube, so considerate, but I don't want lube. I want the force. The grind. The fucking pounding. The filthy fucking joy.

"Beautiful and wet," he says, and his friend grunts and speeds up his ass thrusts. Hell fucking yes. I don't need my clit to come anymore. The way he drives his hand in stokes the fire brightly enough on its own, and I'm grateful.

I tell him so with a *fuck, fuck, yes!*

I'm me again. Creamgirl. The kinky slut who'll serve anyone's filthiest and kinkiest fantasies for the right amount of cash.

Tiffany, the girl behind the whore, *is* Creamgirl now. Creamgirl is all that matters.

I fly high at the sensation as guy number three unloads his first round of cum into my ass and pulls away. I moan for real as the fist in my pussy sinks in all the way, because yeah, the guy's got the hang of it now.

Thank fuck for that, since the night's only just started.

I'm going to take two cocks in each hole once his fist has warmed me up… then three wet mouths on my sopping pussy. They want my curvy girl butt to ride their faces while my tits bounce like beachballs. Man, how I'll bounce for them. They've got a treat coming.

The thought makes me grin, and another glug of champagne cements the happiness. Fuck anything else right now.

"Jesus Christ," the guy who spurted in my ass says, "that was fucking incredible."

"Amazing," the guy turning his fist in my cunt says.

Yes, I am fucking incredible.

I am fucking amazing.

Fuck Carly.

Fuck babies, and happy families and dreams that will never come to life.

I'm nothing but a beautiful whore tonight, exactly where I belong.

CHAPTER 1
Tiffany

I'm a master at hiding both hangovers and holes stretched badly enough that I should be limping. My smile is bright, my laugh at full volume as I walk arm in arm with the girls, hitting the London streets for Christmas shopping. You wouldn't think I was getting pounded by three strangers a few hours ago. They got me good.

I shake my sore butt and let out a cheer when we hear Mariah Carey blaring from one of the store entrances, even though I can't stand that godawful tune right now.

All I really want for Christmas is for Christmas to fuck off. Fuck off and take its jolly fucking jingle bells with it. Just looking at Christmas decorations is like nail extensions down a chalkboard for me.

Usually, my larger-than-life nature embraces almost everything there is to embrace and then some, but the news of Caroline's pregnancy is still twisting my insides like a bitch. Demons run deep and all that crap. I thought they'd have been long dead and buried after a bucketload of therapy, but they're still there, sneering in the darkness, and I hate it. The vulnerability makes me feel sick.

"Christmas is the best," Ella says, squeezing my arm. "Look,

look!" She points to a massive inflatable snowman in front of a mall. "That's amazing! And look at the little boy there. Awww. Oh my God. He's so cute."

Ella's mega babied up now that she's due to be an auntie, pointing out kids, babies and happy parents every other second, but she's twisting knives in me she doesn't know she's twisting. She'd be mortified if she knew.

I don't want to look at the bloody snowman and I really don't want to look at the sweet little boy grinning up at it with his parents crouched at his side. Yeah, it is *amazing*. And he is cute. So cute, I could retch up last night's champagne from the gut punch it gives me, but I let out another cheer instead.

"Oh my God, he's such a cutie!"

My heart pounds when Ebony suggests we go in and get shopping. I'll have to walk right past the happy family, but fuck it. I'll be swimming in happy families and cute little kiddos throughout the holiday season, so I'd better suck it up and get my big girl panties on.

I make sure my smile is convincing.

"Let's go, girls! Ho ho ho!"

Eb joins in with the *Christmas is great* banter as we pass the giant snowman and step into the mall. It's mega busy, with bustling shoppers all around us, which is hardly a shocker since it's a Saturday morning of gift-buying fervour.

I'm glad I've gone for casual today, with my clod hopping boots to keep me steady. I'm in my most comfy tattered black jeans and my huge *Bad Girl* hoodie. Ella is dressed up like she's going to a goth black tie ball, as per, and Ebony looks fresh out of *Vogue*, but not me. I'm just a girl half-heartedly shopping for cards and gifts that'll probably be gathering dust by the time the tinsel comes down. My hair is still in long waves down my back, and my fake

6

lashes are still on from last night. Plus, to be fair I did put on a fresh layer of scarlet lipstick to match my hair before I left the apartment, but that's it. I wanted bed, not socialising. I've got sleep deprivation, double hole burn, and a craving for paracetamol, but I'd already promised I'd go out with Ells and Eb today – three hooker girls hitting the festivities – so here I am. I never break promises.

"Wait a second, I know this place," Ella says, breaking away from me to do a spin. Something hits her, hard, and she looks like a gothic angel as she wells up. "No way! What the hell? I didn't think this was the Central Parade shopping centre. I had a proposal here last year. A new client when I was a newbie myself."

I can't help but laugh, bursting through her tender moment as I point out a sign for a charity grotto up ahead.

"What happened? Did you empty Santa's sack for twenty grand?"

She grins. "No, no. The client *was* Santa at the grotto, actually. But he wanted a plus-one for his work party. He said he was desperate for a companion. He didn't want to go alone."

I raise an eyebrow. "Right... a *companion* for Santa... that he could finger under the table, by any chance? Did you give him a desperation discount? You got suckered in there, Ells."

Ebony gives me a side eye, and I realise I've let my party girl mask slip. I sound bitter.

"Sorry. I had a late one," I say. "I'm a bit yowchy."

"Ah, yeah, I remember now," Eb says to Ella, and takes her hands, so sweet. "This was the client who said he was desperate for a companion, but ended up giving you a lump of cash for charity instead? The guy who wanted to see who would help him if he sent out a load of requests?"

Ella nods. "I thought I was helping him out for thirty quid, I really did, but no. He gave me a shit ton of money. I handed it out, too. I took it out in handfuls from the ATM and gave it to people on the street outside." Her breath hitches. "He was amazing."

Fuck sake. Everything is *amazing* to Ella. I'd usually smile at her humble, charitable soul, but unfortunately two little kids walk by holding hands and I get itchy. I shouldn't have come. I'm so not ready yet.

Eb points to the grotto sign.

"Shall we go and see if Santa is playing Santa again this year?"

"We shouldn't," Ella says. "You know what the regulations say. I shouldn't even be talking about him at all."

Ella is such a sweetie when it comes to the rules. I roll my eyes, because we're long past that. Sure, the rules say strictest client confidentiality at the highest cost, but we all work for the same Agency, with the same bank of clients on the user list. She can tell us she had a 'proposal' with Santa last year if she wants to. It's not as if we're going to blab it on speakerphone, and she's hardly going to broadcast it to the mall that he's signed up for sex services.

"You're allowed to go to the grotto, just like everyone else," Eb says, with a shrug. "It'll be fun. You don't need to acknowledge his dick or the fact you've seen it."

"I *haven't* seen it," Ella says, surprisingly defensive. "He asked me to accompany him to a meal for thirty quid, I turned up because I thought he was lonely, and he gave me thirty grand because I came to help him. That's all. No dick whatsoever."

"He gave you thirty grand without even waving his dick? How rude." I laugh, humour back for real. "I'd want at least a glimpse of Santa's sack if I'd trekked out on a job, charity pay out or not."

Ella looks overwhelmed, tears still welling. Bloody hell, this Santa guy must have made an impression.

"Do you want to see him again?" Eb asks her. "If he's such a great man and didn't so much as pay you for a hand job, I'm sure he wouldn't mind you calling by and saying hello."

"I'd love to see him again, if it's the same Santa." Ella grins. "He might not remember me to be fair, even if he is."

My laugh is a massive cackle. "Who could ever forget you?! You'll be stamped into his spank bank for all time."

My co-worker, Ella – known as Holly to clients – is an absolute stunner, and the girlfriend of my best friend, Josh. She's a leggy, big titted, gothic beauty who climbed the ranks of our Agency so fast when she started last year that she's rivalled my number one chart position in less than twelve months. I have a lot more curves on offer than she does – understatement – but that's about all. Every single item on her 'Naughty List' profile is checked now. No *holes* barred.

But they weren't when she would have done her charitable gig for sweet Santa. She was still a little Christmas angel herself, learning the dirty ropes.

My bitter hangover eases up a little.

"Come on," I say, taking her hand, because screw it. Ella's joy at seeing Santa is more important. "Let's get to the grotto. I'll sit on his lap myself if my butt will fit."

She lets me take the lead, gripping my fingers as I march us through the mall on a mission. I can blank out happy kids' faces for the sake of hers.

The queue at the grotto is so bloody long, I almost suggest we go for midday cocktails instead, but I don't do it. We're surrounded by kids desperate to see Santa Claus, but none of them are as desperate as Ella is. Santa's little home has a cute path leading up to it with artificial grass and snow, and she's virtually jumping on the spot every step of the way. She fans her face as we get close to the grotto doorway, mouthing to us just how nervous she is as she steps inside. Her excited O M G lights up her whole face.

There is no doubt Santa remembers her, because it's nearly ten minutes before Ebony gets called in for her turn. It's supposed to be five minutes tops in with Santa. A lap sit, a quick convo, a hug for a pic, and then out the other side like a conveyor belt, but not for Ella. He's probably been drooling all over her – charitable saviour or not. I stare at a plastic Rudolph figure while Eb has her go, getting my cash ready for the donation at the door, but Ebony's must be an especially quick visit, because I'm called in after her in a flash. I regret my decision to visit Santa myself when I have to duck and squish past cardboard to make it through the doorway. I practically fill up the entirety of this cosy grotto with my massive curves. It's a much smaller little *house* than it looked from outside.

"Hey there, Santa!" I smile at the man sitting in the sleigh chair. He's a convincing actor, with a thick beard and a padded red suit, and he can't be all that intimidated by my size, because he taps his knee and beckons me over. "Sure," I say. "You can have my butt, if you insist."

It's when I drop down into the natural straddle that I get shivers up my back – tiny whispers of WTF that give me goosebumps all up my arms. I drop my ass onto *Santa's* thighs, and his knees dig up into the back of mine in a very memorable fashion – even through my jeans. It's weird. Really fucking weird. But it's not just that which has my memory on autopilot, it's the way he shifts. It's the way he positions his hands on my waist and tugs me back against him. So distinctive... even at the slightest touch.

No.

It can't be.

"Have you been a good girl this year?" *Santa* asks me, and my heart thumps so fast it feels like I'm having palpitations. I must be breaking a sweat.

The way his thighs feel under mine, and the way he shuffles, and the way his hands sit could be written off as coincidence, maybe, but some things can't...

His voice can't. Not in that tone.

I know it so well I struggle to breathe.

He pulls me backwards, and the tiniest bounce is enough for another slammer of recognition.

I've been sitting on Santa's lap plenty of times outside this grotto... I just didn't know it...

"Don't be coy," he chuckles. "Have you been a good girl this year, or a naughty one? Let me guess. You've been a naughty one, haven't you?"

His tone cracks, just a touch, and it's one of those crazy moments of *you know that I know that you know*. I must be open mouthed as the camera flashes. I twist around in the damn sleigh seat and stare into the eyes of the bearded man I should never have crossed paths with. Not like this.

His eyes are dark, mahogany pools with a hint of green. His brows so heavy.

Eyes I've never seen before. Brows I've never admired.

"You're right, I'm definitely on your naughty list," I say, trying to stay as chill as possible. "You should know it though, Santa. You know which of my naughty boxes are ticked, don't you?"

He plays it cool. Calm. Collected.

"What's your name?" he asks me.

My eyes bore into his, my voice barely a whisper. "You already know my name."

Santa gives a *ho, ho, ho* for the guy behind the camera. What an apt expression. Fuck knows what the photographer thinks of this.

I shoot him a glance, but it's just a teenager on his phone, barely interested now that he's flashed the snapshot. My picture is printing out on the table right next to him. Bizarrely, the guy's lack of interest only adds to the intimacy in here. It's baking hot.

"Ho, ho, *no*, Cream. What's your *actual* name?" Santa asks me.

The thought of telling Santa my real name feels like a confession.

"Tiff," I say.

"Tiffany?"

"Yes, Tiffany."

"And what do you want for Christmas, Tiffany?"

His stare is so deep and so firm, even with his stupid beard on. The natural energy floods in and crackles like static between us.

Maybe Mariah's song wasn't so far off the mark earlier.

I want Santa for Christmas. Real fucking bad. I want the man who has ravaged me so hard I could barely move afterwards. The high paying beast who has pushed me to the limits and then some. The only man to ever put my safe word on the tip of my tongue.

"I want... um..."

The brashness of Creamgirl has gone. I'm just Tiff here. The real Tiff.

The Tiff without walls of balls to keep me safe.

I'm still stumbling over my reply when a little girl's screech comes from the queue outside. It's a loud one, a pure wail, and knocks me back to reality with a thump.

I have to get out of here. Now. Before I say something really fucking stupid.

I get up from Santa's lap and grab my photo on my way out with a *thanks, happy Christmaaaaas!*

And then I'm gone.

How I fight for air when I'm out the other side, a mess of

ragged breaths as Ella and Eb step up to join me, both of them beaming. They're oblivious to the state of me. Absolutely fucking oblivious.

"Amazing, isn't he?" Ella says. "You were right, Tiff, he remembered me. Thanked me again for coming to his rescue last year."

Eb sighs. "Damnit. I wish he was an active client. I'd love him to empty his sack for me, even if he is in a pillow suit. Those eyes…"

"What do you mean *if* he was an active client?" I ask.

"He signed up as a newbie last year," Ella says. "He told me he might be using his client profile for bookings, but nah, nothing." She shows me her phone. She's already been looking back through her records. I scan her proposal booking as quickly as I can.

User 5639. Male. 48.

"User 5639 hasn't made any bookings since that one with Ells," Eb groans. "I just searched on the forums. Not one peep about him. Nothing. Nada. Zilch."

But Santa isn't User 5639… they're wrong. He wasn't a newbie client on our list last December… he must have been faking it.

I should know, I was already fucking him by then. I've fucked him so many times, I'd recognise his lap out of thousands… but as for his beautiful dark eyes, I've never seen them before.

I've never seen *him* at all.

I've always been a hooded whore taking absolute filth in his presence, and his actions sure weren't out of charity.

"What is it?" Ella asks. "You alright, Tiff? You seem… weird?"

If only she knew – and I'm so tempted to blab it out to her… until I realise how blabbing about *Santa* really would be breaking the Agency code. I'd be in very deep shit without a paddle if I breached his level of confidentiality.

13

I get flashes of my bookings with him. So much filth. So much money. So much power.

Him and his limit pushing friends.

"Yeah, I'm fine," I lie, putting my fake smile back on. "Like I said, I've got a pissing hangover, and my ass feels like I've been impaled by a battering ram. Cut me some slack, will you?"

Ebony laughs. "A battering ram, now that I'd like to see."

"Actually, it was an enthusiastic three on one, but you get my gist."

"Ouch," she says, "That explains it, then."

Ella doesn't seem quite so convinced as Ebony, her eyes boring into me nearly as hard as Santa's were. She obviously suspects something is up. But I can't let her in on my secrets. It wouldn't be fair. Not about babies, not about being lonely at night, and definitely, definitely not about Santa.

Because Santa isn't just a charitable guy with a dormant client profile. He's our fucking boss. One of the founders of the whole fucking Agency.

One blabbed wrong word from me and I'd be screwed – literally.

CHAPTER 2
Tiffany

I'm in a daze through the rest of the shopping trip. I let out a cringey ho ho ho whenever Eb cracks a *steamy Santa* comment, trying to blank out the memory of his eyes, and the *I know that you know that I know* realisation that burned between us – but it's not easy. Neither of them will shut the fuck up about him. Ella doesn't quit it with the *amazing man of charity* sighs, and Eb wants to empty his sack, and I have to bite my tongue so hard it hurts as we browse glittery cards and debate tinsel colours. I'm glad we don't opt for lunchtime cocktails, because a *Sex on the Beach* never helps me keep my blabbermouth shut.

I'm aching to blurt out what a filthy, powerful bastard Santa really is. His kind of fantasies are off the charts. He's not the kind of figure I would ever have expected to bump into in everyday life. Not a chance in hell. It's never been on my radar that I would be sitting on one of The Agency stakeholder's laps one day with my eyes open wide – let alone in a quaint shopping mall grotto. I want to spill the truth, just to get the WTAF off my chest, but I can't. The owners of The Agency are shielded by confidentiality to the extreme, and hardcore entertainers like us are always hooded whenever we get bookings. *If* we get bookings. Most entertainers haven't got a clue the founders even exist.

Ella and Ebony are going to have to stay in the dark about him. Ha. Ironic.

We seem to circle the whole bastard grotto, store after store after store, and it's like he's a magnet in there. I'd love to rejoin the back of the queue for another five minutes of lap sitting, but I can't. He's off bounds. Period.

I can't bring myself to look at the picture I got from the grotto. I'm hardly in a glitzy ballgown, with my arms wrapped around his neck under mistletoe. I'm in a baggy hoodie, cruddy jeans, and yesterday's fake lashes, likely looking more like a rabbit caught in headlights than one of his star performers.

Me and the girls call it a day with the shopping at just after two, since all three of us have clients tonight. I wish I wasn't such a bloody workaholic – or sexaholic – sometimes, because tonight's proposal involves club dancing and twerking my butt off until I get accosted by a *stalker* in an alley outside. I'm knackered, wanting to curl up and binge reality TV shows with a cheesecake rather than take another pounding, but I never back out of proposals – and this client is a new one for me.

I love playing with strangers, especially when it gets rough. It keeps it interesting.

This one is sure gonna get rough tonight.

I opt for a Jessica Rabbit style dress in red sequins, with a split right the way up my thigh for easy access. Big holed fishnets, and stilettos, and elbow length black gloves that mix class with whore. I don't wear my trademark tiara, but I do use a sparkling hair clip to sweep my long, red curls up on one side. I think my client will like it.

I read through his proposal again before I set off to Club Revelier.

User 2906. Male. 35.

I want to watch you dancing like the boldest curvy bitch in the bar. Flirt with the guys around you and act like you're the prize queen in the room, because I'm sure you will be. I want to watch you perform like a girl after dick, and who knows? Maybe I'll be one of the guys you'll be flirting with. Wouldn't that be a nice surprise? Because you'll have fucking asked for it by the time we cross paths later in the evening.
You'll get a notification from your client app when the time is right, so keep it close at hand. When you do, it'll be time for you to leave, all set to go home, until you pass the alleyway on the right-hand side.
I hope you like to be grabbed and used as much as your profile claims you do, because I'm not going to be gentle. I'll claim every bit of the bounty you've been touting. I want to spread those beautiful chunky thighs of yours and claim the treasure. And as for your gorgeous balloon tits. I'm going to be taking advantage of those, believe me.
I only hope that when you realise you're a slutty bitch who is getting what you asked for, you'll be down on your knees begging for more.
Dirty girls like you should be desperate bitches for cock, no matter how much it hurts.

Duration: 4 hours.
Proposal Fee: £6000.

I smile at his words, hoping that tonight is going to be a fun one. I love being a degraded, cheap bitch who takes it rough – always walking away with a grin on my face and a decent chunk of cash in my bank account. The 6k is a tad low for my taste, but I

17

can't help trying out new clients. Variety is the spice of sluts and I'm getting way too bored lately.

I leave the apartment and send my regular message to Josh. We check in and out of our proposals, finishing them up with D&S texts – *done and safe*. Clients are always checked out and vetted by The Agency, down to every last detail. We are obliged to have STI checks every month, and so do they, and what's set out in the proposals is always to be adhered to, but still. A D&S message is always a good thing to have in the background. Josh would come running if I needed him, whenever I needed him.

We used to be 24/7 kind of friends, and he was the person I'd call on for everything, even to unload my gossip while he was on his treadmill, but I've been giving him some space now he's shacked up with Ella. I've taken the inevitable sidelining of a best friend – my choice, not his, since I'm always welcomed – but regardless of stepping back, Josh is still my number one. The person I'd run to in a storm, and shelter with my life in return.

Cool, the reply says. *Me and Ells are heading out now. Double booking. D&S at 3 a.m.*

I give him *lucky bastard, have fun* and a thumbs up.

Josh and Ella only live a few floors up from me in the West Belgravia tower, but the gap feels bigger as the months move on. It's only natural that they are building more and more of a life without me. They radiate *soulmates* from every angle. I never had to feel this lonely before, because Josh was my constant wingman, and I was getting sex from other places, constantly, but now…

I look in the mirror.

I'm approaching twenty-seven years old. The time I always figured I'd be settled down myself. I dunno, but it seems to be a *nearly thirty, let's get serious* kind of benchmark. I can fob it off with a *pah* all I like, but it's still there, like an alarm bell ringing louder every day.

I don't want to get a pathetic pang of wanting someone, so I shove it back in the depths. It's all about User 2906 tonight.

I get a cab to Club Revelier over in Tottenham. I've been here once or twice before and it's alright. Decent, and a bit of a rave spot with drum n'bass. It's a big enough venue that I can get lost amidst the partygoers without anyone twigging I'm a girl downing prosecco and dancing alone... and flirting with every guy who looks my way.

I scope it out when I get inside, scanning the main dancefloor. If User 2906 is planning on flirting with me, he's bound to be nearby. I open The Agency app and click on *arrived*, and I wait for the acknowledgement response before I go any further.

Yes. I can see you, the reply says.

I suspected as much. Knowing he's got his eyes on me brings me out in a flush. There are so many men around... so many potentials...

I stride to the bar with a smile on my face to order my first prosecco. I've barely taken a sip when a guy steps up beside me and gives me a cocky smirk.

"You alright?"

He's staring at my tits, like most blokes do. It makes flirting so easy as I turn to face him. Piece of piss. I hope my client has his beady eyes on me, watching the way I flutter my lashes.

"I'm great, thanks. How about you?"

I talk quietly on purpose, so the guy has to lean in close, he's got to be barely twenty-one. Not my taste, but oh well.

"I'm cool," he says. "Want a drink?"

Poor guy needs to work on his chat, because he's hardly

original. Still, I down my prosecco in one and put the empty glass on the bar top.

"Sure."

I give him the eye as he gets me another glass, biting my lip when he hands it over with a *cheers*. He's got a beer and chugs some back before he goes in for the usual round of questions.

What's your name, where are you from, who are you here with? Dull as fuck. What I want him to ask is whether he can fuck the tits he's staring at, screw the niceties. I want him to ask if I like being throat jammed like a slut when I'm on my knees, and how much of a pounding I can take in my asshole.

He's midway through another boring question when I finish up my second glass of fizz and walk away with a *thanks for the drink.* My flirting is done with him, no explanation necessary.

I weave my way onto the dancefloor, finding the beat as I sway my hips and lose myself in the groove. The people around me make it hot in here. The stickiness of drunk sweat is welcome as I shimmy my dress up, then pump my hands in the air. I dance, I spin, I jump and groove, and people notice me. Of course they do. I'm not exactly a shrinking violet or one of the bland brigade.

I love the heat of the eyes on me, a blur of people staring as I dance in my own filthy world – knowing full well the dark game lying ahead of me. A stinking alleyway and a dirty fucker who's going to treat me like a piece of trash. That's what I want. I want to be trash tonight.

I hitch my dress higher, twerking my bouncy butt like I'm desperate for action. I've been in this game long enough to send out the right signals, and it works. I feel people shifting. Grooving men getting closer, so thinly veiled, it's ridiculous.

I back into one of them to make it easy for him, grinding my ass against his crotch as his hands come around for some action, but he's shit. This guy isn't my client, I can tell by the way his friends are cheering him on, but he's an easy target for my slut show. I turn to face him and pull him against me, pressing my tits to his chest. He grabs my ass, and some half decent grinding starts. I spread my legs wide enough that his thigh finds my pussy, but it's too early to be getting serious, and nah, he's crap at it. Average, tops.

I pull away and leave him behind, sashaying through the revellers until I get some wolf whistles off to the right. Two guys wanting a piece of me. These two are idiots, dancing with the kind of laid-back groove reserved for Z-listers, but I milk it for all it's worth. Maybe they were on some reality TV show a decade ago and still think they're in it to win it. I act like a girl who thinks they're superstars, fawning as I dance along with them, one after the other.

One of them kisses me, and he's like a wet fish with his tongue, but I don't give a toss. I eat his face like I'm as keen as he is, running my hand down to the bulge in his pants to scope out his hard-on.

Hardly a donkey.

Again. Boring.

Boring, boring, boring.

The idiots protest when I leave them behind, but I carry on regardless, grooving my way into another crowd. This little cluster is hotter. A couple of the guys are tall and imposing. Some girls grip their boyfriends tighter, staking claim, but one of the tall guys is blatantly on the lookout for pussy. His eyes are on my tits from the off, and he knows he's fit. I like that kind of confidence.

I dance closer, giving him the eye as I twist and twirl, and he's straight on it. Coming in close.

This guy has more heat than the others. His moves are more mature. His stature more demanding.

His hands are firm, fingers harsh as they squeeze my ass.

I'd be happy to spread my legs and have him explore my juicy cunt right here on the dancefloor. I'd tug down my dress and set my tits free to let him slaver. But no. Not yet.

More kisses, but these aren't sloppy – just fierce. He wraps a hand around the back of my neck to pull me close, and I figure that this could maybe be User 2906 getting me ready. I'd like that. But no.

"Want to leave, get a cab back to mine?" he asks. "I don't live too far from here. We could… hang out."

I keep up my flirting game.

"That depends…" I smile, my mouth close to his ear. "What would you want to do to me when we got there?"

"Nothing crazy. I'm no psycho, don't worry."

I laugh at that. "Shame."

"Shame?"

"Yeah, shame. Girls like me like it filthy."

He's a decent looking guy. Tall and muscular, with a neat beard and dark eyes. He's in a shirt that fits nicely, and looks like he's packing a hulky dick in his pants.

"How filthy do you like it?" he asks.

"As filthy as it gets."

His smirk is alright. Not an award winner. He's confident, but not a super-ego.

"Shall I at least get you a drink first?"

"Sure. Prosecco, thanks. I'll wait here."

I'm lying. My eyes are already roving around for the next person of interest, but I don't get all that long to mingle. Someone presses up against me from behind, and his hands on my waist put the last guy's confidence to shame. He roves them up to grope my tits through my dress, and grinds his cock against my ass. I work him right back, spurring him on, and I get tingles when his breath lands on my neck.

I can only just hear his words above the music.

"Better get back to loverboy and his prosecco. He wants a piece."

"He's not going to fuck me hard enough."

"He doesn't know that. Be a good slut and appreciate his efforts."

The stranger shoves me forwards, and he's already blurred into the bodies on the dancefloor by the time I spin around. Damnit, I have no idea who that was, and the strobes don't make it easy to track anyone. He's long gone, no doubt eyeing me from a distance.

I do what I'm told, dancing back through the throng towards the guy returning from the bar. He has my drink in his hand, what a sweetie. I thank him and raise it in toast, my eyes locked on his like a siren. He's my target. My minx trap. My job accessory. I want to get him so worked up he's set to ravage me on the dancefloor, and make that plain. The watcher in the shadows is the one who matters.

"Come on, let's stop playing coy," I tell the guy I'm up against. "Show me what you can do, and we'll see about getting that cab."

I guide his hand down between my legs, and it's clear the people around us are too engrossed in their own beat to notice. The lights and noise have ramped up, the club getting headier and heavier.

I've passed off this guy as a half-assed nobody too easily. He's got more dirty substance than I banked on, and if circumstances were different, if he was the guy paying… but he's not.

He's slender against my curves, but he's strong. He hands me his beer, then reaches down to tear the crotch of my fishnets open like it's the most natural thing in the world. He hooks his fingers inside my lacy thong, and damn, he's good… he knows where my clit is, sliding a nice path up and down my slit through my slick, puffy pussy lips.

"I had you down as a hairy girl," he shouts in my ear, and I laugh.

"Nah. Clean shaven. Always." I hand him back his beer.

"Nice and smooth. And wet."

"Sure am." I give him a cheeky grin. "Check it out."

I squat a touch on my stilettos, swinging my hips in disguise, because I want his fingers inside me on the dancefloor. I want him to fuck me to the knuckles, so my teasing means something. I wrap my arms around his neck, being careful with my prosecco, since I wouldn't want to waste any.

"I want filthy, remember?" I say, my mouth on his ear.

His fingers slide to my pussy, scissoring my clit. "Is this not filthy enough?"

"Nah, not even close."

"Fine, let's ramp it up."

He kisses a path from my lips to my throat, and pushes three fingers inside me, hard.

It's easy to use his hand for my pleasure since his rhythm matches the thump of the bass. Good work on his part.

I think about the guy watching from the sidelines somewhere. Through the throng of bodies I can sense him. Watching. Waiting. Viewing me as a slut getting fingered while people dance around me. My scarlet hair must be an obvious spot, no matter where he is in the club. The way I moan like a whore against a random guy's mouth speaks wordlessly above the bass.

But still, amongst it all, I've got my clutch bag held tight to my side, barely anything in there besides my phone – set to vibrate at maximum when my notification comes through. The one that will instruct me to leave this place and head outside.

I wonder if I can come before then. To be fresh from a climax when I get assaulted in the darkness would really make my day.

"More fingers," I say. "Fuck me like you mean it."

I groan as he pushes in a fourth, loving the stretch, even though I'm still sore as fuck from last night's action.

"I'm gonna do you so hard when we get out of here," he says, and I'd get a pang of guilt if it meant anything, but it doesn't. There will be plenty of horny bitches looking for a hookup before home time. He'll strike lucky.

"Show me how hard you can play," I tell him, working myself deeper onto his fingers. "Give me a filthy taster."

I've always loved public playtime, especially when other people are blind to the filthy bitch I'm being, right in front of them. I ride his fingers as I dance, and if the music wasn't so loud, the squelches from my sopping wet pussy would be clear from a mile off. He feels my excitement rising, twisting his fucking fingers as I groan, and then he searches out my clit with his thumb, digging between my pussy lips for the target.

I can come like this, and I know it. I'm on my way quicker than I'd expect, all thoughts of prosecco and beer forgotten as we groove and moan. His pace picks up so it's faster than the bass, and I'm so turned on I'm hardly dancing anymore, just squatting on my stilettos as he gets me off. Fuck, I'm almost there. My breaths are heaving, and my mind is turning blank, and I'm over the fucking moon at the achievement of coming on a packed dancefloor as my client stares on.

I'm sure he can see me. I'm sure he can see I'm serious. This orgasm isn't going to be some bullshit fakery – it never is – and I'm ready, I'm so fucking ready.

Until I feel the buzz of my phone in my clutch.

I could fucking scream. So close. So fucking close. But I know the rules. I know how this story goes.

I stop grinding, stop humping, stop moving. I take hold of my finger fucker's wrist and push him away.

"I need to get this, sorry."

He knocks back the rest of his beer as I grope inside my clutch, ready to resume the action, but there isn't going to be any further action. The notification on my phone speaks loud and clear.

User 2906. Leave the club right now.

I could give the man in the shadows a middle finger.

I shove my phone back in my clutch and down the rest of my prosecco. Hell only knows how there's still any left in the glass after being finger screwed to the crest. My finger fucker looks mortified as I shove my empty glass into the hand that's still wet from doing me.

"I've got to go."

"Go?"

"Yeah, see you around."

I don't wait for the *but* and the awkward questions. I'm out of there on a mission, shoving my way through the other dancers until I get to the edge of the room. I don't bother composing myself. It's going to be straight out of the flames and into the fire, so I march towards the exit, barely bothering to smooth my dress down.

I'm nearly at the doorway when a figure catches my eye, leaning off to the side against the wall. I have to do a double take – a slamming shiver of recognition zipping up my spine.

I get prickles upon prickles. Tingles up my arms.

No. Fucking. Way. It can't be.

I stop dead in my tracks.

My instincts know this man, even though I don't.

He's in a tailored jet-black suit with a glass of red in his hand – and he's staring right at me as the lights flash through his silver fox hair. It's his eyes… his gaze.

I step closer to check him out at close quarters, rationality still doubting my intuition, but I already know what I'm going to see when I get there. I already know they are the same eyes I was gazing into in the grotto. Instincts never lie.

Santa doesn't look anything like Santa tonight. His clipped grey beard is a perfect complement to his easy smile, and he tips his head as I give him another round of open mouthed WTAF. What do I call him? What the fuck do I even say?

He speaks before I do, gesturing to the exit.

"Got somewhere to be, haven't you, Tiffany? Someone waiting out there?"

"I, um…"

My thoughts are scattered. I stare at him, my brain a tumble.

"You'd better go," he says with a smirk. "You wouldn't want a bad rating to tarnish your record."

Santa isn't User 2906, of course he isn't. But he knows where I'm going, he knows where I've been. He knows *everything*, since he's one of the owners of the whole damn Agency.

He's also well aware what I've been doing on the dancefloor, I see it in his stare.

He's likely seen just as much as my client outside…

I don't know why it gives me another zip of a shudder up my spine. I feel more self-conscious than I've felt in years.

"What are you doing here?" I ask him.

He raises his glass. "Enjoying a drink. Nothing more."

27

Nothing more. Yeah, right.

There is no malice in him, nothing sinister. His smile isn't dark or foreboding, it's just surreal – and it gives me the kind of butterflies I like to crush under my shoe, but they won't fuck off. They're stronger than I've known in a long, long time.

There's a twist of bizarre humour in Santa's voice that screws with my insides. It's just the kind of magnetism that makes my stomach tumble along with my brain.

"Have fun in the alleyway," he says. "The clock is ticking."

Yes, it is. I look at the doorway.

My client is out there now, expecting me any second, and as much as I'm loath to tear myself away, I have to go. Creamgirl always comes first.

I smile at Santa before I leave, but say nothing, because for once my big, bold mouth is stumped. I rely on my legs and work ethic to force myself on by.

I daren't look back to see if he's still watching me, because one more flash of his smile would have me crumpling at his feet, and it's not Santa's feet I need to be crumpling at.

I have business to attend to.

CHAPTER 3
Tiffany

I don't need User 2906 to provoke a fight or flight reaction in me. It's already there, loud and clear. Jesus Christ. My head is wired. Spun out to hell as I stumble down the club steps onto the street.

The night chill helps, bringing me back to some semblance of clarity. I suck the cool air into my lungs, desperate to keep a hold of myself. I banish all thoughts of Santa, because I have no time to ruminate or speculate. Not now. I've got to get in the zone.

Creamgirl has to take the reins.

The shadowy alley is just up ahead, running down the side of the club. I figure I'm going to have to 'stall' as I pass by, so reach for my clutch as a pretend distraction, but I don't need it.

An arm bursts out of the darkness, a savage fist grabbing my hair and yanking me from the street as I squeal. My squeal is barely more than a squeak, since a hand slaps over my mouth before I can blink.

My assailant must know martial arts or something, because he takes me in a chokehold – his elbow against my windpipe as he drags me backwards. I don't know how I manage to stay upright on my stilettos, because there's trash all around our feet. I hear the jangle of empty bottles being kicked away, and the crumple of paper under my shoes.

This isn't just an alley, it's the club bin store, and it's a stinking shithole.

User 2906 has already prepped for our session, that much is clear. He slams me into the wall between two big dumpsters and switches the chokehold for a forearm against the back of my neck. My face is flat against the damp brickwork, and the gravel texture could easily graze my cheek, but that's the least of my worries right now.

"Stay fucking quiet, understand?"

I try to nod, but he's got me pinned too tight. "Yes."

He eases up the pressure a touch and I gulp in some breaths.

I stick to my usual script.

"I've got some cash, if you want it... not much, but you can take it."

He laughs, his voice throaty.

"I don't want your cash, you dumb bitch. I want the body you've been slutting around on the dancefloor."

"I was just dancing."

His scoff gives me a pulse between my legs, and I squeeze my thighs shut. I hope this guy is into degradation to the max, because that's what Creamgirl needs right now. The whore side of me needs to come to the fore and block out everything but the dirty games ahead.

I don't want men in posh suits, or Santa smiles to send me loopy. I want to be used like a cheap slut and earn my money.

"Just dancing? Yeah, right," User 2906 says. "You were begging for cock from the second you arrived in that place. Your cunt nearly sucked that guy's whole fist in, you were gagging for it so fucking bad. Dirty bitch."

I love it when my character feels the burn of embarrassment. I could have been an actress in a previous life, since I sink so deep into my roles.

"It was his fault. He made me horny."

"He had fuck all to do with it. You were being a slag, like a piece of beef at an auction house. All it took was one fucking prosecco. You may as well have bought him one, since you were the one desperate for dick."

This client is definitely new to me. His voice has a twang of cockney. I wonder what he looks like, but his arm is pressed too tight to my neck to turn and see.

I say nothing, just breathe. The club is thumping to the side of us, and I can barely hear any traffic on the road. It would be pointless to fight him from back here, even if this wasn't a proposal.

"You still desperate for cock?" he asks.

"No, I swear! Just let me go, please." I hitch a sob. "I'm sorry I was a slut. I didn't think anyone was watching."

"You're talking shit. You can't flaunt it like you do, tits spilling out as you twerk your fat arse, and not know that everyone with a cock is watching you."

"I like attention sometimes, that's all."

His laugh is vile, his weight still hard on my neck.

"Yeah? This attention enough for you?" His free hand goes for my dress, tugging at the split with so much force I'm sure he'll rip it. He finds my thighs closed, and I squeeze tighter. There is no way he's working his hand between them. My thighs are like tree trunks.

His fingers dig, trying to get to my pussy, but he gets nowhere.

"Open your fucking legs, bitch and stop pretending you don't want it."

"No!" I try my best to squirm away but he's way too strong.

"Give it up now, slut. Don't waste my fucking time."

I'm not prepared when he pulls away to set me free, only to slam me back again. My clutch goes tumbling to the floor, and I try to push back with my hands, but he's a big guy. I can't move him.

"You're nothing but a dirty slut who needs cock." He pins me so hard this time that my tits are mashed flat against the wall. "I said, open your fucking legs."

"And I said no!"

I try to fight, but it's pointless. My arms flail, but reach nothing, and the asshole uses the opportunity to lock me in an arm bar. He cricks my arm back so bad I cry out, then I curse, because I know I'm not cut out to fight him. He could break my arm if I dared.

"Fiery bitch, aren't you?"

I both love and hate his snarky laugh at the same time.

My inner fiery bitch battles with my inner slut, both out for the win. I always love this part of the game, where my quest for war has to succumb to my need for dirty, raw sex, but fiery bitch has a sword tonight. Outrage flames up like fucking heartburn and I grit my teeth. I'd punch this guy if I could. I'd fight him, and wrestle him, and claw at his face, goading him through every second he was trying to claim me.

"You're a cunt," I tell him. "A fucking prick."

"You've got a big wet cunt that *needs* a fucking prick." He tugs my arm higher to remind me he's in control here. "Now, open those slutty legs and give it to me."

I groan in frustration. I hiss curses, telling him he's a piece of shit who won't be able to get me off anyway, because he's a worthless asshole.

"You'd have your own choice of pussy in that club if you were half decent," I say. "You wouldn't need to be grabbing me in the fucking dark like a psycho."

"Open your legs and I'll show you how *decent* I am." He slams me again when I refuse. "Open your fucking legs, bitch. I'm losing my patience now."

I get the click of knowing, my experience serving me well. The guy is in the zone himself now, frustrated and sadistic. His character is meeting mine.

My slutty soul waves hello to his in the beautiful depravity.

Finally, I part my legs for him.

"Wider," he says.

I shuffle my feet, but he kicks them further apart. I really am spread now, my flabby thighs parted enough to give him full access. The torn fishnets grant him entry. He tugs my panties to the side and my sopping wet pussy lips are waiting.

I get another flash of delicious embarrassment. It's like he's rummaging through leftovers as he explores me with rough fingers.

"I knew you wanted it," he says. "Fresh and smooth. Yeah, you were out to get some tonight." He pushes his fingers into my slit, rubbing back and forth. "I love a meaty pussy. You're gonna be so easy to stalk, you filthy beauty. You'd better keep one eye over your shoulder, coz one day I'm gonna want to check out this cunt in the daylight."

He grabs my pussy lips in his fist and tugs, and fuck how I moan as my clit springs back to life.

"Dirty bitch," he says and tugs some more. "Like that, do you?"

Fuck yes, I like it a fucking lot.

"No," I tell him, "My meaty pussy loves meaty fingers." I push against his hand.

He likes my words. His thick thumb slips inside me and he

grinds his crotch against my curvy ass. I can feel his hard-on. A decent size.

"I know what you'd like," I tell him as his thumb jabs at me.

"What's that, bitch?"

"My pussy spread open for you. I look so dirty with my legs up."

"Filthy slut, I bet you fucking do." He pulls his thumb away and goes back to tugging at my lips.

I rock myself against his fingers, and the tips start to catch against my hungry fucking hole.

"Go on," I say. "Show me how good you are."

"That wanker in the club was gonna get you off, wasn't he?"

"Yeah, he was."

"How many fingers was he giving you?"

"Four."

"Pathetic." He pushes four right in and Christ it feels good as I sink onto them. "You'll take my cock as well as these, bitch."

I pretend to be intimidated. Tensing up.

"Please, no… I can't…"

"Nah, bitch. I know what a cunt like yours can take. Don't treat me like a dumb fucker."

He doesn't give me a warmup before he lines his thumb against his fingers to demonstrate, and fuck, it's going to hurt. I'm still sore and stretched from last night, so used I'm aching – but my inner whore Creamgirl wins out easy.

I want it.

I shunt back against him so I'm working my pussy against his hand, waiting for the pop as his knuckles sink in. And sink in they do. Just like that.

"See," he says. "You're a fucking liar. You can take it, no sweat."

I moan in protest when he pulls out, but I hear his belt unbuckling, and the zipper on his jeans. He lets go of my arm, and I shimmy myself into position, fight done. My palms are against the wall as I bend for him. Yeah, my *meaty* cunt is on offer. I'll take whatever he wants me to.

I brace myself as he moves up close. He grabs my panties, tight in his fist, and the fucker rips them apart like they're made of paper.

I gasp as they're torn away and gasp again when he slaps my exposed cunt.

"Take it," he says and I take his dick easy as it slides inside me in one. He's deep, but not girthy enough. I clench around him and give a little wiggle.

"You'll need more than that. My cunt needs a pounding, not a poke from a sweet little cock."

"Shut up and take it." His hips slam quick, thrusting in hard, but I laugh.

"You said you know what a cunt like mine can take. *You're* the fucking liar if you think that's going to do the job."

He leans in close. "Believe me, bitch, I'll be giving it to you. You should've asked nicely, because now it's gonna hurt like a bastard."

The initial sensation always pains like a bastard, but I'm an addict. I moan as the piece of shit pulls his cock out to shove all four fingers back inside me. He follows them up with his dick in one big fucking stab.

"Better," I tell him and he stabs me again and again.

It burns like hell, but I'm squelching and bucking, taking it all with a *fuck, fuck, yessss.*

I'm back to the horny bitch I was when I was teasing cock on the dancefloor. I put my hand between my legs to check out the full horny extent of what he's giving me, gripping his wrist to urge him deeper. His balls bounce against my fingers.

"That's so good," I tell him. "You're so much better than the jerk in the club, so much better…"

"He wasn't going to treat your cunt like this. He'd have no fucking idea how to play."

"You know how to play." My breaths pick up. "Oh fuck, you know how to play. And I hope you do play. In the fucking daylight when I can see what the fuck you're doing to me, because you know what? I like watching. I like begging for it. I like to splay my fucking legs and beg to be pounded."

"Beg now, slut. Beg for it."

I circle my clit as he slams me.

"Faster, please. Make me a dirty bitch. That's why I came out tonight. I wanted to be used like a filthy slut."

He speeds up his thrusts, and my tits are bouncing. They come out of the neckline of my dress, hanging free.

"Crush my tits," I tell him. "Play while you fuck me. Please."

He wraps an arm under me, and his hand grapples and grabs. My flesh slaps as he pinches and tugs.

"I'm gonna love seeing these in the daylight," he tells me. "But I'll be in charge, remember that. I'm always in charge."

"That's ok, I don't care… just give it to me. I'll take whatever you want, because you're so fucking good. My God, you're so fucking good."

This time, I'm not lying.

User 2906 is a beast with my tits while his fingers and cock plough my pussy. My clit sparks with lightning bolts. I press my forehead to the wall, not giving a fuck about how I might get grazed. The only thing that matters is reaching the peak, and he owes me one, since he fucking wrecked it when I was about to come on another guy's fingers.

He was right, though. He's better than that. The buildup only made me more needy, full of moans as I get to the edge.

The timing is perfect. My clenching pussy sends him over the edge in sync with me, and we're nothing but a grunting mess of slapping flesh as we come together. He unloads in my pussy with his four fingers still buried deep, and holds them there in the aftermath, squidging them around in his cum as I try to get my breath back.

It's so gross, it's hot as fuck.

"There you go, whore," he says. "I could read you a mile off. Piece of trash cum-slut."

"Fuck you," I say. "I can't help what my pussy needs. That's called biology."

"It's called being a desperate slag with a big wet cunt, and just wait until next time. It'll beg for a whole lot more from me then."

He pulls his fingers free, wipes them on my ass, and can't resist grabbing my pussy lips again.

"Fuck, that was good," he says.

I moan when he tugs.

"Dirty bitch."

I hear him buckle himself back up, but I don't move, just stay bent over like the slut I am while his cum dribbles out of my pussy.

The bottles on the floor do another jangle as he walks away and leaves me there, dishevelled and used up between two dumpsters. I don't move for a while, enjoying the flooding power of the aftermath, with a heady smile on my face as my body comes down.

It really is fucking cold now, and my teeth start to chatter as my adrenaline depletes. My nipples are like frozen bullets and my tits are prickling as I shove them back in my dress.

I scramble around the floor for my clutch, grabbing my phone and calling my usual cab number. They are only ever a few minutes away, given I'm such a regular client.

"Belgravia, please," I say. "From Club Revelier. Tottenham."

I use my phone torch to get out of here in my heels. It's a shit show, with used up wrappers, and battered boxes and broken bottles everywhere. And fuck knows where my ruined panties are. Maybe he took them as a trophy. Damn, I'm glad he didn't drop me to my knees. I'd have likely ended up with far more than a grazed cheek from some brickwork. I brace myself on one of the dumpsters, clenching my pussy to test the aftermath, and fuck it hurts. I take a steadying breath and step back into the street, which is still practically empty since everyone is still clubbing.

The cab lights appear in three minutes, tops, and I hop on in with a *thanks*. My phone is already in my hand, so I get right to typing out my *D&S* message to Josh. But if I'd have waited, just a few more seconds – if I'd have held off on the D&S until my cab was down the street, I might have got more of a glimpse of the man standing at the entrance of the club, directly under the Club Revelier sign.

Santa.

There is no wine glass in his hand. Not this time.

My fucking God, was he outside? Was he watching? Did he hear my filthy begging and the way I took it like a piece of meat who needed a pounding?

Suddenly I'm shaking as the nerves eat me alive out of nowhere. I feel so intimidated, so dirty and exposed as I twist in the cab seat to stare back at him.

Vulnerable.

I feel vulnerable.

Exposed, naked, used, debased and so fucking vulnerable.

Another cab pulls up and Santa glances my way before he gets in.

My heart is fucking pounding as the cab pulls away, but no, he's not telling his cabbie to *follow that cab*. The cab does a U turn and heads in the opposite direction.

Shit.

I don't know whether to laugh or cry.

CHAPTER 4
Tiffany

Central Parade shopping centre, Santa, I type into Google.

The search results come up with some events days, and a mention of Santa's Grotto in a recent news article, but nothing about Santa himself. I scroll down the feed, mention after mention, until finally, there he is.

Santa – minus the Santa outfit – is in one of the pictures, with his gorgeous dark eyes and his side parted silver fox hair. He's standing behind one of those big, printed charity cheques, donating a chunk of money to a kids' support centre in Dagenham. £40,000.

My stomach lurches like a motherfucker as I click the link to see more. I have to blink three times, zooming in on the photo. He's way more gorgeous than the strobe lights did justice. In a suit, in daylight, he's off the fucking charts.

Santa is *Reuben Sinclair*, owner of Central Parade and twenty-three other shopping centres around the country.

Wow!

"*Reuben*." I speak his name aloud, and it sounds like dirty satin. I wonder how it would sound at squeal volume, while he's slamming the shit out of me.

I need to find out.

A search for *Reuben Sinclair* himself hits a lot more results. There's a chunk of interviews as part of his associations with various charities, with quotes on how he had to climb up the ladder from nothing himself, so he knows how hard it is for youngsters out there with nobody to rely on.

I can't imagine him like that. A young boy, desperate. All I can see is the Reuben Sinclair of today. Powerful. Prestigious. Charitable. Loaded. And dirty as all fucking hell.

My stomach drops out with every article click, terrified I might come across either of the two fateful words. Husband or father. I feel ill at the thought of him being a cosy family man behind the scenes, with a beautiful Mrs and some sweet little kiddos. But no mentions turn up. Not in a single article.

A link to an old podcast appears on page seven, and my fingers are legit quaking as they click on it.

He's talking about a particular charity that helps out single mothers.

I, myself, was from a struggling single parent family, and as much as my mother claimed in later years that it was stress talking, not her, she blamed her decision to have me at such a young age for her hardship. She'd throw her emotional outbursts in my direction, and I didn't understand it then. My young mind couldn't interpret her, and all I felt was pain. I had no idea how much pressure she was under to keep our heads above water. It was hard. Very, very hard. I have both huge empathy and sympathy for people battling with similar journeys. It's not easy.

His tone has me entranced, even though it's just a snippet. I replay it over and over, my head whirling. I can't stop.

This is dangerous. It's a familiar road up ahead.

I've been more in control of myself these past few years, '*keeping my head screwed on*' as my nan would have said. I've kept my compulsive *happy ever after* fantasies at bay, confident enough to quit psychotherapy over six months ago. But my grip is slipping so fast by the second, I get tremors.

I had no idea how much pressure she was under to keep our heads above water. It was hard. Very, very hard. I have both huge empathy and sympathy for people battling with similar journeys. It's not easy.

I give myself the excuse of 'just a bit of fun', but I'm staring at the picture of Reuben behind the cheque as his words sound out, and remember Ella's enthusiasm at seeing him. *He's such an amazing guy, so kind and humble, and selfless... and just AMAZING.*

I can't stop.

I had no idea how much pressure she was under to keep our heads above water. It was hard. Very, very hard. I have both huge empathy and sympathy for people battling with similar journeys. It's not easy.

There is another side to the man talking, though. One a podcast and some online news stories will never come close to. He'd have them closed down if they tried.

Reuben Sinclair is a sadistic, degrading, hardcore beast of utter filth. The things I've done with him, along with the other Agency founders would scale the heights of any *naughty list* there could be.

That's one of the reasons it's so fucked up exciting.

Yin and Yang swirl endlessly, the two sides of Reuben's coin unfathomable, and it only makes the man more stunning.

I start chewing on my nail extensions.

Santa.

I need to see Santa.

I need to see him, and hear him, and touch him, and play for him.

I need to play for Reuben.

Yeah. I'm fucked.

I had no idea how much pressure she was under to keep our heads above water. It was hard. Very, very hard. I have both huge empathy and sympathy for people battling with similar journeys. It's not easy.

Dawn is breaking through my apartment windows when I break myself out of the stupid spell. I've been obsessing for hours. For once in my career, I haven't even checked out my review from earlier – my only known time of not giving a shit how I performed.

I drag myself to the bathroom and get ready for bed, giving my used pussy a good soaping, even though it makes me wince. I should have taken some time out between proposals, but oh well, fuck it. I've been in considerably worse states. Even with sore pussy syndrome, the inevitable happens when I get under the covers. My used pussy gets another round as I imagine all the things Reuben Sinclair could do to me, and remember all the things he *has* done to me. I wouldn't want to be hooded... or anonymous. I want to look him right in the eye as he takes me however he wants to.

His voice is still on loop.

I had no idea how much pressure she was under to keep our heads above water. It was hard. Very, very hard. I have both huge empathy and sympathy for people battling with similar journeys. It's not easy.

One orgasm about Reuben should be more than enough to send me right off to dreamland, but my head is too wound up. I drift in and out – my hand sliding down between my legs whenever I picture my perfect Santa. I must be on round three by the time afternoon hits, and I can't stand it anymore. Sleep is lost to me. So is my fucking mind.

I know what I have to do. Call it wacko autopilot.

I go for basic makeup since my hands are too wired to work their magic on contouring. I do decent catflicks and slap on some heavy duty lashes, and freshen up the waves in my hair.

43

I don't want to go hoodie and jeans today. I grab a purple dress with fishnets and lace up my trusty big spiky boots. I wrap myself up in a fluffy leopard print coat, like I'm *Cruella de Creamgirl*. Kind of suits me.

I look good in the mirror. Memorable.

As always.

I almost break and message Josh once I'm out in the open and about to hop on the tube. My fingers hover over the message icon, but I can't do it. I know full well he'll talk some sense into me, and I don't want sense, I want the world of crazy. It's screaming my name.

I'm a fucking idiot on a dangerous mission, stalking Santa, but I don't care. It feels like destiny calling – but it's just me, sky high in fantasy land.

Stalking Santa hardly sounds like a romcom with a cutesy happy ever after at the end of it, but Santa was the one who started it in the first place. He was the one in the club last night with a wine glass in his hand.

Central Parade is rammed, with kids everywhere, but my edginess around happily families hardly touches me as I head for the grotto. I take a seat at one of the indoor benches with a decent view of the grotto. I could join the queue myself, and the temptation calls, but it's Reuben Sinclair I want to see today. Not just Santa.

The grotto closes at five, so I've got forty-five minutes of phone scrolling before I stand a chance of getting a glimpse of him. I barely look at the bullshit on my feed, because I'm too transfixed by the door at the grotto exit.

With only twenty minutes left to go, I give up pretending altogether. I let myself fantasise like a crazy.

Reuben could fuck me in the grotto and slap my ass for being a naughty girl, or he could drag me away and punish me for even daring to cross his path uninvited. He could keep me bound and out of view for a whole weekend straight, like the founders have done before. Hooded and at his mercy.

Or he could tell me to fuck off. Blank me like I'm a nobody, or give me a blasé wave and walk away.

Those thoughts hurt, like pokers in the ribs. The idea of being rejected nearly sends me running for the tube, and I kind of wish it would. I could rebook more sessions with my psychotherapist, and fess up to Josh, and avoid diving headfirst into a muddy pit of my own making.

Still, I can't do it.

I'm already locked in.

The minutes count down, and my breaths get so shallow, I struggle to breathe, but I need to see Santa – *Reuben*. I need to see Reuben.

An assistant elf puts the *closed* barrier across the walkway with a few minutes left to go. I watch on until the last little boy in the queue heads on in with his mum. Five minutes later he's jumping and clapping as they come out from the exit. The little guy really thinks he's met Santa, the greatest man in the world, and I'm shuffling in my seat as they pass me, because shit, this is about to get serious.

The teenage photographer heads out first, with his bag slung over his shoulder. Then it's one of the elf volunteers, a young looking blonde who waves at a man in one of the shop doorways and goes to join him.

Come on.

Another elf comes out – an older one this time – and a woman appears for the bucket of donation cash. Shit. I'm twitching with panic, hyped for the grand finale.

It's like I've been hit by a cannonball, straight in the guts when he steps out from behind the grotto door. He's still in his red Santa outfit, but there are no pillows stuffed inside his jacket. His hat is off, and so is his fake white beard. He's the man I've stared at for hours online – Reuben Sinclair – and he's nodding as the woman with the cash bucket talks to him. They smile, and he puts a hand on her shoulder. Friendly.

Fuck my fucking life, I'm actually doing this. I'm stalking Santa.

I'm stalking a multi-millionaire, charity donating, mall owner.

And oh fuck, when he turns in my direction and looks right at me, it's obvious he knows it.

I wonder if I stand any chance of a last-minute dash for the exit while he finishes up talking to the bucket woman, but I'm stuck to the bench like glue. I hate it. I feel so fucking *sick*, like I'm in purgatory, my heart dependant on some insane judgement from a man I shouldn't even know. I'm ready to hurl when he says goodbye to her and walks in my direction. He towers above me when he steps up to the bench.

"What are you doing here, Tiffany?"

I suck in a breath, dragging my character back in place.

"Shopping," I say, trying to mirror his nonchalance from last night.

"Shopping?" He looks around me. I've got nothing but my pissing clutch, I haven't even bought a takeout coffee. At least he'd had a glass of wine in his hand.

The walls of Creamgirl rise up so quickly I don't stand a chance of stopping them. Her personality takes over mine like a safety blanket.

"I was just browsing. Nothing I fancied. Thought I'd take a seat. Chill out a bit."

"You don't seem very *chilled*."

Crap, I'm twisting the rings on my fingers, my knee bouncing at about 120 bpm. Still, I keep my expression intact.

"I doubt I seemed all that chilled when you heard me getting done between the dumpsters last night."

He looks around us, and I curse myself. There are still customers everywhere. *His* customers.

I've pissed him off, I can see it in the turn of his stare, but I like that. I'm a moth to a flame.

"Cut the bravado, Cream," he says. "Yes, I could hear you between the dumpsters, and I could also see through the grotto door every time it opened. You've been staring over for nearly an hour straight, so I'm asking you again, Tiffany. What are you doing here?"

I have to goldfish it, mute. I recognise his voice more than ever now from being hooded. Bound. At his mercy. His power is so strong, it doesn't need to be overstated. It's level calm.

"Call me curious, alright?" I say, my walls cracking. "I came here because I wanted to see you. But you already knew that, Reuben. You're hardly a dumb fuck."

He flinches at the sound of his name. I should have called him Santa.

"I could be anything for all you know. A man can have many faces, and many secrets."

I'm on dangerous turf here. I see the dance of the devil behind his eyes, and it calls me.

"I'm just glad I've managed to see one of your faces for real." I shrug. "Kinda addictive. Been a long time coming."

He scouts around us, smiling at the nearby shoppers.

"Tell me to fuck off, if you want," I say. "I shouldn't be here. Breach of The Agency rules, I know. Give me a disciplinary, if you like."

"We're both guilty of breaking procedures."

"Good job you're the boss then, isn't it?"

His eyes are so fierce.

"Don't be naïve, Creamgirl. Even those at the top of a hierarchy have rules to follow. The top of our hierarchy isn't a one-man podium."

I get an electric shudder at his words. Flashes of all of the men in the sessions… the founders…

"Were you breaking the rules last night?" I ask him. "At Revelier?"

"Yes, and I'm breaking them now, by speaking with you."

My eyes are consumed by his. The mall blurs away.

"Why don't you tell me to fuck off and stay away, then?"

He holds out a hand. His fingers are long. I've had them inside me so many times I've lost count. It feels eerie when I take them and let him help me to my feet.

"Call me curious," he says. "Now, let's get the hell out of here. This isn't a place for conversation."

CHAPTER 5
Tiffany

The corridors behind the stores are an industrial labyrinth. Back entrances, with pallets upon pallets of Christmas stock being delivered, and staff coming and going. Reuben tips his head to acknowledge anyone passing, but I keep my eyes away from theirs. I must stand out like a sore thumb, and my shield of confidence seems to have vanished into nowhere. It's weird. I feel too like *me* inside *me*.

A few storeys up and we're out of industrial turf. Reuben's office is on the top floor of the complex and has the kind of vibe I'd expect from the CEO of a place like this. His desk is massive, and his monitors are so big they look cinematic, but I'm way more interested in the montage of pictures he has up on his wall. Framed shots of him doing charity work. Presenting cheques, or awards, or helping out at events. There's a gorgeous photo of him surrounded by a crowd of pre-schoolers raising their fists in the air. They look so proud of themselves, and he looks so proud of them.

I get another fucking sick jab, right on the underside of my belly. *The softest part.*

Reuben always seems to work with families… single parents and young kids…

The silver fox Santa clears his throat to get my attention. He's by a closet in the corner, half out of his costume. My eyes can't help but rove as he buttons up a fresh shirt. Crazy, really. He's seen every single inch of my body from the neck down – both inside and out, but until yesterday I'd never seen his face, and he hadn't seen mine, at least not in the flesh.

He puts on a light grey suit jacket which complements his dark eyes beyond belief, and gestures me to take a seat as he steps behind his desk. I plonk my butt down on the chair and spin it from side to side like a naughty kid. I hate corporate bullshit. I'd never make it through a single week in an office job, I swear. Feels like I'm here for an interview, not a forbidden conversation, so fuck that shit.

Creamgirl takes over me. I flash him the eye as I loosen my coat.

"Are we on safer turf now? No hidden cameras we have to worry about, or spies out to strike? No boogeymen lurking in the corners?"

Reuben leans forward, elbows on his desk.

"Don't be a smartass, Tiffany. You have no idea what goes on behind the scenes, and you wouldn't want to."

I laugh. "You so sure about that? I can't lie, I kinda have a thing about the founders. You may have noticed. The more terrifying, the better."

"And you may have noticed you're always hooded," he says. "There's a reason for that."

He may appear calm on the surface, but my attitude is pissing him off. I can feel his energy without needing to see it, which figures. It's always been part of my job.

"Don't worry, Santa. Your dirty secrets are safe with me, *baby*."

I pretend zip my mouth shut.

Creamgirl's walls are scaling high, and my bravado is grating me – so fuck knows how it's grating Reuben with no dick action involved. In a way I wish my entertainer mode would fuck off and leave me alone for a while, but I'd feel kinda floppy without it.

Vulnerable.

Scared.

Reuben doesn't speak, and neither do I. He stares at me, and I stare back, with Creamgirl's smirk still coy on my lips, playing the horny hooker. I figure he'll break first and launch into convo, but his eyes don't waver, and he sits deadly calm, as though he has all the time in the world.

It's weird. Really fucking weird.

I feel more exposed with his eyes on my face than I do in a hood with my asshole stretched open. The way it makes my heart race is ridiculous.

I swing in my chair, finally breaking the lock of our eyes to point over to one of the pictures on the wall.

"You seem like a nice guy."

"Thank you."

"I'd never have expected you to be one of the founders if I hadn't bounced my butt on your lap. I wouldn't have put you down as one. Never. Not in a million years."

"Really? And why is that?"

I shrug. "Just wouldn't. Helping homeless families one minute, then spraying piss all over bound, bruised tits the next. Kinda weird combination."

I lock eyes again to see if my words have hit, but he's still as composed as ever.

"I really can't see how those two interests are related. Everything we do at The Agency is completely consensual and well rewarded. Entertainers can tap out at a moment's notice, as you know." He pauses. "We're not devil worshipping savages, Tiffany. We're a collection of men who like hardcore sex, and hence set up The Agency to facilitate it."

My interest is piqued at that.

"Come on, then. Spill the beans. How many are in this *collection*? How many founders are there?"

He raises his eyebrows. "I'm not at liberty to say."

My mind trawls through some of the scenes I've had with these guys. Sometimes I've attempted to count the number of people around me. I've tried to keep track, even though they've been a blur.

"Seven?" I guess. "Maybe eight?"

"I'll repeat my answer. I'm not at liberty to say." Reuben's tone is no nonsense. He's not going to be laughing with me over this topic of conversation, that's plain to see.

This is such a weird fucking setup – charitable Santa behind a monster of a desk, in his flash suit with his dark inquisitive eyes, and his hero pics all over the wall. You'd never figure he was one of the beasts who use me like a piece of slutty meat for tens of thousands of pounds a go.

"Why did you come to the club last night?" I ask, like this is a round of twenty questions.

He tips his head. "I was curious. Just like you were today."

"Curious of how I sounded in a dodgy scene with another punter?" I grin. "I hope I lived up to your expectations."

"I hated that part, actually. I much prefer it when I'm in control of the scene." He cracks a hint of a smile. "Being on the sidelines of such filth is like smelling impressive cologne in the air, only to find you're not the one who's wearing it."

My mind whirs.

"So, you *are* usually in control of the scenes? You *are* the top of the tree? Caught you."

He laughs as I jab a finger, and his dark humoured magnetism strikes up again. I stop spinning side to side in the chair because the lurch in my stomach can't handle it.

"I'm usually in control of *your* scenes, specifically," he says. "We all have our personal preferences."

My mind spins, trying to catch hold of his implication. *My scenes, specifically.*

"You mean that, you, um…"

He nods before I finish. "Yes, Tiffany. I usually choose you. As I said, we all have our personal preferences. We all have our favourite entertainers. You happen to be mine."

I get a dumbass glow at his words. I must look like one of the kids on the pictures doing an air punch.

I'm Santa's favourite. What an achievement.

I can guess why, of course.

"Ah, you like the plus sized box ticked."

"Yes, I'm very much a fan of curves, but that's not the deciding factor. Far from it. You're not just a plus size girl. There are other elements at play."

I smirk, back on familiar turf. Cream is in her element.

"Ha, yeah. I get it. I'm a curvy girl who also happens to be a dirty bitch who can take just about anything. Especially when it comes to anal. I know you like that, Reuben. Oh, and tit bondage."

I squeeze my cleavage for effect, but steely-eyed Santa shakes his head.

"You put yourself down through your brashness, Tiffany. There are a thousand tiny details that give you the gold star on my favourites list. It's not just how big your tits are, and how much you can take in your ass."

The question *like what?* is on the tip of my tongue, because I'd like to hear every one of those thousand tiny details, straight from Santa's beautiful mouth. *Me,* not Creamgirl. *I'd* love to hear every little thing that's cemented the interest of a man like him.

But I can't ask him. I'm way too fucking nervous.

I start up the chair spinning again, with Cream's dirty grin on my face.

"Well, for what it's worth, you've got a golden star on my favourites list, too. Especially now I've seen your face, you filthy stud."

He cocks a brow. "Is that so?"

"I wouldn't be here if you didn't. You got me good yesterday, Mr Sinclair."

I watch Reuben's face turn serious. Shit. I tense up.

"You shouldn't be here regardless," he says. "I should never have joined you at the club, and I should never have brought you to this office. I should have waved the association away as nothing, and taken you off my click list without hesitation."

A flash of horror zaps through me. A *click list.*

"You haven't done that, have you? Taken me off your click list?"

"Not yet. No."

I've got goldfish gob again. The thought of being ghosted by him unfathomable. I can't even…

Suddenly the temperature in here is roasting. I'm burning up in the flames of WTF have I fucking done.

"Are you going to? That means never booking me again, I'm guessing?"

Reuben sighs. "I should take you off the list, Tiffany. The blindfold has come off, quite literally. That can't be undone."

"Yeah, should, should, should, whatever. But are you *going* to?" I feel sick, and the Creamgirl side of me trips up, losing control. "Because if you're going to bin me off your list, just tell me now and get it over with. I don't want to start getting all fucking jumpy when proposals come in, hoping it'll be you. I don't want to act like a sad, jilted ex or some shit."

He raises his perfect eyebrows. "That's quite a dramatic way of putting it."

I shrug. "I'm quite a dramatic girl."

He smirks at that. "Yes, you are. That's one of the reasons you're *on* my click list, actually. You've got a tremendous range of curses when you're fighting the game."

I want to smirk along, but I can't. I look at my hands in my lap and not at him, because he hasn't answered the question. It's freaking me out, waiting for the Royal thumb to go up or down.

"Tiffany," he says, his serious tone returning. "There is a very strict code that everyone in our organisation adheres to. You included."

I knew it. He's going to bin me off.

"Maybe if you hadn't stalked me to a club last night, you wouldn't have had to strike me off your damn click list at all."

He shakes his head. "That's not true. I would have had to strike you off as soon as you recognised me, face to face."

"But you didn't."

"No. I didn't."

I'm perplexed, flustered. *Out of control.*

"Do you have to? Really? Because I won't say anything. I can be hooded and play dumb, *Santa.* I won't shout my mouth off and scream your name."

His gaze sucks me in, still the calm in the eye of the storm.

"I'd hope not."

The Royal thumb is still hanging, and I can't hack this. I'm already too invested in the fantasy of a man I only discovered yesterday. I'm such a fucking dickhead.

I have to baulk and run, to try to save a scrap of Creamgirl's pride.

"I'll go," I say, and get up. "It's fine, it's cool. You're the boss. Knock me off the click list and I'll get over it. I've got plenty other appointments on my calendar."

"Tiffany," he says as I smooth my coat. "Sit down."

"What's the point if your mind is made up? Go on, strike me off. Sorry I saw your face, okay? I loved those fucking proposals."

"THEN SIT DOWN!"

Holy shit, his voice booms out of nowhere, and the prickles shoot right up my arms.

I'd know that tone a mile off. It's chided me when I'm a hissing bitch, cursing and wailing and protesting before I turn into a dirty little kink slut and suck it up.

I sit my butt back in the chair, but I don't speak. He's seized the power from me in a heartbeat.

"There is no doubt I should adhere to the requirements of the organisation, and refrain from selecting you as our entertainer for the founders' gatherings, but…" Reuben pauses, and I'm fucking quivering, as though he's about to dump me off a bridge. "I do have another account at The Agency. One for more personal use."

"Personal use?"

Ah-ha. My eyes light up, because I get it. I'm as sharp as a knife sometimes.

The account Ella was talking about. The inactive client who reached out to her for the charity gig last Christmas…

Reuben leans forward again, reinforcing his stare.

"Assure me that you will stick to The Agency contract, though. Absolute discretion and client confidentiality at all costs."

I don't even have to think about it.

"Cross my heart and hope to die, so help me God."

Santa's stare cracks into a smile.

"Again, that's a rather dramatic way of putting it."

I smile back. "What did you expect? Pinky promise?" I can hardly believe my own nerve when I get to my feet and offer him my pinky. And fuck, how my pussy flutters when he actually offers his, our little fingers tugging together.

"There now," I say, sitting my ass back down, "all sorted."

It's such a relief to feel Creamgirl back at the fore.

Reuben shakes his head. "You're incorrigible," he says.

I hold my head high. "Which is why you love me so much."

He sits back in his chair and sighs. "I have business to attend to this evening, unfortunately, but make sure to keep an eye on your inbox. You may have a proposal coming in soon."

"Ah, ok. Cool. You'd better get your proposal in pretty quick though, because my schedule is kinda busy, you know."

"Yes, I do know." He smirks. "You're off to play with a couple of guys tomorrow evening, aren't you?"

Fuck, he really has been snooping.

I tap my nose. "That's none of your business. Client confidentiality."

He likes the way I poke my tongue out, I see it in his eyes, and fucking phew for that.

"I guess I'll leave you to it, User Unknown," I say, getting to my feet. "Catch you later. I'll be checking my inbox."

"I hope so."

He raises a hand as I wave him goodbye, and I get out of there, despite his offer to walk me down. I tell him I'll follow the exit signs. Easy peasy lemon squeezy. Truth is, I think I'd fucking combust from just walking by his side.

I manage to navigate the maze and the bustle of the mall with my grin still at the max, but my heart in is my throat as the situation replays in my mind.

He could have said no and binned me off.

But he said I'm his favourite.

His fucking FAVOURITE!

Still, he could have said no and binned me off.

But he didn't.

Not yet anyway...

By the time I'm out on the street my hands are trembling, my screaming soul desperate to call Josh and talk things through. To get his perspective, his opinion, his surprise and common sense... and security.

But I don't do it.

For once, I don't do it. I can't.

I gave Reuben Sinclair a pinky promise, and I'm never going to break it.

CHAPTER 6
Tiffany

User 3081. 34. Male.

My boyfriend and I are seeking a dirty girl to join in on our playtime. We like to share. Primarily we like to share a hot, horny ass that can take two at once. Big tits that can bounce. A curvy butt like a treasure trove. We'll use it hard.

Pussy is a bonus, of course. We enjoy a slick pussy as lube.

Oh, and look like you're a filthy hooker, please. Dress up real fucking kinky.

Duration: 4 hours.
Proposal fee: £4,000.

Mediocre money, but I love double anal, and I like being treated like a treasure trove. My butt cheeks are curvy enough to merit the honour.

I always think of threesomes as two for the price of one. On my part, not theirs.

These two should be a sweet festive appetiser for my rammed pre-Christmas calendar. I've seen these guys mentioned on the Agency forum a lot recently, and they are a hot duo, apparently, with a major liking for double anal – their proposal is playing it down. One of the threads says these guys enjoy lap bouncing. I'll bounce on their laps, alright. I've got just the body for the job, on both counts. They won't know what's hit them.

The booking is at a hotel in Chelsea, and I know it's going to be a night of extravagance as soon as I step into the foyer. It's got a huge crystal chandelier that could outshine the sun – streams and streams of diamonds that light up the room. I gawp up at it, wishing I could slap a huge wedge of cash down on the counter for them to yank it down from the ceiling and hand it over. I could do it, in theory, but nah. You'd need a whole tower block or a country mansion to house the bloody thing.

I click *arrived* on the app and walk on by.

Suite 37 pings back, and I get the elevator with no nerves whatsoever. I'm so used to this game that I could take a decent helping of double anal all night long. I only hope my clients will grace me with a round of two in the pussy beforehand. I'm a spoiled cow who craves it. Creamgirl always loves the cream.

The hotel door opens as soon as I knock. The guy that stands aside to let me in is a suave looking blond, with a cracking smile and gorgeous cheeky dimples. I get the impression he'd be fun on a night out. His boyfriend steps up to his side, and they look kinda similar. Only blond number two is shorter and stockier, and his eyebrows are sharper over his bright blue eyes. I like that. Makes him look like he's ready to rumble.

"Hey, guys," I say, and loosen the belt of my coat, slipping it off as they watch me.

I've gone for a tiny red PVC dress, which highlights every single one of my curves as well as my freshly dyed hair. My tits are spilling so far over the top that they are fit to burst, and the skirt is riding up my ass so far that my cheeks must be showing. They wanted a slut that looks like a slut, and they got one. I've got fishnet holdups on, and a lacy thong that's barely more than a thread.

Blond number one gives his boyfriend a high five.

"Good choice, Jase."

"I think I've hit the jackpot, Cal."

"Maybe." Cal gives me the eye. "Guess we'll find out, won't we?"

Cal and Jase. I assign it to memory. I'm good with names.

Cal takes my coat and hangs it on the back of the door. "We take it in turns to choose our entertainers, Creamgirl," he says. "It's a fun pastime."

Jase puts an arm around his boyfriend's shoulder. "Last time around, Cal made a crap choice. The cutie wimped out and left us twenty minutes in. Talked a good game, but didn't take a good ass fucking."

I give my curvy ass a pat. "You won't be having that problem with me. I think my rating speaks for itself."

I wonder who the entertainer was who tapped out. Probably a newbie, biting off more than her butthole could chew. Happens sometimes.

"What rating did you give her?" I ask, even though it's none of my business.

"Four," Cal says. "She was nice enough while it lasted. We got double pussy out of her."

"Four stars? You guys are generous," I give my boobs a grope. "I'll be expecting a straight up five, then."

Cal's smirk is dirty. "Expect what you like, just as long as you earn it."

I whip him up a dirty smirk right back. "I'll earn every penny, not just the five-star review."

I'm not lying. I never do. Being a hooker has been about more than cash for me ever since I started. Sure, the money was insane, and it took a fuck ton of pinching myself to realise it was really real and in my bank account, but my competitive streak has always been at the fore, in line with my filthy kink cravings. I always relish a five-star review.

I'm pretty safe with these two guys, that much is clear. Two cocks in my ass and I'll get their thumbs up. Sweet, but hardly a stretch for me. Literally. It's a cute but easy one. Just a fun round of filth.

I'm preparing to sink into nothing but the smut when a thumper of emotion hits me in the guts. It's the way Cal looks at Jase, and the way Jase ruffles his hair, like they are sharing a beautiful moment in their fun time. Love. Absolute, unconditional devotion to each other. It's undeniable, even though they're about to fuck a hooker.

These two guys are besotted with each other. The emotion simmers between them.

Just like it used to between me and Kian… or so I thought.

No. I'm not going there.

I give the guys a spin, slapping my butt as I go. I'm Creamgirl, and this is work. No strings, no emotions, nothing but sex.

It always is.

"Come on, lovebirds. Don't let the minutes run away. You're missing out here."

Jase breaks away from Cal and gestures to the mini bar. "Champers first?"

I'd normally say yes, but not tonight. I don't want it. No small talk, no cutesy flirty drinks. I just want to get down to what I'm paid for.

"I prefer cum over bubbly, thanks."

They both raise their eyebrows, then crack each other another grin.

"I guess that's why you call yourself Creamgirl," Cal says.

"Sure is. I never, ever turn down a good helping."

"We can give you a good helping." Jase's gaze drops to my tits. "Shift your hot fucking ass over to the bed, and show us what we're going to be getting."

I do a curtesy. "Your wish is my command."

Their hotel bed is massive, the sheets already crumpled from where they've been sleeping – or fucking. They want to see what they're getting. Sure thing. I wriggle out of my dress as they watch me, keen eyes on my tits as they fall free, then I climb on the bed and lie down on my back, heels up on the sheets as I open my thighs. My lacy thong is on full display, and I tug it tighter, so they'll see the crotch turn into a sopping wet string between my pussy lips.

"Like what you see?" I ask them, rubbing my fingers up and down my bulging slit.

Both of them stare at me, and I get another fucking pang as Cal takes Jase's hand, giving it a squeeze in silent acknowledgement. Two guys in love, sharing some fun.

"You're one hot girl, you know that?" Jase says, clearly trying to be flattering, but I don't need that crap.

"Don't worry about being gentlemen. You can call me a slut. You can call me a hooker, or a whore, or a dirty fucking bitch whose ass is going to gobble up your dicks like candy canes."

He laughs and I watch him shift on his feet, and I read his language loud and clear – another skill of mine. I'm adept. These two weren't talking about a sweet hot girl joining them when they were fucking each other at the thought. No chance. Their real fantasies would have been all about a kinky slut. Dirty, filthy, two on one fucking.

"Come on," I say, crushing my tits together. "Do it. Call me a slut hooker. Try me out for size."

Cal approaches the side of the bed and palms his cock through his jeans. "That's what you like to be called, a slut hooker?"

"That's what I am." I lick my lips as I stare at the bulge in his trousers. "So treat me like one. Take what you paid for."

"Alright. *Your* wish is *our* command."

He leans over and hooks his fingers in the lace of my panties, tugging tighter than I did. My pussy lips are so puffy. So chubby and swollen. It must be a sight.

He smiles over at his boyfriend. "A tit each?"

"They're some tits," Jase says, "she could feed an army." He climbs up the bed on the opposite side of me.

I have two hot mouths on my tits in seconds, lapping and slurping in tandem. They are good, I'll give them that. Jase is especially skilled with the tongue action, giving big wet swirls around my nipple.

"That's so good, guys," I say. "These big beauties are all for you, and they're aching to be sucked."

My words fuel the fire. Their mouths get wetter, and their laps turn to sucks, Cal causing bliss on one of my nipples with his teeth. I hold their heads to me, and my words come naturally with Cal's fingers still hooked in my thong.

"Use my cunt as well. Use me. Play with me. Take everything. Every filthy fucking thing you've ever wanted."

Two sets of fingers pull my thong to the side, and they moan in tandem as their hands join forces, both of them exploring at the same time – pumping thick fingers into my pussy.

"Go on, harder. Deeper. See how much I can take. Because I want

both your cocks as well, you dirty, hot bastards. Both at once, in my face, in my cunt, in my desperate fucking asshole."

Jase breaks away from my tit, his lips puffed up. "Is this really you, or just an act? You don't need to pretend to get us off. We'll love it anyway."

I look him straight in the eyes. Deadpan. "What do you think? Honestly? Think this is an act?"

Our eyes hold contact, burning. He's reading me as he fingers me along with his boyfriend, the love of his life still sucking on my tit like a hungry baby.

"No. I don't think you're pretending," he says, and I let out a laugh.

"You think right. I'm the filthiest fucking slut you'll ever know."

"The filthiest ever?" Jase says. "That's a big claim."

"Yeah, it is a big claim, and I always live up to it. Try it. Give me some filthy action."

That fuels the fire. Jase doesn't give a fuck for complimentary shared exploration anymore. He shoves four fingers in my pussy alongside Cal's, and I groan at the beautiful stretch.

"Shame we didn't put fisting on the proposal," he says.

I buck against his hand. "Call it prep for the main event. Go on! Do it!"

He shakes his head. "The rules say absolutely no deviating from the agreement."

I buck again.

"Fuck the rules. If my cunt is gonna take two meaty dicks, it needs a warmup. A decent fist should do."

I love his grin as he twists his fingers and pushes harder, testing.

"Get your fist in me and quit teasing," I tell him, and his boyfriend breaks away from my nipple. They both look at me as I squirm for them. "You paid for my whore body, so take it. Make the most of it."

They both shuffle down the bed, and I have to close my eyes to blank out the joy they find in each other's smiles. It makes me ache, and it's so pointless and stupid, it's fucking ridiculous.

"Do it, Jase," I hear, and I reach down to circle my clit, hitching up higher to give them better access.

I'm not ready for the stretch of a full fist, but I don't give a toss. I brace myself and take the pressure as Jase works his hand up to the knuckles, moaning like the whore I am as I push back against him. Fuck the pain. I'm going to take two cocks later anyway, and I hope they're girthy. I want them to stretch my cunt as well as my asshole, so let's get with it.

"Need some lube?" Jase asks, but I shake my head.

"No. I want to feel every fucking inch, pure and raw."

"Are you serious?"

"You've never fisted a girl before, have you?"

He shakes his head. Bless him.

I clench around his fingers. "I've had a hundred fists up there. All you have to do is push, and I'll take it."

"Fucking hell," he says. "Really? You sure about that?"

"Oh yeah, I'm sure."

"Jesus, Jase," Cal says, his voice breathy. *Excited.* "Go on, do it. Get your hand in there. Plug her up."

"Now you're talking," I say. "I love filthy words as well as actions. Practice what you preach, boys."

I'm edging them, and that's my job. To set my clients' fantasies free. To break into their deepest desires and let them loose. *That's* what gets me so many glowing five starrers.

"Keep going," I say. "Talk dirty. It's so fucking hot."

The guys look at each other again, words flying between them that don't need to be spoken aloud.

"Plug that needy cunt," Cal says.

"I'm getting there, baby," Jase tells him, pushing a little harder. "Don't fucking worry."

"Nah, you're not. Give her what she really wants. She wants to be a slut who takes it, so make her fucking take it."

Cal's definitely got with the plot. I'd give him a thumbs up if I wasn't so preoccupied with the hand between my legs.

I raise myself on my elbows, straining to see over my huge, spit covered tits. I want to watch Jase's hand working its way inside me. I can't see all of it, since my tits and belly are too big, but I can see the way Cal takes hold of Jase's wrist and urges him on. I like Cal. He's a dirtier player.

"Need a helping *hand?*" he says.

Jase grins and licks his lips. He's fucking drooling.

"Yeah," he says, "help me in."

With that, Cal tightens his grip on his boyfriend's wrist and eases him into me.

I groan as Jase's knuckles pop inside, tipping my head back as my pussy gobbles him up. I'm caught up in my body now, consumed by the pulsing of my pussy as it clenches around a whole fucking hand.

"Twist it," I say. "Please, just twist."

Jase does what I ask, and I cry out as his thumb knuckle hits the spot.

"THERE! Yes. Fuck, yes. Like that. Please, fuck me like that."

He starts slowly, in and out just a touch. I bounce back against him as my pussy relaxes, my tits bobbing against my chin as I go.

"Such a slut," Cal says, and I nod.

"Yeah, I am. Tell me."

"You're a dirty, desperate, cum hungry slut."

It's great how the words sound from him. These guys don't usually play this game, that much is clear.

"Make me ready for two meaty cocks." I buck on his fist. "I want both of you inside me. I want you to fuck me harder than you've ever fucked a slut in your life."

With Jase's knuckle at the spot, it's going to be so easy to come like this, my tits bouncing for them like a horny bitch. I love the squelch as he speeds up. I go crazy for the depth as he pulls his hand all the way out and plunges it back in again.

I shuffle to the edge of the bed when he's out of me, squatting over the mattress as I offer my slick pussy for more. It's great in this position. I leverage my arms and brace myself so I'm practically sitting on his hand when he gets down between my legs, Cal eager to follow him.

It's me riding his fist now. He holds it still as I bounce myself up and down, panting every time his hand sinks in. They are fixated, staring at my pussy as I take it.

"I want a turn," Cal says, and they switch positions.

His hand is dry when his fingers line up, but I lower myself in one, grinning as my pussy manages to swallow him.

"That feels so fucking good," he says.

"You're telling me."

I bounce and groan until I hit the peak, letting out a *fuck, fuck, yes, fucking yes* as I come for the first round. They must have read my profile and know that I'm a squirter, but still, the pair of them start in shock as the gush begins to flow, jetting out around Cal's fist as I lose control. My body is lost to me, my mind blown as the pleasure rocks me through and through.

I'm still on the come down as Jase strips bare and climbs up on the bed. He pulls me backwards, and I know the drill as I lower my back to his chest and wriggle higher, until my thighs are hooked over his. I'm probably crushing the fuck out of him, but that doesn't matter for shit. Cal guides his boyfriend's cock into my pussy, then strips bare himself. As soon as he's naked he's straight on top, pinning me between them as he shoves his cock in for a double.

Bonus. They are both decent and girthy.

I'm still dripping and squelching as they start up with the thrusting. Now it's *their* turn for the pleasure. I clench my muscles to grip them tight, and they both groan in surprise. Yet another thing they weren't expecting. I do so many rounds of pelvic floor every day it's unreal.

I wrap my arms around Cal's shoulders and pull him closer. "Come on, you dirty bastards. Show me what you've got and get this greedy slut fucked."

It's not just me consumed by my body now. These guys' heads are out of the picture, their dicks controlling their minds. They pound me like animals, shaft to shaft as they share one hole. The grunts they make speak louder than words, giving me their all. I can see why the last entertainer wimped out on them. Taking these two in the ass is gonna be a decent fucking challenge.

"Fill me up," I tell them. "Give me two loads of thick, creamy cum."

It pushes Cal over the edge first, and his moan sets off his boyfriend, his shaft being grated by Cal's speed. I'm so proud of myself when they unload after just a few minutes. Cal is so in the groove that he looks kinda dizzy as he pulls out and stares at the mess he's left behind – his boyfriend's cock still inside me. What a fucking view. I push down so he can see the cum dribbling, and feel the horny slop of more when Jase's cock pulls free.

I rub my fingers between my pussy lips, scooping a lovely glob of cum and opening my mouth wide. I let it drip onto my tongue, then suck it all off, murmuring as I go.

"Nice work, guys."

I roll off Jase, and he is nearly as dazed as his boyfriend, but he's grinning. Cal pulls him up off the bed, and they admire me like a trophy as I scoop up another mouthful.

Jase wraps his arm around Cal's waist and they share a look of accomplishment before Cal leans into him for a kiss.

I normally love to watch guys kissing. My fingers are usually straight to my clit. But not today.

I stare at the two of them as Jase takes Cal's face in his hands, both of them smiling, mouth to mouth as they make out like teenagers in love. I get butterflies as Cal runs his fingers up his lover's back, but they aren't the kind of *aww, guys* kind of butterflies I get when something sweet but horny goes down. It's more like a sickening lurch.

They smile down at me when they are finished making out, my legs still spread, with cum dribbling out of me. Jase holds out a hand, and I let him help me up, feeling dizzy myself at being between the pair of them.

"Maybe I'll take a swig of that champers now." I laugh, and they laugh back, unaware of my discomfort. Just like everyone always is.

Just like I usually am.

Jase goes to the mini bar in the buff and the two of them are beaming as he pops the champagne cork. I push off the bed and grab the bottle off him, glugging back the fizz like it's a spurting cock, and it makes the two of them laugh again. Cal pours the rest into actual glasses.

We do a *cheers* together, and I neck my glass back in one. I'd ask for another, but I don't want to get too carried away with the drinking, and I definitely don't want to get caught up in the conversation that generally accompanies it.

Shame for me that they are still waiting for their balls to fill back up, taking a hiatus. They sip their champagne slowly, beaming at me like we're a cutesy trio.

"What got you into being an Agency worker?" Cal asks, and I could groan.

So much for not wanting conversation.

"I don't think you'd have to be a genius to work out the answer." I give them an eyelash flutter. "Sex. I've always been a filthy bitch. Getting paid for it fits my ideal career to a T. It wasn't exactly mentioned by the careers mentor at college, but luckily I figured it out for myself."

"You're a cracker," Jase says with a smirk.

"Thanks." I switch the conversation one-eighty to stop any more probing. "So, what got you into *wanting* an Agency worker?"

They smile at each other before Jase turns back to me.

"I don't think you'd have to be a genius to work out the answer to that either, Cream. Sex. We're filthy bastards who like pussy as well as cock." He looks down at Cal's dick, which is already on the rise, thank fuck. "In the main, cock is more than enough to keep us entertained, but every now and again we fancy a little *entertainment.*"

"Plus, we love sharing ass," Cal pipes up. "Not just fucking each other's. Pussy is an obvious bonus."

"I hope you've been enjoying mine."

"Understatement."

Jase chuckles. "Don't need to be a genius to work that out, either."

I get a nice glow at that.

"I hope you'll enjoy my ass just as much."

Cal puts a finger to his chin, fake pondering.

"Hmm. Somehow I think we'll enjoy it even more."

"More than my pussy?" I spread my legs and tut. "I really need to raise the bar."

Jase still has his chuckle face on. It suits him.

"Don't think you need to be a genius to know your bar is already off the scale."

"Five starrer for me, then?"

"I'd say that was a given. We'd give you a five star on those gorgeous tits alone."

"Then *you* need to raise *your* bar." I mash my beauties together, covered in dry spit. "These bad boys are impressive, but a five-star review isn't to be given lightly."

"Is that so?"

"Hell yeah. Ratings are everything. We have to earn them."

"Ah." Jase nods, twigging. "I get it. Top of the tree and all that. Don't worry, we saw you were at the top. You and another hot goth girl. Holly, was it?"

My mind flashes to Holly – Ella – likely all cosied up with Josh right now, planning their lovely Christmas with his family. Happens every year, and I usually gatecrash.

"Yeah, Holly. She's a superstar. We share the superstar tit vibe as well as the goth one."

"You don't share the curvy, hot butt side, though. You're higher on the chart for us."

I turn to give my ass a slap. "Cheers to that." I look at his cock, on the rise as well as Cal's. "How about you start using it? Cocks are growing and the clock's ticking."

There is no protest when I walk back over to the bed and pat the mattress beside me. The guys simply down the rest of their champers and join me, cocks ready to play all over again – but not just with me. I can read it in their eyes.

They don't just want my ass, they want each other's.

"You know what I love?" I say, tuning in. "Watching guys fuck each other makes me so horny it's off the scale. Seriously. Fancy giving me the honour of showing me how you two get it on?"

Cal takes hold of Jase's dick, working it in his hand like a pro.

"I'd be game. I love being watched with my cock in Jase's ass."

"She may want to see yours filled up with mine," Jase points out with an eyebrow raise, but Cal laughs. His laugh is kinda like mine, actually. If he was really roaring with it, we could sound quite similar.

"Doesn't matter what preference she has." He gives me a cheeky smirk. "She's the slut after all."

"Quite right," I say. "Go for it, boys. I'm dying to watch in either direction."

Cal shoves Jase backwards on the bed and climbs on top of him as Jase mock protests. Within seconds they are all over each other, deep kissing as their hands rove. Cal grinds against his boyfriend, cock to cock, and I dunno why I expected it to be an all fours job with a bit of ass slapping and backchat, but I did. Seeing them like this isn't what I figured I'd be privy to. A dumbass error on my part. As Jase raises his legs and moans against Cal's mouth, it's like watching a movie of true adoration.

Cal is so gentle as he lines his dick up for Jase's ass. He calls him *baby* – just a whisper, but loud enough that I can hear.

I don't touch myself, just stare as the scene unfolds, because it's beautiful. Two guys making love, not just fucking. With my bank of clients, it's normally just filth. Degradation, and kink, and being treated like a piece of meat, but this…

I stamp down another pang and get back into Cream

headspace. I watch Cal's cock moving in and out of Jase, loving how Jase's brown puckered hole takes the invasion. I barely exist here as they get into the groove. I could legit back away and out of the door and I swear the pair of them would barely notice.

I'm not used to this. At all. I'm supposed to be hot in on the action. They're paying for me, so I'm not going to keep my gob shut and let them waste their cash.

"That's hot as fuck," I tell them, and both of them shoot a look straight over to me. I spread my legs and play with myself, resuming centre stage. "I've still got so much cum in here," I say, and give my pussy a decent squelch. "You're making me jealous, you know. I'm desperate for ass action myself now." They pause in motion as I tease my ass with a finger. "Only I want two, not just one."

Cal's eyes zone in on me, clearing as he comes out of his loved up euphoria.

"Good job, since that's what we asked for." He gives Jase's thigh a slap as he pulls his dirty cock out and heads my way.

I'm a major fan of ass to ass with no cleanup. I'm grinning when Cal shoves me onto my back and hoists my legs up.

"Didn't want any lube earlier, but how about now? Going to change your filthy slut mind?"

I hitch a breath. "Nope."

"No?"

"Not a chance in hell."

"Fine. Then take it, *slut*."

He slams his filthy dick into me in one, and I groan like the perfect hooker I am as I eat it up for him. It's not my only hole available, either. My mouth is lolling wide when Jase crawls over the bed to join us. He pushes his cock straight in, bulging my cheek out.

"Her cunt is leaking cum like a waterfall over here," Cal laughs. "Take a look."

Jase's dick is still in my mouth as he leans over me, the two of them examining my pussy like I'm a museum specimen, splaying me open. They finger poke me, and Jase catches my clit with a dream flick. I groan to let him know it.

"Like that, do you?" he asks, like it's not obvious.

He does it again and I give another groan, sucking him harder. Now *this* is a decent fucking three way. They'd get five stars from me if the roles were reversed. Jase rubs my clit as his boyfriend fucks my ass, and I suck his cock like I was born for it, enjoying a damn good spit roasting. My view is blocked, but I can still hear them kissing above me. I'm a flesh toy as they whisper loving words.

I focus on my clit, and the way it's sparking. I clench my ass as hard as I can, and suck Jase as deep as my throat can take him. I'm squirming as I start the ascent to climax. Jase has got some skills. Some real fucking skills. Fuck.

They don't stop pounding me as I come. I splutter around Jase's cock, trying to moan as I choke, but he doesn't let up – his hips keep on pistoning as he drives into my face. Cal's cock slams my ass on a mission, and the guys don't stop it with their intimacy. Still kissing. Still whispering. *Still loving.*

I feel Jase's dick tightening, and I'm close to getting a mouthful of cum. I swallow while he's in my throat, the head of his cock rammed in tight.

"No, it's too soon," he says, and pulls away from me. He catches his breath as his balls hang over my face, and I giggle as I lap at them. "I want to share her ass," he tells his boyfriend, and I groan as Cal leaves my ass void of his girthy dick.

Luckily, it won't be for long.

My clit is on a high as they yank me up and shift me until I'm all fours, then hoist me onto Cal. I straddle him, taking him straight in. I bounce on his dick afresh, because it's where it belongs. Deep in my ass. I ride him like a tit jigging cowgirl, my chunky thighs gripping him like a vice until Jase shoves me forward without mercy and I'm pinned right over again. Freedom gone as Jase lowers his weight onto my back and lines his dick up against Cal's.

"You sure you can you take it?" he asks, and I nod against Cal's shoulder.

"Fuck, yes. Get in there."

I cry out with an *oww, shit* as he strains to dig his way in. My butt is used to two, but my muscles still fight, the strain hurting like a bitch until the spit covered head of him pops inside. After that it's a free-for-all, both guys going for it with grunts and groans.

Double anal is one of my favourites. I've been an ass girl since I first found out what being an ass girl felt like, and I'm in my element as they slam in sync, then alternate, back and forth.

I reach back and spread my butt cheeks as best I can, giving them access to deeper. I want them as deep as they can fucking go. I want to feel them in my goddamn fucking stomach. I want to feel the burn for days.

Shame for me that these two are already well on the way to shooting their load. It's both a blessing and curse for being so good at my job. I get a tick in the box of proud slut when they judder and start to blow, but I could go all night, loving every fucking second.

I encourage them, wanting them to fly high.

"Give my slutty fucking ass your cum, guys. Show me how deep you can spurt. Give me a good fucking load."

I'm still pinned between them in the aftermath, their chests heaving as they catch their breath. Their dicks are still pulsing in my ass, and I relish it with clench after clench after filthy fucking clench. Sloppy and crammed.

Still, it burns when they pull out. Jase opens my ass crack for viewing, and I wink my asshole for him, pushing out their cum in little splutters. Double whammy. Cunt and ass both testament to their cummy efforts.

"Look at this, Cal," Jase says, and rolls me off his boyfriend until I flop on the bed. I raise my legs and practically shit their jizz out of me, both of them staring in wonder before they lock eyes.

"Want to clean our hot slut up?" Cal asks with a smirk. He looks up at the clock. Still thirty minutes to go. "Let's get our money's worth."

"Go for it, boys," I tell them, and push out another slop.

Two hungry mouths dive between my legs, lapping and digging. I splay my meaty slit for them, giving them access to the full butterfly, and my clit is still fucking buzzing as Cal's tongue catches. Goddamn it. I have at least another orgasm in the bank, but no. They finish up with ten minutes left on the clock, kissing each other with filthy mouths and more loving smiles.

I haul myself from the bed, grinning at the mess we've made of their posh hotel sheets. The cleaners are going to get quite a shocker.

I grab my dress and get myself back into it, making sure it's covering my tits in some form of decency, then wriggle until the PVC covers my butt, checking myself out in the mirror. I look as used up as the bedsheets.

My two hot clients are still kissing, fully absorbed in each other when the clock hits the farewell mark.

I call out a *"thanks for having me, guys,"* and they give me a thumbs up and a wave.

"Thanks, Cream, you were one hot fucking slut," Cal says, and he winks at me with his cheeky smirk on his face.

"Still am," I say and pat my sore ass.

I'd definitely get it on with him outside of this place. I can feel it in the vibe.

"Five starrer, please," I say and blow them a kiss before I leave, but I already know I've got it in the bag.

Talking of bags, I pull my phone out of mine as soon as I'm in the hotel hallway, ready to send a *D&S* message to Josh, but a different kind of notification stops me on my stilettos.

No way.

No fucking way.

This User number has been emblazoned into my memory since Ella first mentioned it in the mall.

User 5639. Male. 48.

Santa.

My orgasm heartrate pales in comparison to this one. My fingers are so jittery they can barely click the screen.

CHAPTER 7
Reuben

User 5639. Male. 48.

I stumbled across you, and you took me by surprise.
I have things I need to explore, and I know you'll be just the girl for the
job. Show me you as your natural self, please, however you choose to
present yourself.
Come prepared, with no preconceptions, and be willing to live up to your
profile.

Duration: 10 hours
Proposal fee: £10

*I*t's a ridiculous proposal, and I should never have sent it. Approaching an entertainer for a personal one-on-one booking is against our code of conduct, beyond reprehensible, and an affront to the group of founders who set up the Agency along with me. My stakeholder status should never be worth risking, and neither should the respect of my associates. All of us are high class businessmen with reputations to uphold. We all just happen to like filthy sex – and the revenue that comes along as a result.

We are not running a seedy brothel at the Agency, we're running and maintaining a large network of extreme professionals. We treat both our clients and entertainers with respect, diligence, confidentiality and safety – which are some of my key values in life. Yet, here I am, jeopardising my position with a fake user profile.

Having Creamgirl sitting on my lap with her face on display changed everything for me.

From that moment on she was no longer just Creamgirl – a nameless, faceless entertainer. She was Tiffany.

And she sent me insane.

I could have offered a huge amount of cash for her services, but I didn't. Still, she chose to accept it. One pound an hour for unlimited access to her repertoire is beyond rationale. The girl has clearly bought in to my insanity. She must be going as crazy as I am.

She's travelling a long way out of London to meet me here in Evesham. I booked the bridal suite here at this spa resort for our one impulsive evening, and it's a beauty with its antique four poster bed. I pace around, admiring the period features that are truly fit for a princess.

I get a notification five minutes ahead of schedule. *Arrived.*

Tiffany – Creamgirl – is downstairs in the lobby.

I check my tie in the mirror, straightening it just so. I'm wearing one of my finest suits. A traditional number from Savile Row. A dusty blue tweed that works with both my hair and eyes, complemented by the royal blue tie I've chosen. I smooth down my lapels, and I'm set to go.

I descend the main staircase, my mind still cycling through the options of how she could have interpreted my words. Her natural self, I asked for, and as I step into the lobby and catch sight of her, my question is answered.

Creamgirl has come as Tiffany. The gorgeous creature who sat on my lap in Santa's chair.

There is no way on this planet I'm going to be getting my head together tonight.

She's wearing big boots and torn jeans, with fishnets visible underneath, swamped in a hoodie against the chill with her scarlet hair a cascade down her back. Her expression as she registers me is one of fixation and horror, both at once. She stares me up and down with wide eyes, her fake lashes giving her the appearance of a porcelain doll. I love the contouring on her cheeks as her mouth opens. I adore her bright red lip gloss and the way it looks so inviting.

"Hi," she says, but I ignore the casual and go straight in for a kiss on each of her cheeks, clasping her hands in mine.

"Welcome. It's a pleasure to see you."

She laughs at that and looks down at herself. "Yeah, right. When you said come as *me*, I thought you meant literally. I didn't expect you'd be bringing me to swanky town."

"Where else would I bring you?"

"I dunno. Just somewhere more…"

I smirk at her, because I can't help it. Her smile is already infectious.

"Basic?"

"Yeah, basic. After the alleyway thing, you know."

"I'm sure they have an area where they keep the waste, if you prefer? At least let's have dinner first though, shall we?"

She kicks out a leg so I can see her chunky boot. "Yeah, these are going to be right at home in this place."

I stare at her, and she doesn't shy away from my gaze. "Are you a self-conscious girl?"

She rolls her pretty eyes at me. "Hardly. I was thinking more about you. I don't give a toss what I wear in a restaurant."

"Neither do I."

"Seriously? You look like you've stepped straight out of some *suit porn monthly* magazine, and I look like I've just popped out to grab a meal deal."

I step to her side and offer her my arm. "I think we are very well suited, actually."

She holds back a laugh as a couple walk past and give us a side eye.

"Jeez, *Mr Sinclair.* I must look like I'm your rebel daughter."

My turn to laugh. "I like that analogy."

The flash of a vixen comes to life in her eyes as we start the route to the restaurant.

"Yeah, so do I. I love myself a bit of daddy kink."

The restaurant is relatively quiet when we get there, just a few tables taken. I would usually be scanning the room for signs of opulence and inspiration for my own restaurants, but I have no interest whatsoever this evening.

The waiter is a gracious enough chap, pulling out Tiffany's chair when we get to our table. I watch him as he watches her, clocking his curiosity. She's a striking creature, even wrapped up in a hoodie. She emanates a buzz that can't be ignored.

"Champagne?" I ask, and she nods.

"Yes, please. I never say no to some fizz."

"De Chante, please," I tell the waiter, and he trots off to the bar for the bottle of their finest.

"You could have said we were coming somewhere posh and eating out." Tiffany's eyes are cheeky. "Your proposal was the vaguest one I've ever had. I took it at face value, though. Thought you'd want the Tiff from the grotto."

I put my elbows on the table. "I want *you*. As you. Whether that is the girl from the grotto or not."

I get another flash of the vixen eye. "Yeah, well, I have a lot of different flavours. You can sample them later, if you like."

"For one pound a go?" I pause. "Why did you accept?"

She shrugs. "Dunno. Thought it would be fun."

I know she's playing casual, just like she's dressed casual, but I don't want the outer shell. I want the girl inside the hoodie. Her brains, her beauty, her sexuality, her spice and soul. A taster just hasn't been enough.

"Drop the facade," I say, and lean in closer. "Why did you accept the proposal, Tiffany?"

The waiter returns before she has a chance to answer. He pops the cork and fills our glasses, and Tiffany gives a little *whoop* and raises hers in a *cheers*. She takes a sip as the waiter leaves, and smacks her lips.

"Nice?" I ask.

"Hell yeah. I usually neck the bottle like it's a spurting dick, but since it's De Chante, I'll take it more steady."

I chuckle. "You're deflecting," I say. "Why did you accept the proposal?"

It's a standoff, her eyes on mine. Mine don't waver and neither do hers. She's reading me as I'm reading her, both of us unconsciously probing. I feel the sparks. The static of electric attraction that defies all reason.

"Because I wanted to," she says, "just like I want to do this."

She downs her drink in one.

Cheeky little minx.

"Cheers," I say and clink her empty glass, and then I pour her a fresh one.

"Why did you *send* me the proposal?" she asks me, her big and so beautiful green eyes reeling me in.

"Because I wanted to," I say, and then I down my De Chante as well.

A sudden loud rumble has Tiffany clasping a hand to her mouth.

"Shit, sorry," she says, "fizz on an empty stomach. I should have known better."

I love that she has me chuckling again. I love that her cheeks are burning up.

And I love that my cock is rock hard at the sight of her…

"We best get you fed, then." I hand her a menu.

"What is it?" I ask when she sighs.

"This starter," she says, "Listen to this…" she reads from the menu, "*Creamy garlic portobello mushrooms in olive oil and thyme with crispy bacon bits and a slice of garlic sourdough.* Garlic mushrooms is my absolute favourite and that sounds delicious."

"But?"

She sighs again. "A girl should never eat garlic before or during a proposal. It can be a turnoff should any… *kissing* occur."

I lean in a little, keeping my voice low. "Let me tell you, Tiffany, anything you enjoy devouring would be a turn on for me."

I like that she's speechless at first.

I like the grin that follows.

So does my cock.

"You for real?" she asks. "You wouldn't give a toss about garlic breath?"

"Yes, I'm being truthful. Enjoy your starter. You'll taste divine regardless."

She sits back and fans her face with the menu.

"Posh garlic mushrooms it is, then. Just hope you don't regret it later. At least I know you're not a vampire."

She goes for *the posh* garlic mushrooms, while I go for mussels. She goes for lasagne and chips, while I go for fillet steak. She goes for a triple chocolate sundae, while I go for a cheese board. And we laugh and chat all the while.

We talk about everything from reality TV to the intricacies of cosmology. From tarot cards, to the logistics of running ten shopping arcades, to how long she's had her favourite boots – it all flows seamlessly. Effortlessly. I get sucked in by her flirty giggle as her walls begin to come down, fixated on her big, beautiful tits when she declares how warm she is and pulls her hoodie off over her head to reveal a cami top. I can see the straps of her red lace bra. Layers. So many layers. And I want to see them all. I want to know them all.

And I want to get to the bottom of the well. To the naked Tiffany, in soul as well as body.

I've seen glimpses, even though she was hooded through every experience. I've heard the vulnerability in her naked cries, without needing her face as a reference. I've felt her blissful release, often in the most extreme of circumstances. The glorious creature that's now wiping a finger around the inside of her sundae bowl was at the top of my click list when it came to my booking choice at our founders' gatherings. Every. Single. Time.

She sucks her chocolatey finger into her mouth and I'm transfixed. Two bottles of champagne down, and the glow is alive – *palpable*.

"Where next?" she asks.

I sit back in my seat. "That depends on you. Bridal suite or the kitchen trash dump, or anywhere in between."

She tips her head from side to side.

"Hmm, tough choice. Bridal suite first."

"First?"

"Yeah. We'll save the trash dump for another time."

I dab my mouth with a napkin, then call over the waiter, instructing him to add the tab to my room. Tiffany grabs her hoodie from the back of her chair, and I take her hand, leading her proudly through the anonymity of nowhere. Choosing Evesham was a blessing, far away from London's prying eyes.

"Bridal suite, eh?" she says as we climb the stairs together. "I'm a spoilt girl."

"See if you're still saying that if we do end up in the trash dump."

"If or when?"

She tugs my hand back, stopping me in my tracks as she leans against the wall. I don't need her to pull me in, I'm already on her, my face above hers as I pull her arms up above her head.

"Why are you really here, Reuben?" she asks me. "This is fucking crazy."

"I don't know," I reply. "And yes, it is. I'd get crucified for breaking the code of conduct."

"And so would I."

"So, why are *you* really here?" I ask her, and she squirms against me, rubbing the crotch of her jeans against my thigh.

"I don't know, either."

"How about we go and find out?"

It would be so easy to kiss her here and now. To rip her cami top off and tear down her jeans without giving a shit for passing guests. But I pull myself together. One more flight of stairs and the top suite is waiting. I get us up there as quickly as I can.

"Gosh, posh mushrooms and now a posh suite. Can't wait to see this," she says as I put the key in the lock and let us in.

"This is incredible," she says as she does a spin, taking in the antique decor, but I'm not looking at the surroundings, I'm looking at her. The way she moves, the way she grins, the way her stunning red hair flies around her.

I hang up my jacket and lower my tone.

"Strip off that next layer and get on the bed."

Tiffany, the stunning Creamgirl, is unabashed, her stare strong as she pulls off her cami top without a care. She doesn't break the stare as she kicks off her boots and pushes her jeans down, and there it is. The layer underneath. A lacy balconette bra that raises her gorgeous tits like trophies, and a suspender belt that leads to her fishnets, finished up with a tiny thong that does barely anything to cover her bare pussy.

I've seen her naked so many times I've lost count, but the energy here now is such a stark contrast it's barely comprehendible. My cock is raging for her.

"Get on the bed," I repeat, and she backs over to it, her eyes still on mine.

"How do you want me?"

"However you want to be."

She lies on her back in the middle of the bed and hitches her knees up. Her thighs fall open as she watches me walk across the room. My fucking God, the sight of her pussy. Her lips are already swollen, the clean-shaven mound of hers on show like she's a piece of Renaissance art.

"What are you going to do to me?" Her voice has a slight tremble. She knows what I'm capable of.

"Are you scared?"

She shakes her head. "No."
I break the news to her.
"Nothing."

CHAPTER 8
Tiffany

I prop myself up on my elbows, staring at the gorgeous suited man.

"Nothing? Are you fucking serious?" I laugh, but he doesn't laugh back.

"Deadly."

"Why?"

He doesn't meet my eyes. Instead, he picks up a travel case from the corner of the bedroom and takes out a selection of toys, laying them beside me one by one. Vibrators and dildos in a whole host of sizes, from neat little bullets, to huge towers of plastic with fist sized heads. Butt plugs, and beads – some on loose threads, like shimmering marbles, and others in a hard, thick row.

"Why?" I ask again. "Why won't you be playing with me? We could have so much fun."

"I've no doubt about that, but as I said, I want to see you, Tiffany. I want to see how you play with yourself, when you don't have the rules of a proposal to live up to."

I'm normally adept at reading clients, but with him it seems a whole other ballgame. I don't get it. I'm still trying to figure him out as he pulls up a chair from the dresser and takes a seat at the side of the bed.

"Is this a voyeurism kink? Want to see how far I can push myself for you?"

"No. Not at all. I want to see how far you enjoy pushing yourself, and exactly how you do it."

I grin. "Don't you worry about that, Santa. I'm a very naughty girl. I can push myself a long fucking way."

"I'm well aware of that. I've been privy to it many times."

"So why not get dirty, then? We can do whatever you want. Anything."

He stares me right in the eyes, looking almost angry. It gives me fucking tingles, go figure.

"Because this isn't about me and it isn't about Creamgirl. It's about the girl underneath."

The girl underneath. That makes me shuffle. *Nervous.*

"I *am* Creamgirl. It's not an act. I love everything I do. It's not just for the cash."

"I'm sure it isn't, and I'm sure you do. But you aren't Creamgirl, you are *Tiffany*, and it's Tiffany I want in this room with me tonight."

I can't remember the last time I've fucked around with someone using my real name. I've not ventured into the real world outside of proposals for years. But this *is* a proposal. Kind of. Technically.

Or is it?

The lines are blurry, and I feel like I'm wobbling, the safety of anonymity sailing away into the distance.

"So, what do you want me to do?" I ask.

Reuben leans forward in his seat, his elbows on his knees.

"Whatever you want to do. Those toys are all for you. Enjoy the ones you want to, and ignore the ones you don't."

"Cool." I go on instinct and choose a girthy dildo. Mid-range. I pick it up and run my tongue up the shaft as I giggle.

My giggle sounds empty in the room, because Reuben's expression stays deadpan.

"Drop the act now, please. No Creamgirl, just Tiffany."

I sense the first crack in my Creamgirl armour. Like he's tapped the eggshell on the side of a metal bowl. I look at him and he looks back, and I know there's going to be no movement on his stance tonight. That much I can read.

He wants Tiffany.

Me.

It feels like he's jabbing fingers into my gooey stomach.

I take a deep breath.

"Fine, ok. If that's what you want."

"What *you* want, remember? What I want is what *you* want."

I drop the dildo to my side and shift around on the bed, getting comfortable. I relax and let my thighs loll open like I would at home, with no concern for posing. My heart is racing a helluva lot faster than it would ever be if I was just getting myself off to my own dirty tune, though. Giving him *Tiffany* and not *Creamgirl* is harder than he might think. *Harder than I have ever considered.*

Do I like it?

I don't fucking know.

But I'm willing to find out for him. I'll try my best.

The four poster has an impressive fabric ceiling. A dark red tapestry, highlighted by twists of gold. I've never been a *mindfulness* kind of girl, but Josh used to go on about meditation all the time when he was in his yoga ball phase, so I try to summon up the technique. I follow the golden threads with my eyes and take deep breaths. In and out. I try to forget Reuben Sinclair is in the room with me, and slide my hand down between my legs like I do at home. Just breathe, and play. Breathe, and play.

I'm used to being horny 24/7, and being with Reuben through dinner has already soaked my panties, so my pussy doesn't let me down. My clit is sparking to the touch as soon as my fingers land.

I rub myself more gently when I'm playing alone than I usually do with clients, using nothing more than teasing flicks as a warmup. I tease myself for ages when I'm dancing my own dance, building myself up to a massive spurt since it's normally a one off before bedtime, so I do the same here. Reuben will have to butt in and gee things up if he gets bored and regrets the assignment. Until then, I'll give him what he asked for.

He wants to see what I usually do, fine. I wouldn't be doing it trussed up in lacy lingerie.

I don't look at him as I unclip my bra and toss it aside. My heart starts thumping again as I battle out of my stockings and suspender belt without any kind of flirty performance to go along with it. They go flying off the bed too, and I push my panties down my legs, kicking them off.

Finesse will have to go fuck itself.

Being naked isn't an issue for me in the slightest. I spend a load of my time in sweet FA while I'm with clients, but not usually from scratch without any banter or filth to go along with it.

I always enjoy giving a butt shimmy and crushing my big tits together while I blow a kiss with a *mwah*. But this is nothing like that. Every roll and curve feels under a different kind of spotlight with Reuben's eyes on me.

Practicalities come into play that wouldn't with other people involved. I need decent access to my pussy to play with toys on my own.

I arrange the pillows behind me like I would in bed at home, so

I'm on an incline and able to get past my tubby tits and belly. I can't see my pussy unless it's in a mirror – since I've hardly got the flexibility of a gymnast, and I don't have the neck of a giraffe. They're standard fat girl issues that make no difference to me, but they feel kinda weird when they're exposed to someone watching.

More specifically, with Reuben watching.

I have to turn my mind off from my filthy, gorgeous boss yet again, so I focus back on the golden threads, my fingers only just grazing a path between my pussy lips. It feels like fucking for ever before I'm relaxed enough for this to pass off as natural, but when I do finally cross the barrier it's nicer than I'd have figured. I let out a breath, with a smile.

When I get myself off, I always have fantasies. A stream of things I've done, or things I've got planned ahead in the calendar. Dirty scenes I relive or I crave. And this time there is only one thing I'd be thinking about at home if I was doing this.

Reuben Sinclair, and what the fuck he could do to me if he wanted to.

So, I think about Reuben while trying to ignore him. What a fucking paradox. I circle my clit and think of all the fucked-up things he's done to me while I was hooded and unaware of what a salt and pepper stunner he was.

My fingers speed up of their own accord, and I grab for the dildo, trying not to look his way. I rub the head up and down my slit, closing my eyes as I deny my throbbing clit the rhythm of my fingers. I replace it with frustrating long sweeps of the dildo head instead.

I love this part – almost begging myself to let myself come. I always pretend it's with someone else, and sometimes I even whisper it out loud. *Please. A little bit faster. Just there.* But I never give in to my own wishes if I'm truly trying to work myself up. I can come from clit play in about thirty seconds flat, but when I'm really playing, it's a whole other story.

I moan as I push the cock head inside the first inch, having to hitch myself up for the angle. I always picture myself as younger when I do this – more inexperienced – but I haven't really twigged that until now. Weird. I always imagine it's a dick that's ploughing me, not a dildo, and fuck myself like it's my very first time, inch by inch as I whimper.

I'm whimpering now. Push, push, pushing until it's all the way in.

I don't pull it out and use a thrust method. That's for when I'm with clients. It's not that I don't love it, because I do, but in my own time I have a few different measures. I make big circles with the end of the dick, so it ramps up the pressure inside me, and when I start squirming – building up to a peak – I always pull the toy out with a groan.

That's what I do now, holding true to my own game.

I sink into the fantasy of it being a guy's cock. *Reuben's.* I pretend I'm disappointed as he pulls it out of me. I rub it up and down my slit, teasing my clit with every stroke, but I don't break the rhythm and give my clit what it needs. I fight myself by bucking against it, frog legged as I crave more. *Just there, please. Just there.* But my imaginary lover denies me, and plunges his cock straight back inside.

Fuck yes, being sunk into never loses its thrill.

Over and over it goes. Cycle after cycle after cycle.

I get more frantic with my thrusting, whispering curses as I tug at my nipples, but I don't break my own tease of a rhythm. I keep on going.

When I'm at home and playing like this, I put towels under me. I gush so fucking bad.

When I finally meet Reuben's eyes, my heaving breaths have nothing to do with nerves, they are all about the waves of pleasure.

He's smiling at me.

"That's a good girl, Tiffany."

Tiffany.

I love the way he says it.

"I'm so wet," I tell him. "So fucking wet."

"I know. I can hear."

I give myself some more slit strokes and opt for a thicker dildo. Something dry and raw that will take some pushing to get it in. There's a big flesh coloured one popping with veins lying right beside me, so I go for it. Perfect. It's not so good at slit stroking, but it feels really fucking good when I start inching it into my pussy.

There is never anything fake about how much I love being stretched. *Or how much I love people making me take it.*

"Come closer, please," I say to Reuben. "You don't have to touch... just... watch..."

He gets up from his seat and moves to the foot of the bed, sitting down between my legs. Such a personal view.

I don't change technique, but it takes a more dramatic turn. I deny myself until I'm cursing – begging an imaginary person for more of their dick when it's out, and thanking them when it's plunged back inside.

I've got a very vivid imagination.

I go crazy for clit orgasms, but deep vaginal is a whole other league, and these ones – where I've built myself up for fucking ages – are so off the scale I go crazy.

Reuben seems to read my mind as my hand goes patting around the selection of dildos for the next in line.

"This one," he says, and hands over one hell of a thumper, with a fist-like head.

I nod. Smiling.

"You're in the splash zone," I tell him, "I squirt real bad when I come like this. You should maybe get some towels."

He doesn't move. Doesn't speak. Doesn't do fucking anything as I force the bastard toy inside my pussy and ride the waves of my efforts. My needs are off the charts, desperate as I work that fat fist in hard circles, buried all the way in. I'm moaning for me and nobody else as the sensations take hold.

In my mind I hear the voices of clients over the years, telling me what a dirty slutty whore I am, with a juicy wet fucking pussy, goading me on as I fucking take it. But it's all in my head. There is nobody but me fucking myself with this plastic fist, and I don't hold back when I come.

I grunt and grit my teeth, pushing out against the toy as I crest, but I hold it in position, fighting my own cunt with it, until I set it free.

The gush is a good one, sending waves right through my convulsing body as my pussy releases. I strum my clit and slam that fucker back in again as soon as I'm able, lost to everything in the world but how it feels.

Fuck, fuck, fuck!

Another squirt, and I'm in heaven. A fresh strum of my clit and I have ringing in my ears. I'm bucking against my fingers like a slutty bronco bitch.

And then it's done.

I'm a panting, heaving wreck. Sweaty and sticky, and lying on soaking wet sheets. And there is Reuben Sinclair, seeing me at my most private. Exposed and sloppy in the aftermath, without any attempt at girly flirting or banter.

I get a horrible squirm in my guts, as though I'll have disappointed him somehow, and it makes me scared. *Terrified.* But no, Reuben smiles.

"That was absolutely beautiful, Tiffany," he says, but the squirm doesn't go away, it turns into butterflies. And they dig deep.

"Thanks. I'll clean up a bit." I go to move my fat butt into the bathroom to grab a towel, but he puts a hand on my knee.

The touch is like electric as he shakes his head.

"Don't even think about moving, stay right where you are," he tells me. "It's time to do it all over again."

CHAPTER 9

Reuben

There is no Creamgirl in the room right now, and I won't allow her entry. Now I've seen the true beauty of the sweet slut underneath, there is no going back.

It's all about Tiffany. The siren who has tilted my world on its axis and sent it reeling.

"Again," I repeat, and she tips her head back with a *fuck, really?*

I've never watched a girl play with herself to that degree before, and I need more. I want to see her rise again. To watch her come time and time again until she's out of her fucking mind. Just like I am.

I'm only just managing to keep my cock in my pants. The mastery of self-restraint is a hard fucking task.

I break my rules just a little in order to take her hand and glide her fingertips up and down her gorgeous chubby slit, mimicking what she did to herself at the start of play.

"From the top," I say, and she keeps her fingers in motion when I pull away, even though she's wincing.

"It's so sensitive, Reuben."

"I'm sure you can handle it."

It takes her quite some time to find her rhythm again, but I don't push or rush her. I soak in every glorious moan and whimper as she uses her swollen cunt to level up another gear. The sheets are soaked through from her gushing, clinging to her ass as she squirms. She's more animalistic on this round, like a true bitch in heat when she gets fully into the groove and starts winding her own handle. By the time she has the fist-sized dildo back in her cunt again, she's staring at me as though she's drunk on endorphins. Her body is in control of her mind.

But it's all for her. It's all her own doing. I'm merely an accomplice on the sidelines.

"I normally have more toys than this to help me," she says. "I like clamps, and floggers, and things that make it hurt."

"I'll bear that in mind for next time. In the meantime, make the most of what you have."

"Thank you for the presents, Santa."

She has to haul her butt up from the bed to thread a chain of beads into her asshole. It's glorious how they pop in, one by one, only to be yanked free in one long tear.

"I love ass play when I'm this fucking horny," she tells me. "I have my own set of anal toys at home, but I save them for special occasions. When proposals have been shit, or I'm a desperate little bitch that can't wait for my next booking."

"Show me, Tiffany. Actions, not words."

She stuffs the beads in more quickly, then rips them straight back out of her. So fucking good. She rolls her head back, still trying to fuck her pussy at the same time, but her thighs are straining with the pressure of holding herself in position. Such a big, beautiful girl that she can barely support herself.

"Shit," she says, and gives up. Instead, she rolls over, climbing up onto all fours.

My self-mastery has to rein itself in even tighter, since I've got an incredible hot spot right in front of me. I'm staring at the deep crevice of her ass crack when she reaches back to spread her cheeks. It's beyond tempting to help her out and aim her newly chosen dildo directly at the target. Her beautiful curves make it such a challenge for her to manoeuvre. She has to rub the head of the dildo up and down to find her asshole, and even then, she's slightly out of angle. It takes her three attempts.

Fuck, my mouth is watering. I'd love a taste far more than I enjoyed dinner downstairs.

The beautiful Tiffany groans in relief when the dildo head finally pushes inside her, and she's so horny she's straight off and away, working her ass far harder than she teased her horny cunt.

I lean in closer, to relish the scent of her. I'm out of her view, since she has no wing mirrors. Her bouncing tits and peachy ass block me from sight.

"What are you thinking about?" I ask as she's groaning, ramming that fake dick in real deep.

"What I'm always thinking about when I'm doing this. Dirty things I want people to do to me. Filthy things they've made me do. Filthy things they say."

Her words have the same lilt as they usually do, but there is no gusto behind them. This isn't Creamgirl being filthy, this is Tiffany herself. Tiff and Cream must be practically soulmates – with barely a whisper of difference in between. *But that whisper drives me crazy.*

"Does it make you wet when people call you a slut? Is that the kind of thing you think about while you're playing?"

"Yes. I love it."

"Degradation?"

"Degradation and the truth. I am a slut. I am a whore. I am a dirty bitch. I just love being told it."

"What else do you love? What else are you thinking about right now?"

She pushes a hand between her legs to rub her clit – chubby fingers rough as she keeps pumping the dildo in her asshole.

"Really want to know?"

"Of course. That's why I asked."

She shuffles far enough to the side to be able to see me, and her eyes stay hooked on me. It gives me a strange headrush.

"You," she says. "I'm thinking of you. Of all the filthy fucking things you've done to me."

"You must have a lot of them on your mind."

"Yeah, and some of them I'm unsure of, because I don't know for sure if they were you."

"Oh, the beauty of being hooded. So many mysteries."

She groans again. "I just wish I could've seen you doing them."

I have to swallow as I palm my dick. It takes every scrap of self-restraint I possess not to break out of this scene and launch it into a whole other stratosphere.

"Which parts, Tiffany? Which bits would you want to see me doing to you?"

She's approaching another peak, and her meaty cunt is dribbling. Piss or pussy juices, or a combination. It's absolutely stunning.

"Everything," she says. "Jesus, Reuben, you could do anything to me right now. Anything, and I'd come for you."

"Make *yourself* come," I tell her. "Show me."

The beautiful girl is too far gone to hold back, even if she wanted to. This squirt is less explosive than the last one, but it's still a gush of pure brilliance, running down her thighs as she bucks and squeals.

"Again," I say, before she's even had a chance to catch her breath.

The gorgeous Tiffany does what she's told, rolling back over to start anew.

"It's so tender it hurts," she says, panting.

"Do you want to stop?"

She shakes her head. "No, it makes me want it even more."

I want to share her with those monster dildos so badly it makes my balls ache. I want to shove my hand right into her hungry cunt and take control, but I don't. She does it all for herself.

She shows me how she plays, and exactly how she likes it. She gives me telltale signs all the while, such as the way she turns her head from side to side and grits her teeth as she's teetering, and the way she lashes the bed with her right foot when she's riding the waves.

I file them all to memory. I study the way she touches her own body, like it's an art form.

"I don't think I can take any more," she whimpers after another round, but again, I put her hand back on her pussy, fingers just grazing her beautiful clit.

"Come on, Tiffany. I know you can."

Her eyes are hooded, drifting. The poor creature is exhausted.

"I wish you'd just do it for me. Please, Reuben. Just fuck me. Please."

I'm a hairline from reaching the edge of temptation. I cling on by a bastard thread.

"No, this is about you, not me, remember?"

"Oh fuck, I can't," she says, but her fingers keep stroking herself. "I need help. I need cock. I need you to tell me what a filthy slut I am."

"I don't believe that's true."

"Reuben, please…"

I close my eyes to resist the temptation.

"No, Tiffany." My voice is lower. "Do it yourself. Make yourself come."

"Fucker," she says and it makes me smile.

She's sore, there's no doubt about that. She grimaces as she resumes fucking her pussy, and there is no warmup involved now. She's sweating like she's at an aerobics class, groaning and fighting against the fisty plastic cock like she's giving birth.

Jesus fucking Christ. The thought almost makes me come in my pants.

I look at her big belly, her swollen tits, nipples like the proverbial bullets, and the way she's squatting and pushing down to take it, teeth gritted.

And that's when it hits me, full on in the face.

It sets white lights off behind my eyes. My secret of secrets. The game I never play.

This was what was under my own private hood with her the whole time, and I never knew.

Or at least, I never acknowledged it.

"Good girl," I say. "That's it, Tiffany. *Push!*"

I don't know why the words come out of my mouth, but her eyes are straight on mine, digging. We both heard the underlying meaning.

We both understand.

Time stands still for a moment, both of us locked in a fucked-up version of our imagination. There is a vulnerability about her that strikes me in the heart. Something in her stare that holds secrets as deep as mine.

But then they disappear.

She grits her teeth with more determination and forces that fist sized bastard right into her, holding it in position as she tries to push it back out with everything she has. Her cunt splays like a holy fucking flower, and I see her muscles straining.

Beautiful. Just beautiful.

"Push, Tiffany. Push!"

She's pushing against something that will never come out, because she's holding it in position, but she tries so hard that it makes her face go red and her pussy dribble around the intrusion.

Fuck, she's trying to birth a fucking dildo, and I'm sure my cock is fucking leaking.

"Now come for me! Push and come for me!"

For me.

I shouldn't have switched the focus, but it fucking works.

The sweet chubby cherub sits up on the bed and wrenches her leg underneath her to hold the dildo in position. She pushes and strains, and strums her clit like a woman possessed, pouring with sweat from the effort.

One touch of my cock and I'd be done for. I'd be fucking done for.

"It hurts," she says. "Oh, fuck, it hurts. But I want it, I want it so much!"

"You can do it," I tell her. "Come on, Tiffany, you can do it."

I know her body can come, even when her mind is lost to her, and so it happens. She screams this time, a spurt gushing around the dildo as she rubs her clit like she's on speed. And then she collapses, her whimpers almost like sobs.

"Again," I say, and she barely takes a breath before she starts up rubbing her clit some more. "That's it, dirty girl," I say, and she manages a smile.

"I'll do it as many times as you want, Reuben."

My hands are trembling as I watch her, because I want to touch her so badly. I'm hovering, fit to burst and about to break my resolve when a noise sounds out from across the room.

The alarm is sounding on my phone.

Time's up.

I have to suck in a breath to regain some form of composure. I'm so close to breaking. So fucking close.

Luckily, the jangle of the melody is enough to bring me back to sanity.

Just like I prayed it would be.

CHAPTER 10
Tiffany

I stop strumming my clit, thinking it's the fire alarm for a second, until Reuben pushes from the bed, goes over to the dresser, picks up his phone and switches the alarm off. He puts the phone down and smooths his suit jacket. I'm out of my mind as I watch my suave boss. He's still fully dressed, whereas I'm the total fucking opposite. I'm a heaving mass of naked flesh, sweaty and sordid.

I just tried to birth a fucking dildo.

I played a game I never play. Ever.

My heartbeats are pangs of need, and I hate them… but Jesus Christ, I need more.

"Time's up," he says, and my guts twist so bad it hurts.

Rejection.

Rejection, after that kind of teaser…

I get a wave of sick panic, open mouthed as I stare at him.

"What?"

"Ten-hour timer. Proposal over."

"Proposal over? You can't be serious. I don't give a stuff about ten hours. I'd do this through the whole fucking weekend, and then take it all over again, no problem."

With you. That's the part I leave out.

I'd take it all over again *with you*.

"Yet another thing we have in common." He smirks. "I would too. Gladly."

I sit up and shrug. "So why the hell are you calling time out?"

"Discipline. Common sense. Respect."

He seems so calm, yet I'm anything but. A pair of opposites on different sides of the scale.

I don't know why I feel so hurt, but I do. It's like I've been stabbed in the ribs.

The guy across the room is still the smiling Reuben, eyes full of lust, but his self-control makes me shiver.

I'm not in control. I'm a mess who feels like I've ripped myself open and shown him my soul. I feel so exposed, unsure, and invested but fucking terrified. *With butterflies.* Swarms upon swarms of fucking butterflies.

I don't know when I last felt like this...

Yes, I do. I'm feeding myself bullshit.

Kian.

That's the last time I felt like this. When things were crazy good with Kian.

When I was in love.

I could hurl all over the carpet as I drag myself up and grab my underwear. I'm terrified of some unknown force at play here. A ghost in the room I don't want to face.

I pushed for him.

I playacted.

I wanted it to be real.

"Are you ok, Tiffany?" Reuben asks me.

The walls of Creamgirl come straight back up. I shoot him a cheeky smile.

"Yeah, sure. It was fun. Hopefully you'll book me again, *User 5639.*"

He steps closer as I'm trying to pull my jeans up. My legs are fucking quaking.

"No, Tiffany. Are you actually ok?"

I can't tell him the truth.

No. I already feel like my heart's been cracked open, thanks for asking.

I'm terrified of losing something I never even had in the first place. It's only been ten fucking hours and I'm a pathetic mess.

"I'll be fine," I say, because that's no lie. I will be fine, once I'm out of here and back onto familiar turf.

I throw on my hoodie and it's a relief to be hidden. Covered and safe.

"Why are you racing?" he asks. "Don't you want to shower before you go? You're quite a mess."

More than you'll ever know.

I laugh. "Nah, I'll shower at home, thanks," is all I can say.

He's staring at me as I get my boots. His eyes are burning me as I tighten the laces.

"Anyway, why are *you* racing?" I ask him. "You're the one who called time out."

"I'm not calling time out. I adhered to the end of the proposal."

FUCK THE FUCKING PROPOSAL!

I want to scream it in his face, even though it's ridiculous. I've been doing proposals for four years, and I've had fantasies and infatuations, and morning after syndrome to the max, but I've never felt like this before. It's so fucking stupid, it's embarrassing.

"You're really ok with this?" he pushes, and I could groan at his round after round of bastard questions, but I take a breath and flash another smile.

"Yeah, of course I am. It's only a proposal," I laugh. "We're cool."

He nods, smiling back at me.

"Excellent."

"Excellent?"

I'm so busted up that I can't make sense of things – both inside and out. I'll need a long, hot bath and a bottle of vodka when I get home, never mind a bastard shower.

"Yes, excellent," he says. "That's the reassurance we both need."

I pull a face. "I don't get it. What reassurance?"

His hands are tender as he takes mine.

"The reassurance that we can both handle a proposal without falling into the abyss of insanity."

Ah, ok. The penny drops. I get it now.

He wanted to know if I could stop. If he could stop. If *we* could stop, with no crazy repercussions.

Thank fuck I didn't blurt out a load of emotional crap that would have busted my fat ass.

That knowledge makes it a lot easier for Creamgirl to take back the reins. I shrug as though it's nothing and give his strong hands a squeeze before letting go.

"Yeah, don't worry about that, Santa. We had a good gig, and now it's over."

He looks me up and down. "Unfortunately so. Until next time."

"There's going to be a next time, then?"

A zap of horny delight shoots up my spine at the thought. And now I'm grinning like a love-struck twat.

Fuck sake.

"Of course," he says, "And I'll offer a better rate next time."

I wave the idea aside. "Nah, stick to a quid an hour. It's fun."

With that, Reuben grabs his wallet from the dresser and pulls out a ten-pound note. I try to wave that aside too, but he won't have it.

"Tiffany," he says, with a serious stare. "Take it, please."

"Cool, yeah, alright. Ta for that," I reply, and stuff it into my hoodie pocket. I glance about the place, and it's a right fucking mess. Should have used towels. "Need any help cleaning up?"

"No thanks, that's my responsibility, not yours."

"Good luck."

It's a relief when he laughs along with me, our connection reignited.

"I had a great time. Truly."

"Something else we have in common." I give him a wink. "I'll be keeping an eye out for the next proposal. Get it in quick, my schedule is rammed."

"I'm well aware of that."

This place is suddenly stifling. The heat is from way more than just my hoodie. It's from *him*.

I march straight over to the door with a *see ya*, but he steps forward.

"Wait," he says before I turn the handle. "I wasn't joking about the confidentiality agreement, Tiffany. This is breaking the code of conduct and if anyone finds out –"

I cut him off with a finger to my lips.

"I'm not an idiot. Pinky promise, remember?" I give him a wave before I leave. "See you around."

"Yes. Keep an eye on your notifications."

I make it down to reception before I start to get dizzy. Real fucking dizzy. I lean against the reception desk, trying to act casual as I get the night porter to call me a cab, dabbling in stupid small talk as I wait for it to arrive.

Had a nice stay?

Yeah, thanks. This place is cool. Time runs away when you're having fun, doesn't it? Loved the lasagne by the way. Yum.

The night porter seems a nice guy.

"Saw you in there with your dad earlier."

Holy fuck, if only he knew.

I go along with it.

"We live in different places, you know. Sometimes it's cool to meet halfway, and I get a decent chocolate sundae out of it."

Blah blah blah.

I feel queasy at the thought of Reuben just a few flights upstairs. I've got butterflies upon butterflies wanting to get back up there and throw myself into his arms like a crazy bitch.

I breathe a sigh of relief when the cab pulls up, ready to drive me back to some semblance of normality, but the relief wears off as soon as the hotel disappears around a corner.

Because I don't want a semblance of normality. I don't want my apartment and a hot bath, and my calendar packed with bookings set to whisk me right through bastard Christmas.

I want Reuben.

I send my usual *D&S* message to Josh, since the proposal is marked on my calendar. *Cool,* he replies with a thumbs-up emoji. *Have a good time?*

The butterflies sail into a needy pit in my guts, ready to spill the beans. I want to tell Josh all about it – to talk through the craziness with my best friend and get some perspective. But I can't do that. Not only because of the pinky promise to Reuben, but because he'd tell me I'm fucking insane.

Reuben is a goddamn founder, and this could cost me my whole career.

Josh would get me straight back onto my psychotherapist and have me make another pinky promise. One that states I'll have nothing more to do with this craziness whatsoever. No Reuben Sinclair and dabbling in Agency founder business. He'd say I should never have touched it in the first place.

And he would be right. I should never have touched it in the first place – but my fingers are already burned.

It was cool, I message back to him. *My butt hurts pretty bad, though.*

He sends a laughing emoji.

I'd be surprised if it didn't. I know what you're like, Tiff.

I shove my phone back in my pocket, but it sounds out again. Another message from Josh.

Are you coming over tomorrow? Me and Ells want to see you.

Shit. I've been avoiding this. The inevitable conversation where the two of them try to convince me to join them at Josh's family gathering for Christmas lunch. I usually go, even though Caroline – his youngest sister, who's been a pain in my ass since we were teenagers – is always there, being a pain in my ass, like she always *has* been since we were teenagers.

I've been playing the Christmas Day thing down whenever it's come up recently, saying *nah, I'm busy*. Or *nah, you and Ells should make the most of your first family Christmas in private this year*, but they won't have it. This will be a serious 'sit down and talk about it' job – because Josh knows what the real deal is. Like he said, he knows exactly what I'm like.

He knows full well the real reason I don't want to be there at Christmas dinner this year.

I won't want to see Caroline's baby bump as she sits there loved up with her amazing fiancé. Getting uncomfortable around smiling families at shopping malls is hard enough, but doable. Christmas dinner with Caroline would be off the scale, though. Even the thought of it makes me feel sick. Baby talk, and fawning, and Pinterest boards of nursery décor would take up at least ninety percent of the conversation all day fucking long.

And now I've been playing with Reuben, like *that*.

Even though it was just a small part of the show, I'm already feeling the backlash. The pain I've been burying deeper, year after year.

I won't be able to handle Caroline. No way. So, why beat around the bush?

I'm not coming, I type. *Not tomorrow, and not to Xmas dinner. I'll get an extra special rate for a Christmas Day booking. I'll be coining it, and I'll be fine, seriously. Don't worry about it. x*

'I'll be fine, seriously. Don't worry about it.'

I use that phrase like a mantra, constantly, and it's usually true. It's just now that I'm getting older, with the contrast of cute little Caroline with her cute little baby bump… it just isn't feeling quite the same.

The wrenched apart from Reuben feeling sure isn't helping. Jesus fucking Christ, I feel like such a gooey twat.

I shove my phone back in my hoodie yet again but get another ping straight through. No doubt some pacifying message about how Caroline won't be such a dick, and if I want to talk about anything we can do it without Ella, in the friendship code or whatever.

I love him for it, I really do. I'll tell him so, but I'm not going to change my mind.

Only the message onscreen isn't from Josh. It's a proposal notification.

Fuck. It can't be. Not already.

User 5639. Male. 48.

Suddenly those butterflies have swarmed and my heart is in my throat.

I had a great time tonight, Creamgirl. I wish you could have stayed longer, but I know proposals are proposals, and time out means time out.

This time around, I want to book more hours with you. Go big, or go home, as they say.

I love big, Cream, as you've undoubtedly gathered. So, please consider my offer.

Duration: 24 hours.

Proposal fee: £48,000.

He's having a laugh. Forty-eight fucking grand?!

I'd do it for another tenner. Fuck that. I'd give *him* a tenner. More than a tenner. Maybe not forty-eight grand, but I'd pay him a decent chunk.

I take out the ten-pound note stashed in my pocket from earlier, and it feels like some kind of memento. A sacred trophy.

There's no way I'll ever be spending this. Not a chance in hell.

Proposal accepted I click, and I manage to select my nearest calendar date before another message from Josh pings through.

This time I switch my phone to silent before I stuff it back in my pocket.

I can't be arsed with a Christmas dinner conversation when I'd rather be in a hot bath, dreaming of Reuben Sinclair.

CHAPTER 11
Reuben

The butler takes my coat when I reach Bryson's house. A huge stately manor on the north side of the city.

"Good evening, Mr Sinclair."

"Reuben, please," I tell him for the five hundredth time. "How are you doing, Len?"

"Not too bad. Looking forward to Christmas. We're going to Gill's place for dinner. The kids are coming down from York."

I've known Len for years now. He's been working for Bryson for over a decade, and during that time I've been privy to his major life events, even just in passing. He's from a large family, originally from up north. He's still got a great twang of an accent, and a genuine joy for life.

Nobody would think he was the man responsible for leading hooded whores into the games room and setting them up for sessions of utter filth. But that is the case for most of us in this building. It brings out a side of our coins most people would never comprehend.

"How is Georgie doing?" I ask. "Is he recovering?"

Len grins. "He's desperate to get back to football practice, little tyke. He's speeding around on crutches like a wizard. Got a doctor's appointment tomorrow to see how his knee is."

I've only seen pictures of Len's family, but Georgie always jumps out at me. He's the kind of child I like, full of life and energy, with silly faces for the camera. Such a character. I'm happy for Len that he's going to have such a wonderful gathering over the holidays. Since Jeanette left me, my Christmas Days have been somewhat muted. Lonely, many would say.

I've always marked it as a useful day for introspection and gratitude around my charity work, but there has been an ache over the past few years.

"The group are already set up in the dining hall," Len says. "Everyone is here bar Mr Carson. His flight's been delayed."

"Thanks, Len."

At least I'm not the latest attendee. I always like to be punctual, but on grotto days it's difficult. I hate having to close the line while kids are still keen for the queue.

I walk through Bryson's large stone hall to join the others. The founders are an eclectic crew, but we all have two things in common.

Money, and a penchant for hardcore filth.

I have both in abundance, but still, I'm one of the lower branches on this tree. Some of these men have corporations that span across the globe, and political associations worth billions.

The chatter is still in the realms of casual conversation as I walk in and take my seat at the table. Samuel is gloating about a merger with a major rival, where he's 'raked it in' and come out on top.

"How are you doing, Santa?" he asks me.

"I'm doing well, thank you."

"Should have worn your silly hat and your fat suit."

The others laugh along at the image of me in my costume. They always do, because they simply don't get why a man like me would pour so much time into festive activities for charity. I very much doubt any of them would so much as consider dressing up and sitting in a grotto all day to make children smile – unless it was for a PR stunt, with a crowd of paparazzi buzzing around.

Even then though, the paparazzi can be dangerous.

When we founded the Agency almost twelve years ago, its primary aim was a safe space for us away from the spotlight, where we could all seek our thrills without the risk of being outed. Nowadays the Agency is a multi-million business venture, with each of us taking a cut from every proposal. Officially, it's an organisation in the PR arena. Our faceless persona draws no attention, unless you have reason to know.

We all meet here at Bryson's for quarterly business reviews, and we conduct the occasional social, but more often than not when we cross paths now, it's for one reason only. A proposal with one of our entertainers.

We test out the 'hardcorers', to see if they live up to their profiles, taking it in turns to choose the entertainer and set the scene. Fair trade and all that, since none of us are allowed to use the platform for personal use. It's a code of conduct that we have been adhering to from the very beginning. Anonymity at all costs. Hence why our entertainers are always hooded when they play with us – from the moment they leave for the appointment until the moment they are dropped back at their door.

"Who is it going to be for you next?" Wesley asks me, and my gut twists. It's my turn to call the shots in a few weeks' time.

"Hmm, let me guess." Seb rubs his chin. "Creamgirl by any chance? What's the point in even asking him, Wes? He's practically besotted."

If only he knew.

They all laugh, and I'd normally laugh along with them. It's been Creamgirl every time for me for the last three years straight. Francis pretends to grab hold of a chubby ass with a *take it, slut,* but tonight his humour grates at me.

I know he's imagining ramming his dick into Tiffany's beautiful ass, and so are the others. They have plenty of memories to call upon. They know her screams and whimpers, and the way she curses when she's on the edge. They know how her cunt feels, and how her ass stretches, and how her bobbing tits look when she's bouncing.

They've seen her hung, and hurt, and bleeding. They've lashed her, and tested her to her limits, and put her through filth to the extreme.

But they haven't seen her face. Not once. Not like I have. They haven't seen her eyes light up as she smiles, or the glow of her cheeks as she's laughing. The few cheeky pictures on her profile could never do her justice. Not in a million years.

"I've got the calendar up," Wesley says. "She's rammed full of proposals until Christmas, but I'll get Orla to shift them around. Two weeks Monday?"

I swallow before I nod, trying to keep a cool head. I know exactly what proposals Tiffany has coming up in her calendar, and I have cursed at the thought of her attending any single one of them. I'd hoped that having some one-on-one proposal time with her would cement the relationship into the realms of casual, but I was delusional. It's only made it worse.

Ten times worse, in fact.

I didn't get a wink of sleep last night after she left.

At least booking Creamgirl in for my next session here will shunt back a lot of her other proposals. Entertainers always need some recovery time after they've been to Bryson's, and we always arrange that for them behind the scenes. We exploit the 'naughty lists' on their profiles to the absolute extreme.

"Excellent," I say. "I'll draw up some ideas."

"Make sure it includes piss play, yes?" Bryson asks. "I'll be saving my bladder for that big beauty."

"Ditto," Seb says. "And first dibs on her wholesome cunt for me."

"First dibs on her fat ass," Paul laughs.

The grating of their laughter only gets worse. My smile feels paper thin.

"I'll be getting first dibs on everything, remember? It's my proposal, after all."

"Alright, alright," Bryson says. "You get first dibs on anything, but piss play is going to be in there, yes?"

"Sure, yes. I'll be certain to include piss play."

"And tit punching." Paul jabs the air. "I want to bash her black and blue."

My palms feel sweaty as I notch up my smile. Group meetings used to be so much fun in the early days. We'd be coming up with ideas for hours on end, concocting filthy scenarios that suited us all. What used to be a simple sharing of a whore through an evening edged further to the extreme, little by little. Now it's almost a competition. Who can we push the hardest? Who can take the most? Which of us can come up with the most hard-hitting proposal of the year?

I'm relieved when the attention turns away from Tiffany and how Paul wants to punch her tits. If it went on much longer, I'd want to be punching him.

We have another proposal lined up before then, in just two days' time. Seb has chosen Harlot, and tells us how he wants to bind her on all fours for twelve hours straight, while we all take turns in her asshole. Cocks, then fists. He wants to use the electric wand to shock her pussy into spasming, and clamp her nipples with pincers so hard she'll bleed. It won't be the first time.

Harlot enjoys filth, I've no doubt of that, but she's come close to tapping out on the last two occasions, and Seb seems on a mission to goad her further.

He's revelling in spilling the details of his proposal, banning us all from shooting our loads for at least 24 hours prior, in order to get the most out of her, but for once the idea makes me anything but horny. The thought of fucking Harlot's ass while she's being electric shocked makes me feel nauseous, in fact. And it's not because of Harlot.

It's because of Tiffany.

"What's up with you, Reuben?" Bryson asks me, out of nowhere.

I straighten up in my seat. "Nothing, why?"

"You look like Scrooge, not Santa Claus. Did someone take a dump in the grotto?"

Bryson thinks he's fucking funny. Sad thing is, I used to think so, too.

"Shipment delays are causing some strife," I lie. "Over six of my malls are running low on premium items. It's a nightmare."

"I feel your pain," Seb picks up. "One of our couriers has been an absolute pain in the ass this week. We've had a five percent increase on refund requests."

The guys around the table wince, because we're talking big figures here, and I sweep in on the opportunity like a hawk.

"It's ridiculous, truly. I just don't have enough hours in the day." I pause. "You know, I might not even be able to make it to the Harlot gig. I might be too busy shifting suppliers."

You could hear a pin drop. They all stare at me in shock.

"Miss out on Harlot?" Bryson finally says. "What on earth are you talking about?"

"I'm well aware of what I'd be missing, Bry," I reply. "But these may well be extenuating circumstances. Business does always come first."

"Yes, it does. But I'm certain if you can make time for playing Santa, you can make time for ploughing Harlot's ass." He laughs. "Lighten up, Scrooge boy. Harlot will cheer you up a little bit, if nothing else. Seb might even give you first dibs as a founder favour."

"Shut up, Bry," Seb says. "I'm not handing out a founder favour when it comes to this one."

Their laughter is back, but mine is empty. I feel nothing as I look around the faces of the men who I would call my friends. I'm betraying them as well as scathing their manner. A Judas amongst them, drinking wine.

The code of conduct was set up around this table. I remember it well.

We're all in this together, or not at all. The damned drink with the damned, always.

We could never levy accusations, or use power plays with each other if we are all committing the same 'sins'. That's why we are forbidden to have personal interactions with our entertainers. The power of association is too wealthy to be gambled with.

Everyone is still laughing when Bryson's eyes land hard on mine. He knows me better than anyone else here, since it was him who brought me into the circle. He can probably smell my unease.

"Extenuating circumstances only, remember?" he says and I hold up my sweaty palms.

"Yes, of course. Extenuating circumstances only." My fake smile feels like a crime. "Shipping delays or not, I'll do my very best to be here." I hold up my glass of wine. "Cheers to Harlot, I can hardly wait."

I hang around for as long as I can stomach it, trying my best to join in with the conversation as we discuss Agency figures, but my heart is pounding all the way through. There's an impending sense of doom that won't go away. Part of me wants to confess my sins and face the disciplinary standoff head on, rather than carry the thorns of guilt. But I can't do it.

It would mean never seeing Tiffany again.

But that's only one of the thoughts that's going to see me sleepless, tossing and turning for nights on end. The thought of Tiffany here, being used for other men's pleasure, is sitting like a lead brick in my stomach, and the thought of taking pleasure from another woman does nothing for me at all.

I survey the crowd around the table in horror, masked behind a paper thin veil, because I know the road ahead has hazard warning lights flashing all over it. There's way too much at stake to pull crazy road stunts in this fraternity and come out unscathed.

This is absolute madness, and it should stop, for both Tiffany's sake as well as mine.

If I could pull over on the hard shoulder, I would do, but I'm already too intoxicated at the wheel to entertain the thought.

It's almost midnight by the time my driver arrives and Len hands me back my coat at the front door. The others are still chatting away now that Carson's arrived. They only just opened another vintage bottle of scotch.

"Goodnight, Mr Sinclair," he says, and I slap him on the shoulder.

"It's Reuben, remember? And pass on my love to Georgie. I hope his appointment goes well."

"I'll let you know on Tuesday."

Shit. Of course. Tuesday.

I'm supposed to be fucking Harlot's ass in 48 hours' time.

"Night, Len," I say, and step out into the relief of the cold December air, enjoying a moment of the chill before my driver opens the car door for me.

As we drive away, I know there is no way I'll be able to handle it. I don't want to fuck Harlot, no matter how entertaining an entertainer she can be. There is only one woman I'm interested in, and I stalk her calendar yet again through my founder login.

I don't know what the point is, seeing as I already know what her plans are.

Tomorrow evening she'll be playing *kitty* for one of her regular clients.

I've read every single one of the reviews he's left for her and read every single one of their proposals. So much for having a stalker fantasy, I'm becoming one in real life, and have been from the moment she walked into the grotto.

I could postpone or cancel her booking at the click of a button, and my finger hovers, tempted. I don't want her to be *kitty* for an old man with a pet play kink, and would happily compensate her the £12000 she'll get from the experience ten times over.

But I have no right to make that decision.

Tiffany can be *kitty* all she wants to. The choice is hers to make, not mine.

"Doing anything special for Christmas, Mr Sinclair?" my driver asks.

Tiffany's cheeky smile comes immediately to mind.

"Nothing planned as yet," I tell him.

But that's a lie.

I've subjected Creamgirl to every kink and filthy fetish there is – apart from one thing.

Having our entertainers hooded for the founders has one drawback. There is no access to their mouth.

"If you don't mind me saying, Mr Sinclair, but with the amazing work that you do, Santa deserves his own special time."

Yes, a special time, kissing that gorgeous mouth. Tasting her. Sinking my cock down her throat. My cock swells just thinking about it.

"I'm sure something will come up," I tell him.

CHAPTER 12
Tiffany

User 290. Male. 63.

Here, kitty kitty.

You've been away for quite a while, and I want my pussycat home, where she belongs.

You'll be chastised for being a bad kitty, because good kitties never leave their owners and run away – but once you've learnt your lesson, I've got some treats for you.

I want my pussy cat around for a long evening, and I expect to play kitty games the way we always play them.

Cat outfit, and nothing but meows, please. Food from your bowl only.

Plenty of 'fuss' on the sofa with your owner, and being a good kitty as you sit on his lap.

And not forgetting the litter tray, of course.

Duration: 9 hours.

Proposal price: £12,000.

User 290 has become one of my favourites. I'll be a good kitty for him tonight.

I'm careful as I put my cat headband in my bag, not wanting to damage the fluffy ears, because he deserves the best looking kitty he can get, but I prepare myself with my cat tail butt plug before I go. It's too much of a struggle to try to work that thing into my ass when I'm mewling outside his door.

Pet play was never something on my radar before I joined the Agency. Dressing up as a cat for nine hours straight was never a game I imagined playing, but it's actually good fun. I love being a pussy who is having her pussy used, and User 290 is a very good owner.

It will get my mind off Reuben too, which is a sensible blessing. I have to laugh at myself in the mirror as I give my lip gloss a final check. What the fuck ever. My mind has been on Reuben every single second since I left Evesham. I've been avoiding Josh and Ella like the plague, since Josh would notice my glee in a heartbeat. I'm like a bloody schoolkid crushing over a heartthrob.

My long, fake fur coat hides my butt plug tail alright in the cab, but it's a bastard to sit on. It's quite a chunky sonofabitch, since it has to stay in place so long. Wouldn't want to lose my tail in the middle of play.

My client lives right at the top of a block in Kensington, on a floor of his own, so I get some privacy when I'm outside his front door. There, I prepare myself. I drop my coat on the floor, leaving me stark naked besides my tail plug, and fish my cat ears from my bag. It's high quality, with tight clips that secure it in my hair, so it's not coming out anytime soon. I fasten my collar around my neck, with its tiny bell, and then it's time for the final part of my makeup. I use my compact mirror and my face pencil and get to work on my nose and whiskers. I'm quite practiced at this by now, so it looks kinda cute when I'm done. Being a cat suits me. Maybe I was one in a past life. With a life like this kitty has, it wouldn't be all that bad.

I click on *arrived* before I put my kitty paw gloves on, because I can't use a touch screen through fur. Then it's down on my knees time, with my coat and bag ditched beside me. I give him a loud mewl and push a hand through the cat flap, batting it around in a fake attempt to get inside.

The cat flap gives me enough of a glimpse to see User 290's shoes walking down his hallway. I'm smiling up like a good kitty as he lets me in, crawling past him on all fours and rubbing myself against his legs. He grabs my coat and bag and drops them inside before he closes the door.

"Where have you been, Priscilla?" he says, with his hands on his hips, towering over me. "You've been downstairs again, haven't you? Look how many treats they've been giving you!"

User 290 does love a well fed pussy...

That's a good thing, because so do I.

I rub against his leg again, arching myself like a cat would with a mewl. The bell around my neck gives a little jingle, but it doesn't win *Priscilla* any favours. He kicks me away from him, pointing his finger as he calls me a *bad girl*. I try rubbing myself against his leg again, and get the same result – another nudge of his shoe under my belly as he shoves me away. One more go, and he's rougher, he toes me in the ribs and sends me sprawling.

"BAD GIRL!"

Now is the time to be a good kitty and apologise. I roll onto my back with my gloved hands in a begging position and my legs held up, offering him my belly with another mewl. I give him a flutter of my eyes, staring up at my grand owner as I silently ask for a fuss.

User 290 has to be at least six foot two. He's as skinny as a rake, and his fingers are long and savage. He always looks super stern when he's chastising me.

"No more going downstairs! No more treats from other people!"

I open my thighs so he can see his pussy's pussy, and stretch my arms above my head.

Meow.

I squirm, offering my naked body as a token of my kitty affection. He manages to hold out for a minute or so before he sighs and breaks. He drops to a crouch at the side of me.

"What am I going to do with you, hey? Who can stay mad at such a cutie?"

He tickles under my chin before he runs his fingers down, petting his kitty. I love how zealous he is with my tits, arching my back and mewling for more. It's my tummy next – his favourite. He works my belly like I'm a treasure, tickling and rubbing me up and down. He rubs lower and lower each time, until he's rubbing his pussy cat's horny pussy. Fuck, it feels nice. I clench my ass around my tail plug to let the sensations ripple.

"Do they give you strokes like this downstairs? I bet they do. You'd better start remembering, Priscilla. I'm your owner. I'm going to block up the cat flap unless you're a good girl and stay with your daddy."

He slides two long fingers inside me.

"You've missed your daddy, haven't you?"

I twist and arch against his fingers, with a sweet *meow*. Yes, I have missed 'Priscilla's' cat daddy. I haven't been here in over a month. Being a cat slut is such an obscure, welcome break from being a human one. No words needed, no conversation. Nothing but a cat accepting what her gracious owner wants to give her. User 290 always gives me a lot.

He pets me so well – all the way up and down – from my

slippery cunt, to my belly, tits, chin. He loves to focus on my belly. He gives it a jiggle.

"Look how many treats they've been giving you..." he says again.

I haven't mastered the art of purring, but I've got a range of *meows* down pat. I answer him in cat language, shifting myself towards his touch as any fussed cat would do. I smile as he gives me another tickle under the chin, relaxing into the zone.

I'm Priscilla the pussy, and my pussy wants some action.

"Come on, kitty cat," he says, and gets to his feet. "Let's get you some milk."

I crawl to the kitchen after him, staring up as he gets a bottle from the fridge. I lick my lips with another *meow*, and scuffle along as he takes it through the living room. Priscilla's feeding bowls are waiting on the floor. He fills my drinking bowl up with milk right to the top, *generous*, and I position myself so I'll be facing him when he drops himself onto the sofa.

He's watching me with eager eyes as he takes his regular seat, and my eyes fix on his as I lower my face to the bowl. I use slow, long sweeps of my tongue to lap up the milk. So messy, and yummy, but it feels so fucking kinky.

"That's it, kitty cat, drink up your milk. You must be thirsty."

The filthy smirk on his face and the way he palms his cock through his trousers makes my clit pulse. I want to be a good pet and lick up every last drop.

It's sweetly humiliating being *Priscilla*, on all fours on a guy's carpet while I lap up milk from a plastic pet bowl. It takes fucking ages to drink like this, with milk getting up my nose and dribbling down my chin, but I manage it. I'm licking the bowl clean by the time I'm done, and User 290's eyes are still fixed on mine.

Meow, I say, as though I'm hungry for more, but he shakes his head.

"No, kitty, that's enough. If you're a good girl, you can have some more with your dinner."

I look at the empty plastic bowl next to me – the one for my evening meal, and next to that, just a little way along the wall, is my litter tray. Nice and tidy, just waiting to be soiled. That's one of my favourite parts of this proposal, every single time. Soiling the litter tray while he watches me.

User 290 pats the sofa beside him, and I scurry on over. I know the position he likes me in, and lie down on my back for another fuss, my head in his lap as he smiles down at me.

"Such a beautiful pussy cat," he says, and resumes with the tickles. "You enjoyed your milk, didn't you?"

I give a meow, not a nod, sweeping my tongue around my lips as he runs his hand down to my horny slit.

"Maybe you'll get some special milk later, if you're really good for your daddy."

I know User 290's *special milk*, and I'm always desperate for it by the time it comes. It won't be yet though, since he means pet play when he says it. He wants me to act like a cat for him. He's got pictures of cats all over his living room, and has some cartoon cat magnets on his fridge. The guy is obsessed with them.

It only makes me keener to play the part.

He switches the TV on as though it's just a normal evening with his cat lying at his side, but I'm feeling more demanding than usual.

My mind is drifting to Reuben when it should be here, and I don't want that. Reuben thinking is becoming as obsessive to me as cats are to the guy on the sofa. If I don't watch out, I'll be putting Reuben Sinclair magnets on my fridge before I know it.

User 290 doesn't help with distraction. The TV shows he likes are dull as fuck. I don't want to be watching *Gardener's World* when my clit is throbbing, and tonight I can hardly take it. I want User 290 to be petting his kitty cat with all of his attention, not sharing him with closeups of tulips and honeysuckle. I rub my head in his crotch with a *meow*, and squirm, offering my kitty tits to him.

"Stop it, Priscilla," he says with a chuckle. "You know I like this programme."

Yes, he fucking does, and to be fair, it's not always this bad. Gardening isn't my bag, no, but I quite often enjoy the chill out, lying on my side with my head on his thigh, whittling away the whiles as he strokes me, but I'm more frustrated this evening. I won't stop pawing and mewling and stealing his attention from the show.

"Priscilla!"

I don't stop. I grip his hand in my fluffy paws and playfully bite his arm with catlike games, and his tone lightens up as he laughs.

"You've got a lot of energy tonight. How about we sort that out?"

Crap, I've forgotten about some of the games User 290 has up his sleeve. I know his smirk as he reaches past the arm of the sofa and grabs a stupid battered mouse toy. He teases me with it before lobbing it across the room, and I could curse as I have to jump to attention. I shift my fat butt and leap down onto the floor like I'm on the hunt for a real mouse. I scrabble for it, batting it around the place with my fluffy glove until I pin it down and bite at it.

I chew on a fake mouse as User 290 grins at me.

"Bring it back," he says and clicks his fingers.

I play up for a few seconds at his command, since I'm a cat, not a bloody dog – making him lower his tone before I grip the thing in my teeth and take it back to him.

He loves it as I scurry back and forth, mewling and clawing at the bastard toy every time he throws it. My heart is pounding and my butt is sore from my swinging tail by the time he tells me enough is enough and puts it away.

I'm grateful to be back up on the sofa when he pats the seat again. Tulips and honeysuckle are a welcome contrast to playing mouse games, so I max out the time with my head on his lap, relishing the stroke of his hand on my belly.

But still, my pussy is aching.

I want my owner to touch Priscilla like his good little kitty cat. To play with her with his hands and his cock, not just a cat toy. *Meow*, I tell him, and then I climb up, resting my fluffy paws on his thighs as I meet him face to face. So many words to choose from but another sultry *meow* seals the deal. He knows kitty cat is a dirty feline who wants more attention.

He relishes in my denial, sadistic bastard, giving me nothing more than a token stroke across the back and a gentle pull on my tail. Jesus, how it strains.

"No more fussing until after your dinner," he says, and is if on cue, the credits for the end of the gardening programme show up onscreen. Three in a fucking row, we've played through.

He swats me off his lap. "Move, Priscilla. Let's fill your tummy up."

My tummy almost makes me retch at this bit. It's not my favourite in the slightest. I was hoping I'd get at least a taste of dick before things took this avenue.

I cross my fingers that he's gone for something vaguely palatable, but when he holds up the can, it's the one I hate most. His cold stew, in his fake cat food tin, with the carrot bits I despise. He makes this one on purpose, because he knows I don't like it.

He's testing me. I see the glint in his eyes as well as the swelling bulge in his pants. His dick is rock hard under there.

I haven't come once yet, and no cock has come my way, and I have no reason to resent it. He's paying through the fucking nose for me to be his kitty cat, so I'll be one. I don't know where the frustration comes from as my owner empties my portion of his gross looking *cat food* into the feeding bowl. If Priscilla was a real cat, no wonder she'd be fucking off downstairs.

My heart is in my throat as I line myself up ready to chow down my grim dinner. I have to try my best not to retch and hurl it up whenever he dishes up this load of shit, but he knows that.

Yes, he's definitely testing me tonight.

He switches the TV off and sits on the edge of the seat, watching me.

"Eat up, kitty cat, then Daddy will give you another stroke."

I need something inside me. Fingers, dick, toys – I don't care. No matter how many times I've been touching myself lately, the tingles never fucking leave.

Reuben.

It all comes down to Reuben.

User 290 will have to relieve me, or I'm going to go insane. My cunt's need for play far outweighs the humiliation of foul tasting *cat food*. I keep my stare on him and not on the bowl underneath me. I blank my mind to everything but the way he's watching me, chewing and swallowing, trying not to retch.

When he gets his cock out and starts working his shaft, it's a whole lot easier. I adore how he encourages me.

"That's it, eat up now, good kitty. Lick it, like a sweet kitty. Lick it."

I wriggle my tongue around in the cold gravy, and I can't help myself. I slide a gloved hand back between my legs and rub myself, hard and fast. It helps so much, it's insane. I don't care what I'm eating anymore, I gobble it gladly, mewling and lapping and swallowing, until once again I'm licking my bowl clean.

"More milk for kitty," he says and beckons me over.

I hate how I have stop rubbing myself to crawl over to him. I crouch between his legs when he offers his dick to my grotty mouth, lapping him up and down with my dirty tongue. And then I gobble him with more want than I ate my cat food.

I want *his* milk.

"Good girl, Priscilla," he says as my head bobs. He takes my hair as I lap at him. "Good kitty cats get the cream."

And Creamgirl gets the cum. Always.

I know how to mewl around his dick as he fucks my mouth. I'm well prepared when he gets to his feet so he can drive his cock harder into his kitty's throat. I look up at him as he does it, my chin covered with *cat food* and dried milk. I must be a mess, but I'm his treasured pet serving her owner, and I feel like a superstar as he grabs his balls and tells me to open wide.

The first spurt hits the back of my throat, and I manage to catch most of the rest. Cum tastes so much fucking better than his cruddy stew. I swallow it down, then lap up the remnants from Daddy's dirty dick.

Then I smile for him with a different kind of *meow*.

His kitty cat needs to come now. His kitty's pussy needs his care.

"On your back, pretty girl," he says, and I roll over. I spread my legs and give him feral mewls as he finally gives me what I need, stuffing four fingers in my cunt at once. "Beautiful tail," he says, and I clench my ass tighter. He tugs at it, so I have to fight him to keep it in, brushing my clit with his thumb as he laughs at me.

Then he hooks his fingers inside my kitty cat cunt and really works it.

My tits jig as I do, writhing on the floor. My *meows* are frantic as he fingers me, because I need it so fucking bad.

But it's not about being Priscilla the pussy cat. My mind is still filled with Reuben.

I imagine how it would feel to be Reuben's kitty. Would I lap up milk from a bowl, and play with a mouse toy like a chubby idiot, charging all over his floor? Would I chow down rancid stew, and pretend to enjoy it, and suck his dirty dick like a grateful pussy?

Yes, I would. But more importantly... I'd do it for free.

I'm losing my fucking head.

It's a relief when User 209 changes position and tugs me up onto all fours. When he's behind me, I imagine him as Reuben, bucking back at him like he's the answer to my prayers.

"Let's see what other treats I can give you," he says, and I'm panting, because I could take anything.

Jesus Christ, I mewl when I feel something fluffy gliding up and down my wet slit.

Fuck, it's the mouse toy – I recognise its stupid bobble nose. It's kinda sick, but kinda hot – in a twist of humiliating perversion. I relish that, shuffling my legs wider.

"*Kitty can have her reward,*" he whispers.

The toy isn't fluffy for long. It's soaked in seconds as he plugs my cunt with it, tugging it out by its tail.

This is off script. He's never done this before. But I take it. Fuck rules, and proposal guidelines, because I'm already breaking the most fundamental rule there is anyway. I've been *entertaining* a founder. *Entertaining* my boss.

Entertaining Reuben fucking Sinclair.

Taking a mouse toy in the cunt off script pales into insignificance compared to that shit.

I'm bucking against User 209's hand as he fucks me with it, wanting deeper and fucking deeper. I'm panting harder, building to a crest, ready to squirt and gush around a fluffy bloody mouse when my client reaches across the living room floor for the litter tray.

"You must need to go to the toilet, kitty. Go on, cutie, use the tray for Daddy."

My mewl isn't a meow, it's a moan.

He guides the tray between my legs, and my chubby thighs have to stretch crazy wide to stay in position. Priscilla's owner loves watching her piss in the litter tray. It always drives him fucking wild. But I've never usually got a mouse toy in my pussy while I do it. He pushes it in deep and lifts my tail up, easing the butt plug out just a touch, enough to be torture.

"Use the tray," he says. "Come on, kitty. Use the fucking tray."

The gravel of his voice sets me off. Again, I imagine it's Reuben. Always fucking Reuben.

I push down on both the toy and the plug, trying to focus on pissing. It's just a dribble at first, but it speeds up into jet like bursts – settling into one long stream that soaks into the kitty litter. It sounds fucking filthy. It feels fucking divine.

"Dirty pussy," User 209 says, and yanks the mouse out of me while I'm still dribbling piss from my slit. I'm ready for a decent fucking slamming when he replaces it with his cock, still hoisting my tail in the air so he can see my straining asshole.

Fuck, yes, I'm going to come this time. I *meow* and *meow* and fucking *meow*, rutting back against my owner when he takes hold of my collar and jams in hard. His dick is as long and savage as his fingers, I just wish he'd fuck my plugged up ass with it as well as my cunt.

I'm a mess when I come – literally. Face covered in filth, and a piss filled tray between my legs that I manage to scuff with a thigh while he's ramming me. Litter goes tumbling onto the carpet, but he doesn't let up – just keeps on coming as I do.

We come in sync, the dirty kitty cat with her collar bell jingling and her filthy owner grunting and cursing, and it's fucking perfect. Worth chowing down a bowl of gross dinner for.

Luckily, it's not more *cat food* that comes as a reward this time. It's a fresh bowl of milk. Real milk that will taste like heaven on my foul tongue.

I'm a happy kitty as I lap it up from the bowl, with milk dribbling down my chin and piss dribbling down my thighs.

Priscilla adores User 209.

She's a very happy kitty with a very happy pussy.

"What shall we watch next?" he says as I settle once more on the sofa with my head on his lap.

I give an attempt at a purr, because I really don't care what crap we watch.

He strokes my fluffy ears as he flicks through the channels, coming to rest on a baking programme and the contestants are displaying their efforts. Fuck, how my belly rumbles.

It makes me think back to my belly rumbling at dinner with Reuben. How he smiled. How he handed me the menu.

"If only cats could talk," User 209 says, "what are you thinking about, kitty?"

Another mewl and I nudge his groin with my head.

He chuckles. "Don't you worry, kitty, let Daddy rest awhile, and then we can play bouncing on my lap. I know that you just love that game."

He's not wrong. I do love bouncing on his long dick.

Another purr. Another snuggle.

While Daddy rests up enough for a fresh round, I watch the blonde girl on TV, using her bare hands to slather icing on her cake.

But in my mind, they are my hands, and the cake morphs into Reuben's cock. A cock I have certainly felt but never laid eyes on.

It's going to be a long nine hours with kitty Daddy, but in my head it will be Reuben's cock I'm bouncing on.

Reuben's hands stroking me.

Reuben, chasing me and grabbing for my tail.

Reuben, ordering me to piss in the litter tray.

Reuben, Reuben, Reuben.

I'm fucking doomed.

CHAPTER 13
Reuben

I've been feeling anything but jolly since I left the grotto earlier. I have always loved my Santa days, seeing the smiles on children's faces as they tell me how excited they are for Christmas. It's magical. My own little taste of how festive family life could be, and likely the closest I will come to it. I've resigned myself to that fact.

Or I thought I had.

That's what is hurting today. An unfounded hope I never expected to be feeling.

I'm possessed by the memory of Tiffany's shocked eyes as she entered the grotto. Her smile at dinner. The incredible pleasure at seeing the true woman underneath Creamgirl.

I want so much more from her now. So much more that it's insanity at its finest. I'm having dreams I haven't dared consider in years.

Imagining her playing *kitty* for another man last night churned me up in a way I haven't felt in decades, and that chewed-up sensation came back with a vengeance as soon as my charity time was over earlier.

I battled it all the while I prepared myself for the founders evening, but it's a fight I could not win. There is not a single hint of excitement at the prospect of using Harlot to her filthy extremes, and as my driver turns into Bryson's driveway, the sensation ramps up so severely I feel sick to the stomach.

I've participated in founders' scenes so many times that I should be able to run on autopilot. Harlot is nothing more to any of us than a plaything in a hood, making a fortune out of her session, and for most of it I could be standing on the sidelines, watching on as my fellow founders take their fill. I could focus my attention on the practicalities, like clamping her nipples and binding her in position. I could back away quietly, and remain on the outskirts, barely making my presence known.

The problem is, I don't want to be there at all.

For the first time since I became one of the Agency founders, I don't want to join in on a hardcore scene. The idea repulses me.

My hands are already sweaty when I say good evening to Len and walk on through to join my fellow stakeholders. They are jovial and happy, engaged in dirty chatter when I enter the dining hall. They already have whisky glasses in hand, knocking back vintage shots as they fine tune exactly what they'll be doing to Harlot. Bryson has been obsessed with piss play for months, and he won't shut up about it. He points us out in order of who will spray Harlot when and where like a movie director, and I'm *lucky enough* to be granted the first round in her asshole, but I don't want to be spraying anything whatsoever near Harlot tonight.

I nod along regardless, clinking my shot glass with a *cheers* as everyone ramps up their excitement, but I feel nauseous. Betrayal is never something I take lightly, especially not when it's betrayal to my own soul.

That's how it feels as I stand like a fraud amongst my fraternity.

And it's all because of Tiffany.

The only woman I want to play with is the scarlet-haired

treasure who burst into my world without warning, and turned it upside down.

Bryson fixes me in a stare amongst the *cheers*. "What's with you again, Reuben? You're back to being Scrooge."

"Stock issues," I tell him, regretting how defensive my voice sounds. "Unfortunately, Christmas isn't about pleasure for me, it's about business."

I know Bry well enough to know he isn't buying it. He's trying to weigh me up, and a few of the others join him. A host of eyes examining me.

"Have you been in the grotto today?" he asks.

"Yes, of course."

"Santa takes precedence over business concerns then, but sharing an evening with your fellow founders doesn't?"

I don't like the edge to his words, because regardless of Harlot, my priorities would be the same.

"My charity efforts do take precedence over business concerns, yes, as far as they can do. But getting my dick wet? No, Bry. That's on the other side of the spectrum."

Seb steps closer to Bryson. "Wouldn't have imagined you saying that a few years ago."

"Things change."

People change, is what I mean.

"It's a few hours with Harlot." Seb shrugs. "I'm sure your stock issues can wait. Come on, man. Don't spoil the party."

"You'll thank us later," Bry tells me. "Once your cock is in Harlot's ass your priorities will swing."

He's wrong.

I pull my phone from my pocket. "I'm waiting for an urgent email, actually. It should be arriving any time now. Either that, or a supplier phone call. Preferably the former, as the latter would be conveying much more serious news."

"Right," Bry says. "Well, we have another forty-five minutes until our hooded whore arrives, so hopefully you'll have it sorted by then."

"Yes, hopefully."

I despise having to lie, even if the lie is a shallow, white one. It's true that I do have stock issues – any mall chain is bound to have them at the busiest time of the year, but the fictious email or phone call is nothing but fabrication.

I try to talk myself into reason. Tiffany is an entertainer, and I am a client. There is no relationship, no due loyalty, no exclusivity. In fact, I know she will be in as extreme a circumstance as Harlot will in a few hours' time. *Creamgirl* is attending an infamous proposal at a members club not all that dissimilar to ours – a friend of Bryson's who enjoys the filthy scene with his own group of filth buddies. She won't be hooded, but she may as well be.

He has a *glory wall* fixed up in one of the backrooms of his manor, and invites up to thirty guests at a time. He pays well for it, and we get a healthy cut of the proceeds. Tiffany will have a massive payout for her attendance later, and her reviews around the proposals have conveyed nothing but praise at her enthusiasm. She enjoys it. There is no good reason I should be so uneasy at the thought. So *enraged* at the prospect of other men treating her like a slut.

It's a ridiculous outlook, because she is one.

I can't wait for my next booking with her. For twenty-four hours straight, I'll be the one she'll be entertaining.

The week in the interim is going to feel like a lifetime.

I feel sweaty, even though Len has taken my coat. The room is stifling, despite the chill of December outside. Instead of accepting another whisky top up I take my phone back out and scroll through emails as the crowd watch me.

I sigh, and shove it back into my pocket.

"Still no news," I say, and Bry looks at the clock.

"Thirty minutes left to go."

Thirty minutes of hell.

I force myself to get in line and stop drawing attention, but I can't keep composed. I take another look at my phone, scrolling through already opened emails as I pace up and down the room, cursing loud enough that the other guys can hear me.

"Jesus Christ, man," Seb says. "Can you give it a rest now? You're dampening my fucking hard-on."

I force a smile. "Sorry. But needs must."

"Fuck stock issues. My needs are to get on that dirty little bitch as soon as Len has trussed her up, and make the most of our playtime. So sort your shit out, will you?"

Seb has grown in arrogance since his last merger. It's notched up to another division. He was lighthearted when I first met him, excited as his empire grew one step at a time, but he's a different man entirely now. My eyes scan around the group, and it's with startling realisation I realise how true that is of almost everyone.

The men I shared companionship, business rapport, and the creation of The Agency with aren't the men in this room anymore. They are hardened and ruthless now. Often crass and always greedy.

Yet, I'm not.

I'd rather throw myself on my own sword than turn into a shallow, egotistical narcissist.

In fact, I want the very opposite. I want to put my Bentley in reverse and drive back to earlier days, when this place used to be fun.

Or even further. Back into the distant past before I banished my dreams.

"Give me a moment," I tell them, and turn my back. I set up an alarm with the same tune as my ringtone for seven minutes' time, then thrust my phone back into my pocket. I rejoin the group and raise my whisky glass. "Fine, I'm done with emails. If it's urgent, they'll call."

Seb is smiling as he tops up my drink.

"Thank fuck for that, workaholic."

I force a smirk. "Sorry, sexaholic. Wouldn't want to impose on your boner."

"You'll thank me later."

I'm used to keeping a mask up when it comes to conversing in business, so I use the same tactics through the next few minutes, joining in at every possible opportunity despite the thunder in my guts. I've managed to blend back into the crowd when my alarm sounds out.

"Goddamnit." I shake my head in frustration as I take my phone out. "Sorry, guys. I have to take this."

I swipe the alarm to silent and press the phone to my ear, pacing away into a corner.

"What? Four days? But that's impossible. Fourteen stores are already out of stock, and twenty are at virtually zero. It needs to be sorted now. NOW. No. Not tomorrow. I need to speak to him now!"

My heart is thumping so hard I fear it could be palpitations. I know the entire room is staring at me.

"I'm not going to be accepting this, Margaret. Absolutely not. The terms have been in place since July. I'm calling him directly."

My cheeks are burning when I *hang up* my call and step back over to the group. I'm scowling as I shake my head.

"Fucking idiots. Honestly. It's a piss take. I'm not going to be standing for this bullshit a moment longer."

I check the clock, and then I go for it.

"I'm going to have to bail, everyone. My apologies, but I have business to attend to. This has to take priority."

"Get on it here," Bryson says, and gestures to the room next door. "Join the party when you're done."

I get a wave of panic at the prospect, wanting to get the hell out of here and be gone.

"Yeah," Seb says. "We'll only be down the hall. Don't miss out on the show for the sake of one bloody phone call."

I can feel my escape closing up around me. The other guys are nodding, but I'm already stepping away.

"I'd love to, but it's going to take a lot more than one bloody phone call. This might well be an all-nighter. It's global." So many hawk eyes are on mine, perplexed as I gesture to the exit. "Have a good time. I wish I could join you."

Seb shakes his head, looking at me like I'm a madman.

"At least we know you'll be joining us for Cream's hungry butt in a few weeks. Wouldn't want to miss out on that fun time, would you, Santa?"

A few of the men laugh at that, and I laugh along. "You've got me there, Seb. As if I could resist." I do my very best to keep my composure. "Good evening, gentlemen. Give Harlot an extra spray on my behalf, won't you."

My breaths quicken beyond reason the very moment I close the door behind me. I stay in the hall, leaning back against the wall as I message my driver. I wipe the sweat from my brow, pacing on a mission for the front door, but stop in my tracks when the grand entrance appears.

There is the sweet Harlot, hooded and shaking as Len strips her bare. She looks so tiny in comparison to Tiffany. You could play a tune on her ribcage. And her hip bones are clearly visible as Len slides her panties down.

He raises his eyebrows in surprise as he sees me there, but doesn't say a word. Neither of us do. I communicate as best I can by pointing to my phone and then to the door, mouthing *I have to leave* as I grab my coat from the rack.

Harlot flinches as I step up close to her, and my fears solidify to certainty. The idea of playing filthy games with such a willing participant does nothing for me whatsoever. I'm numb as I look at her naked body. Not a hint of animalistic lust in my veins.

I'm quiet as I open the door and mouth a *bye*, and then I'm out of there.

I need to go home. I need to get out of this place. I need to get away from the seedy den that used to satisfy every filthy craving I had.

It's only a week until my booking with Tiffany, I remind myself – but my resolve crumbles.

I don't bother waiting for my driver before I call up the Agency app. I click through to the calendar and call up *Creamgirl's* profile.

So many bookings. One after the other. Client after client expecting the beautiful slut to arrive for their appointments, ready to serve. But I can't take it.

It's madness. I know it is. But I do it anyway.

I click *postpone* on every one of them *due to personal circumstances*, selecting random dates in the new year for fresh bookings.

There is one I can't move, though. Not without scrutiny and a whole host of ramifications.

The founders' gig.

I can't change that without approval from at least three other members.

Fuck.

It won't be Harlot standing hooded in Bryson's hallway in two weeks' time as Len undresses her, it will be Tiffany, and there is nothing I can do about that. My hands are tied.

But they aren't entirely tied tonight.

We do need to be responsible advocates of the Agency after all. Entertainers are our primary assets, to be supported at all times.

I click on the address of the Glory Wall.

Just for reference...

And then I log in as User 5639.

CHAPTER 14
Tiffany

User 3980. Male. 39.

It's your time for the glory hole wall.
Can't wait to get you bound up and ready for it, you kinky bitch. Make
sure you're hungry for it.

Duration: 9 hours.
Proposal Fee: £18,000

The glory hole is another one of my favourite bookings. Nine hours straight of being trussed up and used by whoever wants me. These nine hours are a different league of hardcore than playing kitty and watching gardening shows. These guys always milk it for every fucking second, and I milk them for every fucking second right back. Nine hours of pure sucking and fucking is no easy feat, but that's why I'm top of the leaderboard. I don't give a toss if my cheeks hurt for three days straight. They always get prime service.

I wear a cup-less bra in black lace, and stockings and suspenders with no panties. This is a late nighter, so it's gone 9 p.m. when I get my cab. I wrap myself up in my long leather coat, but it won't be staying on long. The glory wall is in Chelsea. Some rich millionaire has turned their gothic manor into the ultimate seedy sex den, but it suits the place.

The cab drops me at the bottom of the driveway, and I walk on up in my red gloss stilettos with a sashay of my hips. I give the butler a coy *hey* and a wink, like usual. I know his smile by now, a half smirk that lights his face up. Only this time, it makes my guts flip.

He's a silver fox, and he's got to be in his fifties. He's nothing like Reuben whatsoever, bar his beard. The trim of it. The shape around his chin. But fucking hell, just that one pathetic parallel is enough to give me a rush.

The bullshit rush makes me giddy when I hand him my coat. He hangs it up like it's just another day at the glory hole wall, but I have major fucking butterflies. Beard be damned. Stupid comparison.

Reuben, Reuben, Reuben, fucking Reuben. I hate myself for this bullshit. If I didn't have a whole night of action ahead of me, I'd consider calling my therapist this very second. *Consider.* Yeah, right. That'll never happen. I'm lying to myself. I'll be *Reubening* myself to death before I make that call.

Me and the butler don't speak as he leads me to my destination. The glory den is along the hallway and off to the right, in a room literally split in half by a plasterboard wall. I know which side of it I'm going to be on and take my position – just another day at the office. Time to focus and get into Creamgirl mode.

I have to banish at least some of my Reuben related thoughts this evening. Any distraction would be a welcome relief. The more dicks the better, as far as I'm concerned.

I focus on the way the butler tightens the collar around my

neck, trying yet again to ignore the way his bloody beard looks. He isn't Reuben. He's nothing like bloody Reuben.

I get down on my knees and the chain from the collar is fed through a gap in the wall, it's length and tightness controlled by the user at the other side. I'm just a puppet with an open mouth in this spot. I get up on all fours, where the chain is at its tightest, and spread my legs open wide. Clients have full access to my ass and pussy whenever they want them, and the door they enter from is to my rear. I never get to see their faces.

It's like one of the founders' meetings in some ways, but the anonymity is less… extreme. Less formal. *Less terrifying.*

If I saw one of my client's faces in this place it wouldn't be the end of the world, but with the heads of the agency, it would be a whole other matter. Reuben has only reinforced the severity, and it should put me off since a breach of anonymity has my entire career at risk. *Should.* I'm a dumb cow sometimes though, always attracted to the forbidden – tonight I'm going to use that to my advantage. I'm going to channel that sensation into the job at hand, sinking into the beautiful black hole of slut space with a smile.

Or at least try to.

It's not going to be a smile for Reuben tonight. No. It can't be. It has to be about the clients. Just a shame that I'll be able to picture every single one of them as him.

I lick my lips as I wait for my first arrival. I shuffle my knees wider apart and rock myself, teasing my own pussy with my motions. I want cock inside me, and I want it rough enough to smash my schoolgirl butterflies to smithereens.

The overhead lights are bright in this place on purpose, highlighting every action and every move. I enjoy that. A lot of plus sized women are embarrassed by their curves, and I get it. Self-consciousness is a goblin of the fucking soul, but I love my body the way it is. I love how fat my ass cheeks are, and how it feels to have them spread wide open. I love the way my tits and belly bounce and slap when it's playtime. I love the way people see me as a chubby slutty mantrap, and how I'm so fucking good at exploiting it.

I'm so desperate today that I'm almost calling out for my first punters. I'm fixated on the hole, waiting for the first cock to present itself. My mouth is watering to fuck by the time one appears, and I'm straight on it like a dribbling bitch, slurping like I've been offered a triple chocolate sundae. I smack my lips, and trail my tongue up the shaft, then pop and suck in a rhythm that has him cursing. I can hear him on the other side, and my heart drops a little, since he doesn't sound like Reuben at all.

Fuck it. It's all still about fucking Reuben.

"Swallow it all," the guy behind the wall says, and I keep my mouth closed tight around his dick when he spurts for me, downing my first load.

It's the first of so many, I'll lose count by the time my shift is done.

I'm on cock number three, bobbing my head on a decent girther when I hear the door open to my rear. Judging from the footsteps and the heavy breaths, I think there's three of them.

I hear one guy getting down on his knees behind me. He shuffles up and gives my chubby booty a decent slap before his fingers get to work, sliding their way between my legs to feel how wet my pussy is.

"Love this juicy cunt," he says, and I recognise his voice. I've done him plenty, but nope. He sure as fuck isn't a Reuben type. He pushes three fingers in, and I'm so gagging for it that I nearly abandon my duties and neglect the cock in my gob. All I do is moan around the other guy's dick when a fourth finger slides in, pushing back as best I can.

"Nice to see you're as horny as ever," he says, but he has no fucking idea. My head is spinning with Reuben, and the founders, and it only makes me more needy. I imagine this setup is theirs, and Reuben could be one of the men either behind me, or on the other side of the glory wall.

If only he could see me, I'd make him proud of his slutty employee.

Or even better than that, I'd make him jealous.

That's what he said after all – another man's cologne when you're not the one wearing it. Oh fuck, how I wish he could smell just how many scents I'll be taking tonight. And maybe he will be...

Just like he was, watching me in the club, maybe he's watching me right now...

That spurs me on more than any other thought in the world.

I groan like the true whore I am when the first cock of the evening pushes its way into my pussy. A spit roast is always a winner for me, especially when the collar around my neck pulls tight enough to have me gagging. My eyes water as I choke on thick cock, but there is nobody staring down at me to witness the stream of my mascara.

I don't get any warning when the client at my rear shifts from my pussy to my ass. The surprise makes it hurt when he shoves his way inside me. I cry out around the cock in my throat, but it's muted. I manage a smile to nobody as I work my curvy butt back and take it.

I want to enjoy the burn of the tightness before I'm fucked so many times they slip in without restraint.

There is no rhythm to the fucking from either end. Each guy

works to their own different tune. It's hot like that, so amateur in its fucking filth. I'm just a girl on offer for anyone who wants a piece in this place. I get my first round of cum in my ass, and the dick gets replaced by another in my pussy and it's very welcome. He spreads my ass cheeks as he goes, and I've got his game. He's one of those guys who likes to see another man's jizz dribbling from my asshole. Hell fucking yeah. That turns me on. I push it out so he gets a better view. *My pleasure.*

I don't get an instruction to *swallow* through the wall this time, so I keep my mouth open when the guy spurts for me, happy when it splatters all over my face. I'm always such a fucking mess at the end of these sessions that I never get a cab back home – the butler usually drives me with a plastic seat cover to protect the Merc. It's not just jizz that I get through the hole – it's whatever the cock poking through wants to give me. Whatever comes out of the hose...

I always get some dirty surprises. I always get some filthy laughs from the other side when someone sprays my slutty face and leaves me drenched, but the laugh is on me, too. I don't get toilet breaks in the entire nine hours I'm collared here. I don't get to hold up a hand and go to the bathroom like a sweet little schoolgirl, oh no. I have to go right on the floor where I am, on my knees in my own wet mess.

The clients always love it that way.

That's the kind of proposal £18k gets them, and I'm more than happy to accommodate. Little do they know I'd probably do this shit for free.

Or I would... for Reuben...

His outrageous proposal comes slamming back into my mind. Forty-eight grand for twenty-fours with the man himself.

Only seven days until I'm playing for him – *with* him.

Only seven days until I get to see his cock for the first time.

I wonder what he'll do to me – if he'll aim for super hardcore.

My pussy floods at the thought.

Floods at the image of me with my mouth wrapped around his dick and looking up into his lusting eyes.

Jesus fucking Christ.

I wish my brain would shut the fuck up.

I've had five rounds of cum in my mouth when the first hose spray greets me through the wall. No matter how many times I think I'm prepared for it, I always jump backwards and strain against my collar. Instinct.

The guy feels the pull and tugs the chain tighter.

"Open your fucking mouth," he says, and I do as I'm told, making sure he can hear me slurp and swallow. But I'm too late for a clean go. My tits are already drenched, nipples dripping. The guy fucking my pussy gives a *fuck, yes* and picks up the pace, thumbing my ass at the same time.

I could be so dirty for him if he asked me...

If he's one of the *fuck, yes* gang when he sees the spray coming through the glory hole, then he's likely one of the long stayers who sink into the deep end of the filth pool by the end of the session. But it's too early to know that yet.

The next guy through the hole is so big he makes me heave when he fucks my throat, and he's paired up with a guy from behind fucking my ass from a high angle. Both of them strain and grunt like sin, and I feel myself sinking into my whore mind. The place where Creamgirl truly becomes Creamgirl – the puppet slut, out to serve her clients and nothing more.

It's a wonderful place to be.

Away from thoughts of Reuben, just a little bit.

My ass is a deep playground. Fingers, cocks, and a hefty slap of lube as they work me up to a dirty fisting. My needy whore cunt eats up three rounds of cum in ten minutes tops and I'm begging for more around the dick I'm slurping on.

More, more, more, always fucking more.

I get offered a drink of water and down it gladly when a set of dicks switch over, but then it's back to it. Cock after cock after cock, until I'm dripping jizz from my chin, and my tits, and my ass crack. My pussy is slimy wet by the time I need to go to the toilet myself.

I give notice with a *need to piss* warning, groaned around the dick in my mouth, but it only fuels them further. I've got a cock slamming me deep when I break and let it go, and his fingers are on my clit spurring me on as I piss around his cock.

It drives me out of my fucking mind. I'm out of my head when I come while pissing, grinning around a glory hole cock as the pressure subsides.

It's not the guys who usually start up with the degradation, it's me.

I'm a dirty fucking bitch, so take me like one. Fuck my slutty cunt, that's it. Just like that. Slap my chubby ass and get your dirty fucking fist in there, make me take it. Make me.

My mouth talks trash around cock and laughs along with the guys when more spray comes through. I come for the second time when one of the pussy fuckers pulls out and finally works a fist into me. It must be so creamed in jizz, it's crazy easy to take. I can hear the sloppy mess over my throat quacks as his fist thumps at my insides so beautifully.

One of the clients changes up the position. He rolls onto his back and shuffles on the piss wet floor so his face is under my cunt, and when the fist is yanked free, I cry out and ride his mouth like my life depends on it.

"Yeah, clean me up. Fucking clean me!"

I cry out again when the guy behind me slams his dick into my ass in one hard thrust.

And fuck, my cry turns to a whimper when the guy underneath me locks his mouth around my clit. He's got an advantage, since my clit is already swollen tender and ready to go, but he's good at it. Fair play to him. His sucking tips me over the edge, and his friend thanks him, since my spasms of joy clench the cock in my ass like a vice. I get another load of jizz to treasure.

The dicks blur, the sensations blur, everything blurs as I get wetter and wetter – caked in cum and spit and piss as I do my job. The glory hole gets dirtier, and the cocks need sucking harder, the dirty bastards tasting more and more filthy as the hours go by.

Another two glasses of water later and my bladder gives in again. The early attendees have disappeared, and I've got a new round of players. Still, none of them sound like Reuben as they cheer on the slut pissing on the floor.

Shame.

I'd love to hear his voice right now.

Halfway through the proposal and my knees are killing me and my arms are aching. My ass is on fire, and my pussy is full to the brim, and my cheeks hurt from sucking, but still I keep going. I never stop and flake out of a proposal, not ever.

I'm on auto slut mode as I beg for everything they have to give. My hair is soaked, dripping wet. I've been hosed by so much piss, I get chills, but it all just adds to the thrill. I love the insults they sling my way. I love my ass being slapped before they use it, voices merging together in cheers as they make me fuck myself on hand after hand, and cock after cock after cock.

Do you know how much of a filthy, cheap, slutty fucking bitch you are?

I get asked that quite often, and yes. I do.

It's what I want. It's what I love. It's where I lose myself and find myself, both at once.

Yet deep in the pits of me, something else is stirring tonight.

More than being a filthy, cheap, slutty fucking bitch right now, what I really want is to be with my silver fox Santa.

I'd give up all these cocks for just one go with his.

And if he was here... if he could see me... would he feel anything? Even for just a moment? Would he feel even the slightest pang of jealousy? Would he drag me away from the glory wall and hose me down for real and take me for himself?

I come again with a random cock inside me, but that's where my mind is.

The fantasy of Reuben storming in here and tearing me from the wall, claiming me as his and his alone.

I'm sleep deprived, and delirious. I have to be.

I've never wanted to be with just one man before. Ever since I became an entertainer, it's always been the more the merrier...

It's as though the earth is shifting under my dirty knees, minute by minute. Unstable as my feelings morph inside me. The dick in my throat means nothing. The people jeering and fucking me from behind are a blur of whatever. I just don't care.

I just don't care *anymore.*

I get a rush of terrifying freedom as the iron clad persona of Creamgirl finally cracks and falls away.

It's not Creamgirl I want to be in this room tonight. It's Tiffany.

And all Tiffany wants is to be with Reuben.

I want Reuben so bad it hurts.

Seven more days until our proposal and I wish like crazy that it was tomorrow.

I'm fucked. Really, fucking fucked. I should call my therapist for real.

But it feels so good...

I'm barely conscious by the time the session is over. The butler offers me a towel and I clean myself up. In the silence of the aftermath, he wraps me in a blanket and guides me out of this place into the hall outside. It's 6 a.m., nobody left around bar me and him, and even though I've been fucked half to death, all I can do is stare at his beard, still possessed by the fragment of similarity.

"All done," he says. "Ready for home?"

I can't help my usual banter.

"Kinda. Could do a few more rounds, you know me."

I swap the blanket for my coat and bag, and wait for him to get his car keys, but he doesn't put on a coat, just looks out into the courtyard as a flash of headlights show.

"Your cab is here," he tells me.

"My what?"

"Your cab," he says, like it should be obvious. "You booked it, yes? We got the confirmation via the app earlier."

I haven't got a fucking clue what he's talking about until he opens the door to reveal a Bentley parking up outside.

That's no fucking cab.

My heart drops through the floor, then zooms up into the fucking sky.

It can't be.

The driver gets out of the car and I was right. He does have a similar cut of a beard to the butler. Only better.

One billion percent fucking better.

The grin on his face makes my insides melt when he steps up to me.

"Time to go, Creamgirl," he tells me, and links his arm in mine.

CHAPTER 15
Tiffany

The morning sky is still dark as Reuben leads me towards his flash Bentley. I'm so fucking tired, it's untrue – but so excited that the adrenaline is spiking in my veins. I can't comprehend this is happening.

I wait until we're down the steps and out of earshot before I start firing questions at him.

"What are you doing here? Why did you come and get me? Was there some kind of Agency emergency or something? What's going on?"

"Get in the car and I'll explain."

He opens the passenger door for me, and I stare at the luxury leather seat. The idea of soiling it horrifies me.

"Have you got a seat cover or something?"

"No, I don't have a seat cover, but I do have a valet company. Don't worry your beautiful head about it."

"Beautiful head? Yeah, right." I laugh and give a *mwah*. "I'm covered in cum and my hair is in piss soaked ringlets, in case you hadn't noticed."

"I'm well aware of that, *Creamgirl*."

"You must be bloody bonkers then."

My own brash voice is grating at me, but I can't help it. I'm so nervous, I rely on my usual manner, where it's safe.

I slide my throbbing ass into the seat and suck in breaths once Reuben shuts the door for me, trying to stay calm. My stare is fixed on him as he walks around to get in the other side. He fastens his seatbelt, starts up the car and turns out of the drive without so much as breaking a sweat.

"Seatbelt please, Tiffany," he says, eyes on the road.

Seatbelt, right. I pull it over my big tits and buckle up.

This is so fucking weird, it's insane.

"There's a bottle of chilled water for you in the glove box," he says.

"Thanks."

I'm so thirsty, I down the whole thing in two long slugs.

"That really hit the spot," I tell him. "Thanks for that."

"Not a problem," he says. "Are you ok? You've had quite a night."

I narrow my eyes, still trying to comprehend this level of craziness.

"At the glory wall? Yeah, no big deal. I've been there plenty." I twist in my seat a little. "Seriously, Reuben, what's going on here? It's freaking me out."

He indicates right at the next turn, his eyes on the road.

"Check the Agency app, and things will make a little more sense."

I fish my phone from my bag and see an Agency notification waiting for me. It's from User 5639, asking for his proposal to be rescheduled.

To this morning.

Now.

"Why did you need the proposal moved? Did something come

up? I could have fitted you in somewhere else, you didn't have to grab me on the back of the glory wall."

"No. Nothing came up. It was all on me."

He's smiling at the road, not wound up or pissed at me. It's another wave of surreal that has my heart thumping.

"The question is," he says. "Are you going to accept it?"

"The proposal? That's hardly a question." I click accept and show him the screen with a *tada* as we pull up at some traffic lights. "So, where are we going?"

"I have nowhere pre-booked."

"Nowhere?"

"It was an impromptu decision. So it might be a more traditional affair of *your place or mine* this time around, unless we grab a standard double."

There is no chance I'd want Reuben bumping into Ells or Josh in the elevator at mine, so Belgravia is off the cards, and a standard double hotel room when I'm covered in piss? Not the best after the night I've had.

That isn't the real reason I'm having stomach flips, though. I'm too fascinated by the other option on the table. *His place.* Where does Reuben Sinclair live? What does his home look like?

"I think we should try yours, if that's ok, User 5639?"

"That's more than ok with me, Creamgirl. Do you want to swing by yours first to grab anything? Belgravia isn't too far out of the way."

I have to laugh, even though I'm knackered, because it's another straight up round of *what the fuck?*

"You know I live in Belgravia?"

"Yes, I do. I am your boss, remember."

"Are you turning into a stalker boss? Want to do a stalker play scene next?" I grin. "Do you know what my apartment number is?"

He shoots me a side eye. "West tower, number 27, if I'm correct?"

I laugh. "Jesus. Do you know what colour my living room carpet is, as well?"

He tips his head. "Not yet. Shall we go take a look? Like I said, we can swing by."

"Nah. I don't expect I'll be wearing my favourite PJs for our booking. You're alright. I'm hardly there at the moment anyway. They're probably still in the washing machine."

"I did notice your calendar is extremely busy," Reuben says. "I'm surprised you get any time in there whatsoever. Do you ever even take an evening off, you kinky workaholic?"

"Workaholic? Says you who practically lives at the grotto as well as running a multi-million-pound empire."

He smirks. "I guess I'm not the only stalker in this car. Have you been checking me out?"

I hold up my hands with another laugh. "Guilty as charged."

"We seem to be two very bizarre fitting peas in a pod. You're not the only one who rarely gets to spend time at home, Tiffany. It will be nice to spend some time at mine, actually."

"Aren't you in the grotto today?"

"I am indeed, but I'll be back this evening."

My head feels fuzzy – glory wall catching up with me. My timings must be screwed.

"That's when the proposal will start? This evening?"

Reuben smiles. "You blindly accepted without so much as checking the details, didn't you? How unprofessional."

He's got me there.

"What can I say? Guilty as charged. Again."

"Take a look."

I get a hint of something underlying in his tone, but I don't know what. He's still a mystery to me. The man seated beside me is a beautiful oddity, and comes with a chemistry I don't understand. I'm alight with it. It's like a layer of static under my skin.

"Go on," he says. "Take a look."

I take a look at the proposal again and have to blink twice. The booking started at six a.m. sharp, exactly when he picked me up. Twenty-four hours for £48k, and it started when I stepped out from the glory wall. Jesus.

But why? What the fuck?

Reuben just stares at the road as I stare at him. His profile as he drives is fascinating. I'm drawn to the way he grips the wheel, and the way he's so straight in his seat. The very opposite of a show off boy racer.

The static builds, and it's addictive. I get crazy waves of want – obsessive to the extreme. It reminds me of my younger days when the mega attractions I had really meant something.

This static is so much better than feeling numb.

I'm glad we're going to Reuben's place, because I don't actually want to go back to mine. Even Josh doesn't know quite how much I've been avoiding my own company lately. It's been getting worse. I was mainly at his place before Ells came along, but lately I've been becoming more of a third wheel. And then there's Caroline's news... her sweet little baby bump...

As much as I tell myself it doesn't matter for shit, things have changed. I cram in proposals, and binge watch TV, but the pang of loneliness has been jabbing me. I nearly booked a holiday over the holidays, it was doing my head in that much. But I have nowhere to go. I'd still be lonely on a beach in Timbuktu.

"This is mental," I say. "You don't have to pay me for sitting in a car with you."

"I know I don't, and you don't have to be sitting in a car with me. This is at my request, not yours."

"So you're paying forty-eight grand for what? Me chilling at your place while you hand out goodie bags in a Santa costume? You won't be getting a go with my goodie bags for hours."

He chuckles. "You could see it like that."

"How else is there to see it?"

He takes another turn, towards Mayfair. "I see it as a fair proposal. You catch up on your beauty sleep, I do my grotto shift, and then we take it from there."

The butterflies in my stomach are on overdrive. I feel like such a state in this car. A piss soaked hooker, next to a suited, booted millionaire. But when I study him more closely, there are some telltale signs I haven't noticed before. His hair is slightly dishevelled, and his tie is a bit loose. He looks tired, not fresh after a morning shower, ready to hit the mall for the day. Mr Sinclair looks drawn. His eyes hooded.

"Did you have a late night?" I ask him.

"Maybe."

I check the app for the exact time his proposal landed in my inbox. Hmm. Just after I arrived at the glory wall. Interesting.

"You didn't pull an all-nighter yourself, did you?"

He keeps his eyes on the road. "So many questions from a girl who desperately needs a shower and some sleep. Just relax. Have a good long snooze if you want to."

A snooze is the last thing I want. All I want is to touch him. To talk to him. To *be* with him.

He pulls into a Mayfair driveway, and it's hardly a surprise that his place is one of the impressive red brick manors that cost multi-millions. It only reinforces how much of a messy shit show I am when I drag my soggy butt out of his car. I stare up at the Mayfair palace as he opens the front door. Impressive, and full of character. Another opposite to my side of life. The Belgravia towers are uber flash and fresh. Glass fronted and modern chic. Gorgeous, but not homely. Not for me anymore, living solo. Ever since the opulence and the wow factor wore off, it's been cool but bland. Like my personal life.

I'm sure I shouldn't be here in Mayfair. This is fucking madness. But as I step into Reuben's hallway, I feel weirdly at home. It's Reuben's energy as he slips his jacket off, and the tenderness with which he helps me with mine. I'm in nothing but foul smelling lingerie as I kick off my stilettos and put them on the shoe rack, but his smile doesn't waver at all.

Guess he's seen me a lot worse.

"Let's get you in the shower," he says, and takes my hand.

The details around me are blurry as he leads me upstairs, because all I can focus on is him. The strength of his hand in mine. His smile as he turns on the shower in one of his grand bathrooms and checks out the heat until it's ready. "Nice and hot."

I giggle. "Me or the shower?"

"Both."

I don't take off my lingerie before I step under the running water, just step in and lather myself up with soap as Reuben watches. This lingerie needs a clean before I'd let it even make an appearance on Reuben Sinclair's deluxe marble floor. Once it's lathered and drenched, I take it off, tossing it to the side of the shower as I start work on myself, shampooing my hair and sighing at how good it feels as the pool of filth disappears down the plughole.

"May I join you?" Reuben asks. "Santa needs a morning shower before he gets going."

"You're the client, User 5639. You can do whatever the hell you want with me."

He loosens his tie and unbuttons his shirt, and I curse the fucking steam on the glass for blurring my view. This is my first sight of the man beneath the suit. The unsurpassable Reuben Sinclair. I want it etched into my eyeballs for ever.

I've given up on shampooing my hair when he steps inside, my eyes roving up and down his naked body. He's muscular, but lean, and his skin is remarkable for a man approaching fifty. The main giveaway are the few grey hairs on his chest. Just enough to count as hairy.

His cock is hard, standing tall and proud and begging to be sucked. And fuck me right now, please, but it's got some girth on it. It's pussy-fluttering instinct that has me dropping to my knees to get a taste of it, but he takes my shoulders with a *no, no.*

I stare up at him. "Santa doesn't want his sack emptied before the grotto? Don't I at least get a token taste before you leave for the day?"

He coaxes me up, supporting me with an arm as I push myself back to my feet.

"No, Tiffany, because it's me who wants the token taste. I've been waiting for it all night long."

He puts a finger under my chin and tips my face up to his, moving in slowly.

"What the fuck? I haven't brushed my teeth yet," I say, but he smiles.

"I couldn't give a shit about that."

User 5639 is in the dust the very second Reuben's mouth lands on mine, because this isn't a client I'm kissing. I wrap my arms around his shoulders and kiss my idol like he's the saviour of life itself, diving into the tangle of tongues as I moan.

Once it starts, it doesn't stop. He pushes me against the tiles and brushes a thumb across my cheek and I'm done for. A therapist would have no chance getting me out of this state. My obsession is off the charts, fantasies flying high.

I reach for his cock that's nudging my belly, but he says no between kisses and pins me tighter. I groan in protest, but he gives me a firmer *no* and pulls away to look at me.

"Santa needs to get to the grotto."

"Yeah, and this naughty girl needs a goodie bag before he leaves."

"Patience is a virtue."

"Says he who drove across the city to pick me up from a proposal the very second I was done."

He holds up two hands.

"Guilty as charged. Patience hasn't been my virtue these past few days."

His face is so close I can feel his breath, the water cascading over both of us. I pluck up the courage to ask the question that's burning my soul.

"Past few days as in since the second I left the hotel room?"

He pauses. His gorgeous grey eyes scorching mine.

"Guilty as charged. Again."

I run my fingers down his shoulder. "Yeah, well, I guess we'll be sharing a cell together. I'd be convicted of the same crime."

Our next kiss is a total frenzy, soapy hands desperate as we make a mockery of sharing a shower in favour of flesh on flesh. His eyes are magic, his hands are strong and hard, and his lips... oh fuck, his lips feel so good against mine that I could kiss him for a lifetime and never get bored.

Finally, he breaks away.

"Sorry, but I really must make a move."

"On me?" I say with a giggle.

"To get to work," he says, not laughing at my joke.

The thought of being left alone hurts.

"One last kiss," I say, but take at least five, stepping out of the shower with him. His mouth is still peppering mine as he grabs me a towel from the rail. My hands are on his cheeks as he wraps me up and takes one for himself.

"Can't you call in sick?" I ask.

He smirks as he towel dries his hair. "Santa never gets sick. You need to sleep, and I need to bring Christmas joy to the mall. Ho, ho, ho."

"All I need is *you*." I tell him, and pull back as my stomach tumbles.

Jesus Christ. I sound so needy. So fucking real.

That was much too soon. Much, much, much too fucking soon.

I grin like it was no big deal and start towelling myself off. But Reuben doesn't move, just stares.

"Sorry," I say. "Got a little goofy there. It's been a long night."

I'm so embarrassed that I look down at my thighs as I towel them, knowing that my cheeks are beetroot red. I'm cringing, terrified I've just broken some stupid code of *sweetness* that a founder like him doesn't want from an entertainer like me.

My heart feels exposed and on the line.

"Tiffany," he says, and I want to apologise and let Creamgirl take the floor. I want to flutter my eyelashes and go for his dick again, but no. His hands take mine.

"Say that again," he tells me.

I attempt a giggle. "What? *Sorry?*"

He doesn't laugh along with me. "Don't play Cream here. She may have been the entertainer I booked, but she isn't the woman I want here."

I can hardly breathe.

"Want or need?"

"I think you already know the answer to that question. I don't usually offer personal cab services in my Bentley."

My heart is pumping so fast, it's thumping in my ears.

"So, say it again," he says. "If you meant it, then say it. If you didn't, then don't."

I take a deep breath, teetering on the edge of loved-up madness.

"I meant it. I knew it from the very first moment we locked eyes in the grotto."

"Then say it. Tell me."

My heart screams, truly alive for the first time in years as I bare my soul.

"All I need... is you."

CHAPTER 16
Reuben

$\mathcal{I}$ make a sleepy Tiffany a hot chocolate before I depart for the mall. Shame I don't have any squirty cream that she requested on the top.

"I'll rectify that with my next groceries delivery," I tell her, "I'll order a crate of the stuff, and we'll use it for considerably more than hot chocolate."

"Promises, promises," she says, taking a sip of the hot drink.

I shrug my jacket on and grab my keys, and I can't resist the temptation.

I take the mug from her hands, place it on the counter, take her beautiful face in my hands, and kiss her.

She rakes my hair and our tongues dance a wonderful chocolatey dance.

"If only you could stay," she says as I break away.

"I'll be back before you know it," I stroke her hair, "you rest up. I'm sure you'll need plenty of energy for later."

Her pout is so quirky, it gives me a rush of adoration. It's so *her*.

It's so hard to say no. But I can't let the kids down.

Still, one last kiss won't hurt.

That one last kiss lasts all the way to the front door – a giggly dance and biting of lips that has my cock hard all over again.

"You're incorrigible," I say and give her ass a slap before I step outside.

"Hurry home!" she says as I get in the car.

Home.

Home is where the heart is, they say.

My home – big and empty – but not right now.

I watch her in the rearview mirror, waving as I turn out of the drive. I give a toot of the horn and a wave back.

Shit, I'm going to be late.

I'll have to throw my Santa costume on like a madman and sprint to the grotto.

Evelyn and Jen will manage the line until I get there. They are as tireless when it comes to charity work as I am, turning up without fail whenever we have an event on. Jen is a wonder with children, having had five of her own – all grown up now and flown the nest. Her face always lights up when the festivities start, engaging with the youngsters.

If she was twenty years younger – and single, not married – she could have captured my heart when I first met her. *Could have.* Her curvy figure would have driven me wild, and I can't deny I would have been fascinated by her huge tits and voluptuous ass. Still, even if she *had* been twenty years younger and single, not married, when I met her, our incompatibility would have been obvious when we first walked past the kink and lingerie store at the top of the mall together.

I don't get it, she'd told me. *Why would people be into all that stuff? Imagine being hit by something for fun. Weirdos.*

That would have been it for us.

I could never deny the man I am – the real Reuben Sinclair. I attempted that with Jeanette, my ex-wife, for far too long, and still she left me. If I was ever lucky enough to find 'love' again, I'd have to be certain it would be someone who could 'love' and accept all sides of my nature, for better or worse. The idea of a soul that could ever match with mine has grown more and more obscure.

I'd given up on the idea of ever meeting such a woman until I found Tiffany sitting on my lap, and now…

I have no idea.

Traffic isn't too bad through London, lucky for me. I pull up at the mall with just enough time to park up, grab my holdall from the boot and dash in through the rear entrance. I change into my Santa costume in the nearest toilet cubicle, and make sure the fake beard is in place over mine.

"Ho, ho, ho," Evelyn says as I arrive at the grotto. "Looking good, Santa baby!"

Oh, if only she knew how much this Santa wants a baby of his own.

Playing Father Christmas is a beautiful torture – the stream of happy children passing through is like having a carrot dangling continuously at the end of Rudolph's nose. Even the sliver of hope that Tiffany could *need* me the way I've been needing a woman like her, is a terrifying carrot to contemplate. The thought of that sliver of hope disappearing already gives me shivers.

I'm smiling at Evelyn but in my mind, the image of Tiffany standing at my door morphs into a cock-swelling beauty – she's pregnant, almost full term, and she looks like a goddess with a baby inside her.

"You okay, Reuben?" Evelyn asks. "You look a bit… lost?"

I laugh at that. "Yes," I say, "supplier problems. You know how mad it gets at this time of year."

"And yet you're still here, doing your bit."

And in my mind, I'm doing Tiffany, getting her pregnant and stroking her growing belly.

"Always," I say with a smile.

Fuck, I've fallen into the realms of insanity.

Dangerous insanity.

I attempt to pull myself together, concentrate on the queue of children and giving them Santa's full attention as they tell me how they're going to leave me cookies on Christmas Eve. I'm not going to be wanting cookies this year, though. I'm going to be wanting cream.

"I need you."

Her words still sound loud in my mind, the honesty in her eyes so naked as she said them.

Once again, I'm guilty of the same crime. I need Tiffany. I need hope. I need dreams. I need aspirations beyond business and charity, and the animalistic lust of the founders' circle.

Problem is, my heart has been captured by one of the most forbidden dreams there could be.

A little girl comes into the grotto just before lunchtime, and the sight of her takes the breath out of me. I'm practically winded.

She has red hair – auburn, not scarlet – but it's a close enough resemblance. Her big, wide eyes and cute chubby cheeks remind me of a tiny Tiffany. Her smile is bold and bright, and she has two teeth missing on the bottom. What a cutie.

As she sits on my lap, she tells me a joke about Rudolph with a cackling laugh, and I laugh along with her, trying to banish the idea that Tiffany's daughter could resemble a girl like this. I stare into the little angel's eyes as she tells me about how she wants a puppy for Christmas. A Dalmatian with lots of spots. She points out how tall he would be, grinning as she says she would call him *Popeye*, and assuring me she would take very, very, very good care of him.

Please, Santa. Can I have Popeye for Christmas? I've been really good, I promise!

If she were my little girl, she could have 101 Dalmatians, just to see her so happy.

The girl's mother winks and nods. It seems this little girl is going to be very happy on Christmas morning.

I tap my nose. "I'll see what I can do," I tell the grinning cherub.

I find I'm choked up when she leaves, watching her take her mother's hand and disappear into the bustling mall. I breathe deep through the ridiculous emotions, praying nobody sees me. Luckily, Mark – the youngster in charge of the photos – doesn't notice. He's too busy scrolling on his phone between taking pictures.

When our ten-minute break comes, I check my own phone as I sip the coffee Jen has kindly provided. I have a whole host of emails about work, but no interest in looking at them. There's an Agency founders' thread running, with comments about last night's filth with Harlot. Bry sure got all the piss play he was after. That much is clear.

Harlot must have been as soaked through as Tiffany was when I collected her.

Creamgirl next, one of the comments reads. *Can't wait to spray some over that big beauty. I'm going to get some better clamps for the next session, btw. The ones on Harlot may have cut, but I want some that will pierce Creamgirl's chubby cunt lips straight through.*

I want to retch as I see that comment.

I don't want any of them spraying any fucking thing over Tiffany, and they can stay the fuck away from her cunt as well. The fire burns like embers in my gut. My finger hovers over the chat thread, trying to find some reason to interject and suggest another entertainer. But I can't do it. It would arouse too much suspicion.

After my departure last night, everything I do will be

scrutinised, and I've already taken some hefty risks with Creamgirl's calendar. I muted her notifications of her calendar movements, so she wasn't bombarded, and blocked them from admins' view, so as not to draw attention. But it would be obvious under investigation. Nobody would have to be Sherlock Holmes to find out who was guilty of the interference.

Only I don't feel guilty. Not in the slightest. Even a sliver of hope can outweigh sensibilities, and this sliver of hope has been a long time coming.

I'm going to enjoy every second of this dream I can, because the likelihood is, that this ridiculous wave of optimism will all turn to dust. Creamgirl will still be Creamgirl, and I'll still be one of the founders, with a five-million-pound stake in the business, and my reputation on the line.

In two weeks, Tiffany will be hooded and ready for a founders' night that will put the glory wall to shame, and there is sweet fuck all I can do about it.

Not without risking everything.

CHAPTER 17
Tiffany

I know a thing or two about beds – since I've slept in more than a few over the past four years – and this one is fit for royalty. Five stars from me.

Hardly a surprise though, since this one belongs to Reuben Sinclair.

His mattress is huge and so comfortable it's like floating on a cloud. His pillows are perfect and his sheets are the kind of high-grade cotton I love. But it's mainly the scent of him I'm addicted to.

It's clear which side of the bed is his. There's a paperback on the nightstand, with an alarm clock and phone charger, but the sheets give more away than his nightstand does. They smell like him.

I can't help myself lolling further over, even though it's against some of my wackier principles. Sleeping in someone's space has always held a sacredness to me.

I hate people sleeping on my side. Ever. Not even Josh ever did it on bestie nights. It's just one of those things. My side is always my side, and Reuben's should be Reuben's – especially since he isn't here to invite me into it, but I can't resist. I hold his pillow tight and breathe him in. I don't know what makes scents so powerful, but I get an animalistic rush at the thought of him lying here, sleeping.

Sleeping next to me.

I *want* him next to me.

I want to share this bed with him, and hear his deep breaths in the night. Feel his arms around me. Touch his naked skin while he's far away in dreamland.

I've actually managed a decent few hours of shut eye since Reuben left for the grotto. As tempting as it would be to hole up here under the covers straight through until he gets home, I'm going to have to shift my butt. My mug is empty on my nightstand, as well as the water glass next to it. I need a pee and another round of painkillers to help combat my aches and pains from the glory wall. I always keep a stash in my handbag for such occasions.

Plus, I have a whole manor's worth of curiosities to explore. The home of the man I'm obsessed with is here for the stalking. It'll give me a lot more insight into him than an online grotto calendar and *Reuben Sinclair* search terms ever will.

There's a robe on the back of the bedroom door that just about fastens around me. Maybe I should have taken the opportunity to drop into Belgravia this morning since I have little here with me. Just some half washed lingerie still discarded in the shower, and a dirty coat and stilettos downstairs.

I'm making my way downstairs when I hear my phone ringing. Crap. I don't remember where I left my bag. Probably in the kitchen, on one of the worktops, or by the breakfast bar while I was drinking my hot chocolate. It cuts out while I'm dashing to the kitchen, then starts right back up again… behind me.

Turns out my bag is hung up in the main hallway. My gentlemanly client must have put it there for me. My phone is still ringing when I fish it from my bag, and my loved-up smile disappears when I see the name on screen. It rings out again before I can answer.

Josh.

Oh, fucking hell. FUCK.

There are eighteen missed calls from his number in the notifications window.

I didn't check back in with him this morning after the glory wall. I forgot to update him on my next proposal!

I call straight back with my heart in my throat.

"Hey," I say.

"Tiff?! What the fuck? Where are you? Are you ok?"

I could slap my own forehead. "Yeah, I'm cool. All good. Was just tired. Sleeping. Sorry, my bad. Should have let you know."

"Should have let me know?! No fucking shit! I've been worried sick. So has Ella. We figured you were asleep, so called around your place to check, and you weren't there. So, where the fuck are you?"

Bollocks.

I picture Josh in my apartment, searching for me, scared shitless to find I wasn't at home. We have a key to each other's places, and I didn't send him a fucking D&S message when I finished last night. He didn't know I was done and safe.

Fuck it.

"Where are you, Tiff?"

"I'm, um... busy. I'm on another proposal."

"On another proposal? After the glory wall? Are you fucking serious?"

"Yeah, something came up. An urgent one."

"Really? Why the fuck didn't you let me know? I got onto Orla a few hours ago and it looked to her like you were busy. Then she sounded weird. Said there were some things she'd investigate on your calendar, but hell knows what. She wouldn't fucking tell me. Agency rules and all that, so I know she couldn't give me more, but I was about to call the fucking police, Tiff. I thought you'd been fucking kidnapped!"

My gut lurches. Josh has spoken to Orla. About me.

Orla is one of the Agency team admins, managing entertainers, and schedules and clients. She can see calendars, she can see locations, and bookings histories, and FUCK. I feel like a criminal on the run.

"Why the fuck did you get onto Orla, Josh? I'm fine!"

"Because I figured she'd know where the fuck you were, or who the fuck had kidnapped you!"

"Urgh." I rub my sore head. "Look, I'm sorry, Josh. Seriously, I'm sorry, alright? I should have let you know, but please, next time, don't freak out and definitely DON'T get onto Orla! Why bring the Agency into this?!"

I hear him scoff.

"How about because they are the ones who know what the fuck you're scheduled in for? It was either them or the POLICE!"

Remorse and fear are a nasty combination. If the situation was reversed and I'd been the one freaking out about Josh, I'd have sure as fuck have gone to Orla, and everyone else in the damn place I could get hold of, including the police, but at the same time, my pulse is racing... because if Orla looks too deeply...

"Look, I'm sorry, babe," I tell Josh. "Forgive me, hey? I won't do it again."

"We ALWAYS send D&S messages. ALWAYS. That's what we promised each other."

"Yeah, and I screwed up. I'm sorry. I'm really sorry." I take a breath. "But I have to go. I'm at another proposal, and this isn't great timing."

"Isn't great timing? Are you for fucking real? You're the one whose timing's gone all to shi–"

"Yeah, sorry. I know. Listen, I had an urgent proposal, literally started the second I stepped out of the glory wall. It was a really good deal. I said yes, the proposal started right there and then, and…" Fuck, I'm rambling.

"What proposal?" he asks. "What kind of good deal?"

His questions push a button they never usually push. My voice is a hiss of a whisper when I answer him.

"That's fucking classified. Non-disclosure!"

"Seems to me that everything is becoming non-disclosure with you at the moment. We need to talk about what the fuck's going on."

I want to bang my head against the wall. It won't just be about Caroline's baby and Christmas now, I'll get a proper grilling on all levels, because he's right. I have been hiding things.

"Yeah, ok. We'll talk. I'll let you know when my calendar is clear, alright?"

"Alright. Fine. Send me a D&S when you're done."

I hate how hurt he sounds. He hangs up before I can even say goodbye.

Maybe I'd call him back if my heart wasn't thumping like a bastard on other matters.

Orla.

She might be digging into my bookings right now.

I call up the Agency app and log into my account, calling her name up in the chat window.

Hey, sorry, Josh was freaking out. It's all cool, just a misunderstanding. I took a client on at short notice, no biggie. It's in the calendar.

I see the typing icon and my gut lurches.

Hi, Tiff. Good timing. I was just looking into your account. Is everything alright? Are you ill or something?

Ill? Fuck yes, I am. My jowls just went and fucking tightened and I'm gonna puke. My fingers are trembling as I type...

Yeah, I'm fine thanks, why?

I swallow the bile as the typing icon shows up again.

The postponements on your account. There are quite a lot of them.

The postponements on my account... what the...

No way.

My heart races. An instinctive rush of panic as I click my calendar to find my schedule has completely vanished after tonight. It's clear. Right up until the founders' proposal in a few weeks' time.

You moved them? Orla asks. *We haven't had any client complaints, but if you are ill or need any support or anything, please do tell us. We prefer to manage it from this end.*

I don't know what the hell to say to that. I type, then delete, type then delete. I can't tell her the truth. I'm still reeling with my lack of bookings myself, because I sure as fuck didn't empty my calendar... and apparently the Agency didn't either... which only means...

Shit. Sorry, Orla, I type. *I should have brought you into it. I'm having some personal crap going on around Christmas. Just need some headspace, and want to make sure I'm fit for the founders.*

My head fucking pounds as she types.

That's no problem. You have a client booking now, though? Are you going to be ok with that? And have you managed to postpone everything else that needed postponing?

Again, I feel like a criminal as my jittery fingers type lie after lie...

I'm on a booking now. Just taking a break. Client is a newbie, but he's going to be a big player, I think, so I'll keep him happy, but some of my regulars got shunted. I'm sure they will be ok. I'll be back and booming soon! Nothing else needs doing from your end, honestly. Thanks, though. You are a star.

Lies don't suit me. Just as well she can't see my face, or my burning cheeks would give me up in a heartbeat.

Great, she says. *Let me know if you need anything. Speak soon x*

I hope fucking not.

Telling white lies to Orla has made this situation all so real. She could have been such an ass to me for breaking cancellation rules like that, and not giving her updates. But I didn't have any to give her. They weren't my fucking updates.

Thank fucking God I'm one of their star performers, or I may have got ten times more of a bollocking.

I scroll through my empty calendar – so many appointments gone. Not a single gig between now and the founders one.

Not apart from today, of course.

My head is spinning with so many questions.

Are my clients gone for good?

Is the Agency going to find out?

Why did Reuben do this? Is he pissed at me? Have I fucked him off?

Has someone found out what's going on between us?

More to the point – what the hell IS going on between us!?

And what's going to happen to my income?!

Jesus Christ, I could do without this right now. I grab my painkillers and down a couple with some iced water in the kitchen, and then godfuckingdamnit, I feel the paranoia rising. I feel the shakes, hating the lack of control... because without Creamgirl... without my job...

I check the clock. About an hour to go before Reuben leaves the grotto.

I scroll through my *postponed* bookings, assuring myself that I have options at my fingertips right here. I could click and offer to reverse the postponements. I'd get a load of them back. My regulars.

The safe option.

It's only been one night since they were messed around with. I could tell them it was an error or something. I could sort it out. I could ease my mind, and tell Orla I've changed my mind, no problem. I could tell her I'm feeling just fine now.

But I don't click anything and I don't type a word. Not yet.

I need answers from the original *finger clicker* the very moment he walks in through the front door. He is the boss after all, and I'd best have the sense to remember it.

All it would take is one click of Reuben's finger clicking fingers, and my whole fucking life could come tumbling down.

CHAPTER 18
Reuben

It's been years since I've been excited to pull into my own driveway. I take the bouquet of roses and orchids from the passenger seat, smiling to myself as I grab the can of squirty cream. My heart is thumping as I put my key in the lock. I resist the urge to shout *honey, I'm home!* as I step inside, although that's how I'm feeling.

This house feels like home again.

Or so I think until I find the gorgeous Tiffany sitting at the breakfast bar with a stare like thunder. Her eyes are red, and she swipes a fresh tear from her cheek as she glares at me.

"Why did you do it?! What's going on?!" she shouts, and my heart sinks as I hear the crack in her voice.

I lay the flowers down on the counter and place the can of cream by their side.

"What do you mean, what's going on? Has something happened?"

She holds up her phone, even though the screen is blank, and the pieces slot into place as she jabs a finger at it.

"Don't play dumb. You cancelled my bookings! I had Orla on my case about it, asking why, and I had nothing to tell her, since I didn't do it. YOU did, didn't you?"

Shit. I hold up my hands.

"There is nothing to worry about, Tiff. Let me explain."

"Nothing to worry about?!" She wipes away another tear. "I've been shitting myself, Reuben. Absolutely fucking shitting myself!"

I approach calmly, battling the urge to grab her and hold her tight.

"You can reinstate your bookings if you want to. Every single one of them. You won't have lost any revenue, I assure you. There will be no comeuppance from Orla or the team." I pause on the other side of the breakfast bar, swallowing as she tosses her phone on the counter and puts her hands over her face to hide her tears.

"Why did you do it? It could have pissed everyone off so bad, I'd lose my job."

"Yes, it could, but it wouldn't have. I'd have taken the fall myself, if I needed to."

She stares at me in disbelief. "Why would you do that?! You'd be breaking worse rules than I would! It's fucking insane!"

She has me on that. It *is* fucking insane.

"May I?" I ask and point to the breakfast stool at her side. She nods, but pulls hers away to create some distance between us. It hurts, because that's the last thing I want. I take a breath.

Trying to get my words in order while my thoughts are scattered all over the place is quite a task, so I take my time. She lets me, her breaths hitching as her eyes burn mine.

"I apologise wholeheartedly for interfering with your calendar. I should have asked you first," I say, and the red-haired goddess rolls her eyes.

"No shit, Sherlock. No wonder you're the owner of an empire. Your IQ is off the scale."

Even now, I love her dark humour. The cheekiness of her mouth, even in her pain. She folds her arms.

"So, why?" she asks. "Spit it out, Reuben. What's going on?"

I offer the truth.

"I don't know."

She raises her eyebrows. "You don't know? What do you mean you don't know? You postponed every one of my bookings click after click, then blanked the notifications."

"Yes, I did, and I shouldn't have. Not without asking you first."

"I was so fucking scared. I thought Orla was going to go ballistic, and call me out, or cancel my account. And then what? I'd just be Tiffany, a girl living in a tower with no fucking job."

"As I said, that would never happen. I'd have admitted my actions and taken the fall myself."

"But WHY? What the fuck?!"

She flails her hands in the air as though I've lost the plot, and the sight of her, frazzled and barely covered by my night robe only stokes my insanity. In a moment of madness I reach out and take her hands in mine.

"Because I HAD to. I couldn't bear the thought of you being with anyone else. That night, at the club, when I heard you getting fucked like a slut behind those bins, I wanted to burst in and push him the fuck off you. Because *I* wanted you! ME! Not HIM! And ever since then, since our first *proposal* together, it's all I can think about." She's wide eyed as I take a breath. "I didn't get a wink of fucking sleep knowing you were at the glory wall, on your knees being taken by a load of clients who don't mean a fucking thing. So I lost my mind, ok? I called up your calendar and put in a proposal of my own, and then I abused my authority. I used my founder login to postpone everything else I could, right the way up until Christmas. Because I wanted to. That's why."

"Wanted to or *needed* to?"

"You already know the answer to that, Tiffany. You said it yourself in the bathroom."

"I want to hear you say it for yourself."

The fire in her eyes has dimmed to glowing embers. The tension in the air is so stifling I can barely speak.

"Needed to," I tell her. "I needed to. And so fucking help me, if I was back in that moment, staring at your jam-packed calendar with my heart in my hands, I'd do it all over again."

I feel like a defendant awaiting a verdict. Vulnerable in ways I haven't felt since Jeanette left me, my heart on the floor, exposed, with the potential to get trampled to shit.

"You should have told me," she says.

"I agree, yes, I should have. Or more specifically, I should have asked you. I can only offer an apology and assure you it won't happen again."

She looks up at the ceiling. "We're both going mental."

"No doubt about that, but as I said earlier, it feels like we're two very different peas in the same pod. And so help me, I love it. I haven't felt this way in years."

I let my words sink in, her hands still in mine. She blinks and more tears fall. Her bottom lip trembles.

"This could fuck us both up so bad."

"I know."

"Why me?" she asks. "You must have been with hundreds of women. You're a founder, and a businessman, with years under your belt to find someone perfect, so why me?"

"Because my idea of perfect doesn't come along all that often, Tiffany. The only taste of what I thought was perfect was an ex-wife who didn't want my *perfect* in return, and walked away."

Her eyes slam into mine.

"She left you?"

"Yes, she left me. Differences, arguments, growing apart. *Irreconcilable*. That's how the divorce papers term it."

"Did you want her to leave?"

I hate talking about Jeanette. I usually avoid it at all costs.

"Yes, and no. No at the time. I was a wreck. Later, I felt it was for the best. Good riddance, I'd tell myself. Then slowly, the loneliness crept in. It's easy to ignore it when you're busy. Work and charity, the Agency. All good reasons to forget that you're coming home to an empty house and bed every night. Christmas is always hard. I do the grotto to ease my own pain as well as give people joy. And then you walked in."

She smiles. "Walked in and plonked my butt on your lap."

"Indeed. It wasn't your butt that turned me into a madman though, it was your face. Your smile, your eyes, the way you raise your eyebrows when you laugh."

The goddess takes her hands from mine and points a finger at her watery eyes. "Looks great right now, yeah?"

"You will always look beautiful to me, Tiffany."

"Yeah, well, like you said, we must be two very different peas in the same pod."

I dare to smile. "Am I forgiven? I assure you, I won't do it again." I push her phone towards her. "Please, cancel the postponements, if that's what you want."

"And what if I don't want to?"

"Then I will compensate you for all of them."

"With proposals, or just cash?"

I lock my eyes with hers. "Whichever you want. Just forgive me, Tiffany. Please."

She looks at her phone, but doesn't take it. She sighs, and rubs her eyes on the cuffs of my robe.

"How about neither?"

"Neither?"

"Yeah, neither. I don't need the cash, Reuben. You've stalked my account enough to know that. I've got plenty stashed away. I don't need to be paid, and you don't need to book me up with proposals. So let's just…"

"Let's just what?"

She shrugs. "Do what we need to. Hang out together because we want to, fuck because we want to. Be around each other like normal people."

I have to laugh at that. "Normal people? That's an interesting phrase."

It's a relief to hear her laugh along with mine. "Yeah, alright, maybe not normal people." She takes my hand. "Be around each other like *us*. Just us. Reuben and Tiffany with no bullshit."

I pull her into me, fuck the distance. I hold her like she's a jewel, brushing her hair away so I can press my mouth to her ear.

"That's exactly what I *need*, Tiffany."

She relaxes in my arms. "Same. I'm getting used to being Tiffany, you know? I'm kinda liking it."

"I'm getting used to being alive again. I didn't know how dead I was until you lit up the grotto." I smile against her cheek. "You could say I'm *kinda liking it*, too."

The scarlet haired beauty pulls away again, tears drying. "So, what's the deal? We're gonna be Christmas sweethearts, are we? Have a *happy holidays* and go from there?"

"That sounds excellent to me. I can cook a really good turkey, you know. I just haven't had the motivation for quite some time."

"I can eat a really good turkey, you know. Can you do Yorkshire puddings with it? And mashed potato?"

"Carrot, peas, parsnips."

"Roasters."

"Cranberry sauce."

"Gravy."

"Christmas pudding for afters."

"Twenty-seven boxes of festive biscuits."

I chuckle. "At least."

Her gaze turns serious. "Don't you have anyone you usually spend Christmas with?"

I shrug. "Charities mainly."

"What about family?"

"No. Unfortunately not. Jeanette took a lot of that with her. You stay in contact for a while, but it grows more distant." I look her in the eyes. "How about you?"

"Nope. My stepdad is a douche, and Mum gets on my tits. I'm usually with Josh, but he's with Ells now. His family are cool, but with them being together it's different. I don't want to be a third wheel."

"I'm sure you wouldn't be."

"No, they'd say not, and they'd mean it, but..." Her words trail off and I sense a wall there. A gate closing on the conversation. She looks over at the flowers on the counter instead. "They for me?"

"They are, yes. Didn't quite get the grand entrance of romance I was intending. I'm sorry about that."

She gets up from the barstool and walks over to them. The fabric of my robe is tight across her ass, highlighting her hourglass curves. She grins as she picks them up and sees the beauty of the flowers. The roses are bright red, like her hair.

"Thanks."

"Take them as an apology bouquet rather than a romantic one."

She laughs. "Nah, I prefer them as romance. Apology is already accepted anyway. I've chilled out a bit now I know I'm not about to be kicked out of the Agency."

I sit and face her, soaking her in as she plays with some of the petals.

"Let me ask you something, Tiffany."

Her stare shoots across at me, wary. Yes, there is definitely a closed gate in there somewhere.

"What?"

"If the roles had been reversed, and you'd been the one with my booked up calendar in front of you, would you have done the same thing I did?"

Her cheeks flush red. "I, uh. Would have been tempted, yeah."

"Tempted, or overcome with insanity?"

She cracks a smile. "I was the one who stalked you to the grotto, remember? My strictly anonymous boss, dressed up playing Santa, and I stood and watched you like a soppy teenager. I'd say that's a symptom of insanity, wouldn't you?"

"Maybe."

"Definitely." She puts the flowers down. "Talking of which, there's one proposal you left in there. The founders. Why?"

My gut churns at the thought.

"Because I don't have the power to postpone it. I'm only one of a faction. My stake is five percent."

She nods. "Ok, so what are we going to do about it? I'll have to play really fucking dumb when I'm hooded. I'll know exactly who you are."

I don't back down with the honesty.

"I don't know," I tell her. "If the other stakeholders find out, it's going to cause havoc."

"Yeah, I figured. For both of us." She fluffs her hair up, giving a flash of Creamgirl. "I'll manage it. I'll play the game, don't worry."

Only that's not what I'm worried about.

The thought of sharing her with Bry and the gang seems

192

horrifying. I've been avoiding the group thread all day. But that's not a concern for now, and it's one for me to come to terms with, not her. She's grinning as she picks up the squirty cream.

"This for me as well? Gonna make me a hot chocolate, are you?" She lets the robe drop open, displaying her gorgeous tits, and the mood changes. The power of need takes a different direction as she teases her nipples. "How about we have a sample first, Mr Sinclair?"

I'm already walking over to her as she shakes the can and sprays cream all over her tits, but it's not her tits I'm interested in right now.

I take the can as I pin her to the counter.

"Open your mouth," I say, and she does as she's told, parting those gorgeous lips nice and wide. "Don't swallow," I tell her as I fill her mouth up with cream in a sugary explosion.

And then I kiss her.

I taste that sugary cream straight from her tongue, sucking it from her mouth before my tongue dances with hers. She moans along with me, grinding against me as I kiss her with desperate, wet need.

"Look at you," she says when we stop for air, her face and tits a wonderful creamy mess.

My tie and shirt and suit jacket are smeared with the stuff, so is my beard.

She swipes a finger across my beard and licks it. "You look like the cat that got the cream."

I'm grinning like the proverbial cat when she threads her fingers through my hair and pulls me in for another kiss. A slow, languorous kiss that has my cock swelling against her belly.

Just like I've been dreaming of all fucking day.

CHAPTER 19
Tiffany

Squirty cream and hot kisses. What a perfect combination.

I press my tits against Reuben's smeared shirt, loving the warmth against my nipples as my mouth meets his for another round. I can't get enough of him, raking my hands through his silver fox hair.

My fears have disappeared under the lust. My need for closeness pours out of the closet like a broken dam.

He kisses me like we're underwater and I'm his only source of air. I kiss him back like my life depends on him, pushing his jacket from his shoulders until he shrugs it to the floor. My fumbling fingers work at his tie, our mouths inseparable. I undo his shirt buttons one by one, practically tearing his shirt from him to feel his hot flesh against my creamy tits.

We're still kissing as we fumble our way to the kitchen door, my back sliding against the hallway wall as I giggle against his mouth.

"We could just walk," I tell him, but he shakes his head.

"No. I need your mouth too much for that."

He keeps on kissing me, guiding me backwards, and when we

reach the stairs I fall back, my ass landing on the third step with a thump that makes me giggle.

I reach for him, expecting him to help me up, but no.

The gorgeous man lowers himself on top of me. I wrap my arms around his neck and his mouth is back on mine as I bump myself up, a step at a time, my tits bouncing and sliding against his creamy chest. My legs wrap around him as we reach the top, gripping him in position as he devours my mouth.

I want to beg for his cock, but it seems I don't need to beg.

He breaks the kiss and I let go of my grip, panting as he unbuckles his belt.

And I'm buzzing like crazy when his trousers and his boxers are shoved down.

His cock springs free.

Fuck me. It's long, it's girthy, it's popping with veins and...

He kicks his trousers and pants away and my legs open for him. He climbs on top of me, right there on the top stair.

I'm not used to straight up fucking without filthy games as a buildup. It's an unusual sensation to have him ease his cock into me sensually, an inch at a time. Such a beautiful tease. He kisses my chin, my cheeks, the corners of my mouth. He licks smeared cream from my neck as I finally get the full length of him, and then he captures my mouth for a whole new round as I moan with his cock buried deep.

I expect him to slam me right now. I want him to slam me right now.

I want him to fuck my brains out till I'm screaming.

I give a little buck against him but he pins me tight, our tongues still dancing.

"Fuck me," I say into his hot fucking mouth.

His mouth mashes mine and he fucks me. Slowly. Withdrawing

all the way and sliding in deep and it's... torture. Fucking amazing torture.

And my fucking God, he knows the perfect angle.

He circles his hips like a master, in line with my body so well it feels like he's known me a lifetime. But then I remember how intently he watched me playing with myself that night...

As if on cue, he varies his circling with three deep thrusts, then pulls out and slides the wet length of his cock up and down my slit, toying with my clit like I go wild for.

I'm already groaning *please* against his mouth when he pushes his cock back inside me, and he circles again, sucking my tongue as I whimper.

Please, please, please...

He picks up the pace, not by much but fuck it burns so good. Feels so good.

Then he stops. Circles some more. Pulls out. Fucks my clit with his hard cock end.

And Jesus Christ it's so good.

When he slides back into me and thrusts hard and fast, I'm fucking done.

I try to turn my face away to grunt and groan as I reach the peak, but he doesn't let me. He grips my cheeks and licks my open lips and keeps on fucking me. And I smile as I'm coming, darting my tongue out to meet his. And it's a crazy kinda coming... weirdly smooth as it waves through me and stokes the need for more.

I turn my attention to bucking against his cock, still inside me, but he doesn't react, just holds it in position.

"You not gonna come? Give me some more cream?" I ask, and he smirks.

"Your pussy is a work of art, Tiffany, but I've used the wonder plenty of times. It's your mouth I'm interested in. I've got years to catch up on."

"We've both been missing out, then," I say, and pull him in for more. Kiss after kiss, after fucking kiss. I can't stop.

My eyes are open to stare into the deep pools of his, and his are gazing straight back. It's an intimacy that makes my heart flutter, scared as well as entranced. I'm on display, in soul as well as body. He's well and truly broken down Creamgirl's walls.

There is nothing left but me. Myself. Tiffany with the smears of Cream left behind.

"Let's get to the bedroom," he says and I could cry when his cock slides out of me.

Fuck knows how he manages to help me to my feet with his mouth still peppering mine, but he does. My arms are around his neck as he guides me backwards, step after step. I collapse with a squeal as he shunts me down onto the mattress.

"How about you give my mouth something else now?" I ask him, eyeing up his dick as he climbs on top.

"Not yet."

"I'm so hungry for your cum. I haven't even had a sample."

"Patience is a virtue," he says, and kisses my puffy lips like a starving man.

I bite at his kisses as he pushes his cock back into me. The bounce of the mattress makes it easier to buck against him but he glides his hips so slowly, it's a crime. He teases me to the brink and back like a fucking wizard, because he's cracked the code.

More circling. More pulling out and nudging my throbbing clit with his cock end. More sliding deep and little thrusts at just the right angle.

"Fucking hell, Reuben. What are you going to do to me when

you ramp it up?" I ask him as he's circling fresh. "You're such a filthy, dirty bastard. We both know it."

"That depends. What do you want me to do to you?"

I suck in a breath as he sweeps his cock between my pussy lips.

"Whatever you want. I'm yours. This is your proposal."

His eyes are stern when he grips my chin. His stare is piercing.

"Fuck proposals. This has nothing to do with sex for cash, or filthy plans set out in stone. What I want is *you*."

"Want or need?" I ask with a cheeky smirk.

"*Need*," he says, and kisses my neck. "Did you hear that? *Need*."

"Yeah, well, that makes two of us. Another case of two peas in a pod, because I *need* you, too."

"I'll never get tired of you saying that," he says.

"Same goes, Santa. So give your naughty girl some dirty treats. She *needs* them."

The smile on his face is so honest, so full of the moment, it makes my heart sing.

Fuck, I'm turning into a fucking poet.

"My naughty girl deserves some filthy treats," he says and lifts my legs back, spreading me wide.

The lust in his eyes as he stares at my pussy makes me want it even more. I push down, and I know my chunky lips are moving for him.

"I adore your beautiful cunt," he says. "I've made it gush many times, but I've never had the honour of watching your beautiful face as you spray my cock."

Oh, Jesus, fuck me now.

With my legs pinned back, my sexy Santa ramps it up, fucks me like I know he's fucked me before – the heat, the friction, the angle, and in no time my ass is jerking off the bed and he pulls free to a generous fucking spray that soaks his stomach and his cock.

"Fucking incredible," he says and pins me back again, slamming his cock deep.

I gush on his bed twice over, and the covers are fucking soaked, but he doesn't get me a towel, he's right back to it. Whenever I'm on the comedown from a round of fucking, his fingers are straight back on my clit, building me back up, even when I'm tender to the max.

It's such a relief to have someone else do it like this, and not me. My body is his, and the pleasure is all mine. It's selfless to the extreme – all he wants in return is my kisses. My moans against his mouth.

My mind wanders in my headiness. Flashes of memories coming back to me as the highs make me almost delirious. I remember his cock so well, snippets of filthy recollections. But he was always blurred amongst other men.

Now it is only him. Him and me.

This man is like a smudged palette of eye shadow. Colours in every direction. Santa, Reuben… and one of the filthiest fucking founders known to man.

I want to know the real Reuben, just like he wants to know the real me.

"You going to share some info?" I ask as his fingers stroke my pussy lips. "Is this a one way street, or do I get to find out what drives you fucking crazy as well? Sex for me is never just about my pussy, and you know it. You've read my proposals."

"Yes, and you've played my filthy games."

"But I've never *seen* you playing them."

I get a glimpse of the beast in the silver fox. He's rough with my hair as he pins me to the bed, and instead of his cock this time, he uses his fingers, lining them up so they'll be bigger than the raging hard-on he's been using.

"Which of those dirty games did you like?" he asks.

"All of them."

"All of them, really? Even when you were fucking screaming?"

I nod. "Especially when I was fucking screaming. Like I told you, I'm not just a whore for the money, I'm a whore because I love the filth, too."

"Does it make you feel good to be a slut?"

"Yes."

"To be a dirty, naughty girl?"

I nod, and smile, inching myself down against his hand.

"You have no fucking idea. I love everything, I fucking swear."

He puts his mouth to my ear.

"Yet another thing we have in common, because so do I. You want to know the real me? You have it. I'm the man you knew in the proposals, as well as the man outside of them."

My soul soars at his words.

"You're blessed with tits big enough to take the punishment I like to give," he tells me, but there is no malice about it, just power.

"I know," I say. "And I'm blessed with an ass big enough to take one hell of a lot of fucking cane stripes." He curls four fingers inside me and I groan. I'm so tender.

"You've bound my tits before, haven't you?" I ask him.

"Yes."

"Were you the one who hung my entire weight on them when I was struggling to stay on tiptoes?"

"I was one of them, yes."

"It hurt so fucking bad."

"I know. I heard you cry."

"Have you fisted me? Do you know how much my cunt can take?"

"Yes."

I push down harder. "So why aren't you giving it to me right now?"

"Because I'm enjoying your gorgeous face as well as your gorgeous cunt."

That makes me smile.

"Were you the one who used the speculum that stretched me open until I was begging for it to stop?"

"Yes."

"Were you spreading it? Were you in control?"

"Yes."

"That's so fucking hot. I thought about that for days after. I couldn't get it out of my mind. Was it you who did what came after?"

"Plugged your ass up while you were gaping? Yes. I love anal play."

"How about the nettles? Did you fuck them into my pussy?"

"Yes, and your ass, too. Multiple times."

"Did you piss in my ass? Was that you?"

"Many times. Amongst others."

I kiss my boss, my filthy hero, my lover, lapping at his mouth with a grin.

"Are you going to do it again? Are you going to give me everything all over again... but just me and you?"

"Yes. If you'll let me."

"I'll *beg* you, not just let you."

"Good job we have a few weeks left until Christmas, isn't it? We've got a lot of ground to cover."

I'm so desperate for his fist in my cunt that I'd offer him my heart on a platter. I raise my hips to show him. "How about we make a deal for tonight? You stretch my needy pussy, and I'll show you how much I want your cock in my throat? I want you to watch me sucking you."

He must be fit to burst right now, he's been fucking me for so long. My pussy is sore from coming, and my lips are swollen from kissing.

My dirty hero shifts his position, so he's kneeling up by my head. He's stunning from this position, the underside of his cock a waiting promise. He strokes my huge, sweaty tits, then tugs at my nipples.

I imagine the way he fixed the clamps and tightened them when I was hooded. I imagine watching him while he's doing it. I want to see his face while he watches me struggle to bear it.

Tonight, I only get a few token tit slaps before he reaches back down to my pussy.

Fuck, he's going to fist me from an angle. Jesus Christ, I tense on instinct.

"Changed your mind?" he says. "That's ok. Say stop and we'll stop. I'll give you my cum regardless."

I smile as myself, not as Creamgirl.

"I'll never change my mind, Reuben. I never do."

My mouth is already open as I struggle to take his fist. He groans as he pushes his cock in my mouth, bulging out my cheek.

"Take it," he says and twists his fingers and thumb together, stretching me to the max.

I grip his cock in both hands, suck him in deep, and push against the stretch of his knuckles. He knows what to do. Knows how to twist side to side with just the right amount of pressure. And as his cock pops from my mouth, his fist pops into my cunt. Just like that, and it's a fucking delight.

I look up at him in pure adoration as I show off my cock sucking skills. He strokes my hair as he fists, with little nudges back and forth, telling me what a beautiful girl I am as he fucks my throat.

A beautiful girl isn't something I hear all that often.

Horny bitch, dirty slut, hot, filthy. Hell, I've even been called a cute piggy girl in degradation play, but *beautiful girl* feels so different.

I'm so comfortable as I dribble and groan. I'm so proud of the way my tits and belly bounce as I work myself against his buried hand.

"I love this," he says as his balls tighten. "I love this so much, it's driving me out of my mind."

Part of me wishes the *this* was *you*.

That's the part of me that's driving *me* out of my mind. Because ever since meeting the real Reuben Sinclair, my dreams have been morphing into reality.

My heart cries out with a different kind of need as the man I adore gives me the very first taste of his cum. The greatest reward there could be.

I love *you*, is what I want to hear from him. Crazy but true.

But instead, I get a different round of creamy kisses, and he makes me come all over again.

CHAPTER 20
Reuben

I wake up to find Tiffany sprawled like a starfish next to me. I can barely see her with just the hint of dawn shining through the crack in the curtains. She's got a cute snore which hitches at its loudest, and the covers are right up to her chin. I love the way they rise and fall with her breaths, relishing the sensation of having someone in bed with me. It's been years.

I watch her while she's lost in dreamland, wondering what fantasies are rolling through her mind. Are they happy dreams, or terrifying nightmares?

I hope they aren't like mine. Recurring sensations of loss that have my heart panging whenever I wake in the morning to realise what's missing all over again.

Love. Companionship. The commitment of two people believing in a future together.

I resist the temptation to reach over and pull Tiffany close, or to snuggle up to her side and hold her like a treasure. I don't want to disturb her. I don't want her to start in shock as she wakes up in an unknown space with someone beside her.

More than anything, I don't want her to sit up in confusion and back away – Creamgirl's walls back up on instinct.

Dare I believe that this beauty really does need me as much as I need her? That her soul is ready to embrace mine the way mine is craving to truly let go and embrace hers?

Maybe she senses me staring at her, because the hitch of her snore morphs into a sigh, and she stretches her arms above her head. She does start in shock, but it doesn't send her spawling to the opposite end of the bed, it sends her moving towards me, patting the covers as though she's searching.

"I'm here," I say and take hold of her hand.

"Phew." She giggles. "Thought you might have gone."

"Gone? Why?"

"Dunno. Work. Grotto. Downstairs." She pauses. "Anywhere."

There's something in her voice I can't ascertain. I pull her towards me so her head is on my chest as I wrap her in my arms.

"You're nice and warm," she says, and this time as her hands rove there is nothing sexual about it. She doesn't slide her fingers down to my cock or hitch herself closer against my thigh like a horny minx. She just breathes, and relaxes. "Don't you need to get up?"

"Soon, yes. I've got to get my Santa hat on for the day."

"Do you ever take a day off?"

"From the grotto or just in general?"

"Either."

I answer honestly. "No."

"Nah, me neither. Not unless I can help it. Workaholics, both of us."

Sexaholic is how the founders have referred to her before, not workaholic. She must have enough cash in her bank account to live a life of Riley – I've seen the value of her proposals, plus I've used my status to check the property register. She owns her place in Belgravia, and those apartments don't come cheap.

There are so many questions I want to ask this beauty as I run my fingers up and down her arm.

Why?

Why is she such a workaholic?

Is it really her sex drive that keeps her busy night after night, apart from when she's recovering?

"Why do you work so much?" she asks me. "Does the business need it? You could be living it up on a yacht somewhere, bathing in the sun."

I have to laugh, because it's like she can read my mind without me saying a word.

"Like you said. Workaholic. How about you? Why aren't you on a yacht somewhere, bathing in the sun?"

"Don't think I earn quite as much as you, Reuben. I'm pretty minted, but I'm not in millionaire territory. Not yet."

"You're surrounded by plenty of clients who are. I'm sure one of them would whisk you away for a trip whenever you wanted one. And you'd get paid for it."

She strokes my chest.

"How about you? Would you whisk me away for a trip in the sun? You wouldn't have to pay for it. Winner."

The idea of relaxing in the sun with this goddess gives me a pang. I haven't taken a proper vacation since Jeanette. Breaks with my 'friends' involving whisky and business chatter, yes. A true holiday, no.

I have nobody to share one with.

Had.

I *had* nobody to share one with.

"I'd gladly whisk you away for a trip in the sun, as long as your calendar would allow it."

"Hmm. In that case, I guess we need to book some shared leave."

The thought of her resuming her client bookings makes me feel sick to the stomach. I don't want anyone else to touch the treasure. *Least of all my founder friends with all their filthy plans.* It's on the horizon and I know it. The founders' thread has been blaring on in the background without my input, and I know fresh proposals have been landing in Tiffany's inbox almost constantly.

"After Christmas," I say. "Keep your calendar free for a while when your proposals allow it, and we'll go away?"

She stiffens in my arms, and her tension terrifies me.

"Sure, yeah. I'll leave some bookings free. No problemo." With that, she rolls away, planting a kiss on my shoulder on the way. "I need a pee."

That was Creamgirl talking and not Tiffany. I know it.

I follow her to the ensuite, adoring the sight of her naked body as she drops herself onto the seat. But I don't have a hard-on. I'm not out to fuck her senseless as I stand in the doorway.

"What?" I ask her. "What triggered that?"

"Triggered what?"

Yes, that's definitely Creamgirl's tone.

She spreads her legs as she starts pissing. "Want some playtime, or do you need to gallop off to the grotto?"

"Come on, Tiffany. Don't deflect the question with your pussy."

Her eyes flare at me, walls up high.

"I'm not triggered by anything. I'm cool."

"Did I say something to upset you?"

She gives me a Creamgirl cackle. "No, of course not. You just offered me a yacht trip, I should be giving you a high five, not crying in a bathroom."

I note the word *should*, but I don't push it. *Should* be giving me a high five, not crying in a bathroom.

Crying.

She wipes her pussy and flushes the toilet. Her naked body looks incredible under the harshness of the bathroom lights. I love how her tits jiggle as she washes her hands.

Unfortunately, the grotto opens at ten, so I ease back on pushing her.

"What are you going to do today?" I ask. "Put your feet up, watch some TV? There's practically a cinema downstairs."

She shrugs. "Sure. I'll find something to do. Always something to scroll through on social media, or who knows? I might even grab a book." She gives me a smirk. "Don't worry though, *Santa*, I'll be ready to empty your sack when you get back home."

The sparkle in her eyes would normally fill me with lust, but for some reason it grates at me this morning. I don't *need* my *sack emptying* every minute of the day. I might enjoy it, but I don't *need* it.

I guess it's me who's been *triggered* as I give a 'great stuff' and walk away.

She's out of the bathroom as I take down one of my robes from the back of the bedroom door and wrap myself up.

"Jeez, Reuben. What's up this morning? It's like we're a married couple in a mood with each other, not a hooker and a client."

It's my eyes that are like fire as I switch on the bedroom light to look at her.

"You are not a hooker, and I'm not a client. Not here. Not now."

I head downstairs and put the coffee machine on. I need my caffeine. Fuck it, I hate feeling like this. Walls are there for a reason. It hurts like a bastard when they have to come up after being broken down. I take out a mug for Tiffany as well as myself, taking advantage of the squirty cream to make her a hot chocolate. I know she enjoys them in the morning.

She's been rummaging in my wardrobe when she comes down. She's dressed in a pair of my loose joggers and a big hoodie, which looks like she's wearing a huge onesie. The hoodie is way too long for her.

"Sorry," she says. "Can we just start over? I don't know what this bullshit is, but I don't like it."

The eyes that are looking at me aren't Creamgirl's now, they're Tiffany's. Her gaze drops as she fake examines her nail extensions.

I force my own unease away for the sake of her smile. And my own.

"Of course. Good morning, Tiffany. I've made you a hot chocolate."

Her grin is bright as she heads over and takes it from me.

"Thank you, kind sir." She raises herself on tiptoes to plant a kiss on my cheek. "Aren't you off to the grotto soon? The kids will be desperate to see you."

"Yes, I am, and yes, I'm sure they will be." I take a chance on impulse as she sips her hot chocolate – giving herself a cute cream moustache. "Why don't you come along? There are always elf vacancies."

Her eyebrows raise. "What? To the mall? With you?"

"You could come to the grotto, yes. Get in costume."

She puts a hand on her hip. "Do elf costumes come in plus size?"

"We have plenty of elf costumes in plus size, Tiff. You'd make a cutie."

"And what if someone saw us..." She looks right at me. "Someone, you know, who shouldn't."

I get a shiver, because her concern is well founded. Sometimes my associates do call in. They like Firenzo's – my restaurant at the top of the mall.

"You could put your hair up, leave off the catflicks for a day."

She giggles. "I think catflicks are done for me for the day anyway. Have you seen the state of them?"

There are barely any traces left to see. I kissed her so many times last night, licking and sucking that there is barely a hint of makeup left on her gorgeous face.

"It's up to you." I sip my coffee, grateful for the caffeine since my head is thumping after last night. My fuel tank is running on empty after playing with the goddess for so long. "I'd best go get ready anyway. Books, scrolling, TV, they are all there for your attention. Explore the house. Have a snooze."

"Reuben wait," she calls when I reach the stairs. She bites her lip, and my heart dares to race. "I'll come. I'll be an elf for the day. You're right, nobody will recognise me. Not with my hair up."

My heart soars as I grin.

"Great, we'll be pleased to have you. So will the kids. They're going to love another elf on the team, especially one with a smile like yours." I hold out a hand. "Come on, let's go get ready. I have clothes that will fit you better than that, at least until we get there."

"Phew," she laughs. "These joggers are going right up my butt crack."

My cock hardens at her laugh. *Tiffany's* laugh. Her real smile. The true humour in her eyes.

"I'll be going up your butt crack later, missy. But I'll be diving a lot deeper than those joggers."

"Promises, promises," she says as she takes my hand.

"A promise I intend on keeping." I give her ass a good slap.

That sends her giggling and shooting up the stairs ahead of me.

"Look at you!" she says from the landing.

I look down at myself, wondering if my growing cock has escaped my robe.

It hasn't. Not yet, anyway.

"This," she says.

When I look back up the stairs, the gorgeous Tiffany is grinning wide, pointing at her huge smile with both hands.

"I've never seen you smile like you are right now," she says.

And she's right, I'm grinning so wide, I must look like the Cheshire cat.

"Come on, Santa," she says and whips off the hoodie, "Santa's baby needs dressing."

It's my turn to go running up the stairs, still grinning as Tiffany casts the hoodie aside and runs giggling to the bedroom.

I've never rang in sick for the grotto before, but hell, it does cross my mind.

This amazing girl has got me hooked, and I intend on never letting her go.

CHAPTER 21
Tiffany

I'm wracked with nerves when Reuben pulls up at the mall. I take a deep breath as he puts his hand on my knee and gives it a squeeze.

"You ok? Looking forward to being an elf for the day?"

Part of me wants to be honest and say no, not in the slightest. Being around kids gives me the heebies. Especially the cute, curious ones at about six or seven years old, gripping their parents' hands as they skip along, excited for Christmas.

My baby would have been six now, skipping along by my side.

Fate's a bastard, though. It chewed me up and spat me out, and since then it's been safer not to dream at all. To avoid horrific memories at all costs.

There is no way I'd be here now, about to be an elf, if it wasn't for Reuben. In some ways I want to curse my dumbass soul for daring to believe.

"I'm cool," I tell him. "It'll be an experience. I've never played an elf before. Cats, yeah. Naughty daughters, playing up for their *daddy*, yeah. Even girls who get turned on by radiators." Reuben laughs, and I laugh along with him. "For real, one guy loves radiators. The hotter the better."

"I know. I read your proposals, remember?"

Proposals seem miles away. I have a shit ton of them stacking up in my notifications, but I've been ignoring every single one of them.

"Let's do this," I say, trying my best to sound happy about it.

He gets out of the car and I follow suit. "Does being Santa's elf bring any perks?"

"You get free coffee and cookies," he says, coming to stand next to me.

"I was thinking maybe a turn on Santa's lap between kiddie visits."

"I'm sure that's a given," he reaches for my hand.

I take a step back. "Maybe it's best if you go ahead."

He nods. "Good thinking."

I follow him as he leads the way, keeping my distance as we head through the mall. Being here together feels so risky, in case there are prying eyes. I'm probably being paranoid, but the combination of nerves upon nerves makes me especially on edge. The last thing I want at risk is my career right now. If things went tits up, my job would be the safety zone I'd run back to at full speed.

If.

There it is again. That sliver of hope. I'm daring to believe.

I'm a stupid ass sometimes.

Reuben brought his Santa suit in a holdall. I wait by the toilets as he dashes to get my outfit.

He presents me with a bag and I open it to take a peek. Stripy red and white tights, a green dress and a cute little fluffy hat with a bobble on top. I've got my red stilettos on under Reuben's fresh pair of joggers. And I've got a pair of his boxer shorts on to stop my butt crack showing.

"You sure this is my size?"

"Positive," he says.

"Really?"

"I know body shapes like a professional, Tiffany. Especially curvier ones."

I get dressed up in a cubicle, and I'm impressed. Reuben has selected my outfit perfectly. My stripy tights fit nicely, and my elf dress doesn't show too much cleavage – just a taster. The hem is a decent length, almost to the knee.

I put my hair up in the scrunchie I always keep in my bag and pop my hat on top. I check myself out in the mirror and it's convincing. I kinda like it.

I'm about to leave when the door opens, and a little girl bounces on in with her mum. She's one of my beautiful nightmares, about six years old, with red curls, and freckles dusting her cheeks. She has bright blue eyes – like Kian, and I get the familiar hit, right in the heart.

She stares open mouthed at me, her eyebrows high.

"Mummy, look! It's an elf! An elf in the toilet!"

Her mum grins bright. "So it is."

I fight the urge to freeze as the girl dashes over and wraps her arms around me, linking them tight around my thighs.

"Hey, elfie! Are you helping Santa?" She looks up at me. "I'm going to see him, you know? I'm going to ask him for a reindeer for Christmas. He's got loads, hasn't he? Do you think he'll give me one?"

I can't help but break into a smile. A reindeer, wow. Her mum gives me a silent grimace, and I come up with an answer on the spot. I drop to a crouch to meet her daughter eye to eye, my heart thumping.

"I don't know about that, sweetie pie. Santa's reindeers have to work really hard every Christmas, and I'm not sure he'll be able to do without them. Especially not Rudolph." I keep smiling as her grin drops. "But… he might be able to get you a really nice pretend one. A fluffy one that looks just like Rudolph. They are so good, almost like the real thing. PLUS, you can give them a cuddle. Real reindeers can be a bit grumpy sometimes, and they are hard to fit in your bedroom."

Her face lights up as though I've just given her a revelation.

"That sounds really cool."

I give her a pat on the back before I get to my feet, and her mum mouths a *thank you*.

"Right, toilet time, Penny," she says. "The grotto opens soon!"

I leave them to it, fighting the urge to burst into tears once I'm out of sight. I take deep, slow breaths and tell myself I can get through this. I can do it. I always fucking do.

The sight of Reuben waiting by the grotto allows my fears to fuck off a little. It brings back the rush of pure *oh my fucking God* as I see him like that again, trussed up in his red suit and silly beard.

"Ho, ho, ho," he says when I reach him, and I almost dive in for a hug before I remember that this is the grotto, and I'm just a helper here. A volunteer – not someone who woke up in Reuben Sinclair's bed this morning, still feeling the shape of his fist in her pussy.

He introduces me to Evelyn and Jen, the other elves, and takes his spot in the Santa cavern. Evelyn is young, in her early twenties – tall and energetic with her long blonde hair in a plait. Jen is a lot older and has a real motherly quality to her. I like her from the off. She's about the same size as I am, and we are in identical outfits. Ah-ha! No wonder Santa picked my costume just fine.

I get a shiver of panic at the thought there might be some history between them. She has a great smile, and shimmies her ass in her costume, joking as she says she could be my elf mother. She leans in and whispers '*My husband thinks I look like an idiot in this garb, but he can piss off. I love elf time.*'

Phew, she has a husband. I feel the relief in my bones.

The pair of volunteers direct me well and put me at ease, talking me through how they manage the queue and engage with the kids waiting in line, to make sure they don't get bored. We have a bucket of candy canes each to hand out, and Jen takes the entrance while Evelyn and I stand on each side of the queue. Within no time, it stretches way beyond the grotto entrance – it's like a bloody snake through the mall. I stop darting my eyes to Santa's cavern every fifteen seconds in an attempt to catch sight of Reuben, because the hustle and bustle just doesn't allow it. I have no chance to let my emotions overtake me as I chat to the kids as they pass by, and in no time at all I'm laughing and joking with them.

I get so many questions on what it's like to be an elf, and I come up with elaborate stories about my experiences with reindeers, and how silly Rudolph can be when he's in a mood. The kids love it, and the parents appreciate the effort. I get more *thank yous* mouthed at me than I've ever known, and it feels good to be appreciated like this. Really fucking good.

The kids' happy faces don't pierce my heart after a while, they make me grin. My silly elf costume doesn't make me feel like an idiot with my waves of scarlet hair scrunched up in a bun, it makes me feel magical. By lunchtime, I've kicked my stilettos off in favour of going barefoot, since they're so bloody uncomfortable, and with that I start to do silly elf dances and I sing along to *jingle bells* with groups of kids. It's hilarious.

"You're doing a fantastic job!" Jen gushes as we grab a ten minute break. "Where the hell did Reuben find you? I've never seen you around here before."

Fuck, what a question. I turn it into a joke and give her a slap on the arm.

"He found me feeding Rudolph when nobody was looking and snuck me into the grotto!"

She laughs. "No, seriously. Where did he find you?"

Shit.

I can see the way she's digging.

She gestures to the grotto.

"Come on," she says. "I know Reuben pretty well. I've been working with him for years. I saw the way he looked at you when you appeared in your elf garb."

Fuck it. I'm not wearing foundation today. I feel my cheeks burning up like hell.

Her smile turns into a full on grin.

"It's so good to see him like this," she tells me. "Honestly, I've been waiting to see him find happiness for a long, long time. You must be one special elf, put it that way."

I don't know what to say or do. My heart is racing, as though I've committed a crime, because she knows we've got *something going on*. She sees it.

"I hope you feel the same way about him," she says. "He's one of the most incredible men you could ever know. And if it wasn't for my husband, well." She swats my arm. "He's quite a dish, isn't he? I hope you appreciate being Santa's baby, because there would be a queue longer than this one to get a chance at that."

I've no doubt about that.

Thank fuck the break is over before I get more of a grilling from her. I'm back to Rudolph chatter and singsongs, and I try to play it as casual as possible in front of Jen and Evelyn when Santa takes some time out for a coffee. It's no bloody wonder Jen cottoned on though, because he can't stop looking at me, and I can't stop looking at him. My heart flutters, and the butterflies soar, and I'm so fucking glad I braved my fears enough to join him at the grotto today, because it beats anything I could have done back at his place. A million times over.

It's not just because of him, though.

It's because of the kids, too.

The joy on their faces, and the sound of their laugher, and the way they are so happy to speak to me. So excited to see the amazing Santa.

There is no point hiding the truth from myself any longer. My guard has been up so high for so long that it's touched the sky, but now it's breaking. Crumbling.

I want to be Mrs Santa, not just his elf. I want to have Santa's babies, and build a family with the stunning, charitable, dirty, powerful, loving Reuben Sinclair. Screw proposals, and a life filled with smut for cash, I've had my filthy fill.

All I want for Christmas – is him.

"You are an absolute superstar of an elf, I hope you know that," he says as soon as we're back at the car. "I caught sight of you, singing and chatting with the kids. It was magical."

I feel so proud of myself, it's ridiculous, and so hot for him, it's insane.

"Yeah, it was pretty cool. I liked it."

He grins as he reverses out of the parking space.

"Cool enough that you'll come back here with me tomorrow?"

Fuck the charade, I laugh out loud.

"Cool enough that I'll come back *every* day to elf it up with you, how's that sound?"

"Now *that* sounds magical. Thank you."

"On one condition," I say, and hold up a finger.

"Go on."

"You give me the fuck you promised me earlier. I'm gagging for it, Santa."

"Don't worry about that, my sweet elf princess." He gives me a side eye that sets my clit on fire. "You've been on the nice list all day. It's time to get real fucking naughty when we get home."

Home.

Yeah. Home is where the heart is.

And mine belongs at Reuben's.

CHAPTER 22
Tiffany

$\mathcal{I}$'m absolutely gagging for it when Reuben opens the door. I'm prepared to rip off my clothes and get right down to the filthy action as soon as we're in the hall, but Reuben hangs up his coat and takes off his brogues. Cool, calm, collected.

"Hungry?" he asks, and walks through to the kitchen.

"Hungry?" I laugh. "I'm fucking ravenous. But not for dinner. For dick."

I catch up with him at the fridge, and wrap my arms around him from behind, sliding my hands down to his crotch, but he doesn't react to my advances. He simply turns to me with a raised eyebrow.

"You have to eat something first. You haven't eaten since breakfast."

"Not true. I had at least six cookies." My hands move to his tie. "I'm sure I'll cope."

He takes my hands and stills them, rubbing his thumb over my knuckles. He's still in Santa mode. I see it in his eyes. Such care.

"Six cookies aren't enough for the energy you'll need when I fuck you into another dimension later. Eat, then I'll fuck you senseless, I promise."

I'm not giving up. I pull my hands free and go back for his cock.

"You promised you'd fuck me senseless when we got home. And now here we are. Home." I flash him a dirty grin. "So fuck me senseless now please, *Santa*."

He tips my chin up and looks me in the eyes. "You've been on your feet all day, helping like a star performer from the very moment we arrived at the grotto. Eat, please. Enjoy some calm before the storm."

I don't know why I feel so resentful of him trying to help me. Bigging me up, rather than tearing me down. His Santa eyes are filled with affection. His smile is a winner. His intentions are real fucking pure.

Too pure.

Maybe that's it.

Because without the superpower of my sex prowess being my ace card, what do I have to fall back on? What do I have to keep me safe?

"What is it?" Reuben asks. "Your expressions always speak volumes. Even louder than your words sometimes."

I shrug and pull away from him. "Nothing. I'm cool."

I sit down at the breakfast bar and take my phone from my pocket. I feel myself trying to disconnect, wanting the butterflies to fuck off and flutter somewhere else. I'm too consumed for my own sanity.

I've got a couple of missed calls from Josh as per. Another message saying we need to meet up soon, which I give a thumbs up to. Then I'm on to social media. Aimless scrolling.

"Tiffany," Reuben says. "What's going on with you? Why does the switch flick from hot to cold so suddenly?"

I call on Creamgirl's swagger.

"I was trying to set the switch to hot actually, but you were more interested in the fridge. No prob. My pussy can dry up while I'm waiting."

"I wasn't proposing a three-course extravaganza from the Firenzo menu, I was thinking pasta."

"Pasta's cool, thanks. Yummy."

I know I sound like a petulant kid, but it's easy with Reuben in Santa mode. He's the ultimate *daddy* figure like this. So kind and generous and fucking lovely. But I don't want a daddy for *myself*. I want a daddy for –

My scrolling finger catches me off guard.

I've been barely paying attention to my social media feed until a post shows up that both Josh and Ella are tagged in. Caroline always likes to tag everyone in the world, the attention seeking cow. She's tagged them, along with the rest of Josh's family.

Her baby bump is on proud display and she's holding up a blurry scan image.

Can't wait for our little bean to meet her family! You're going to love her, guyssssss!

Her post has a massive chain of hearts and happy emojis in the comments. It sucker punches me right in the guts.

I don't want to see Caroline's baby. I don't want to hear about how happy she is, and how blessed she is with such a sweet little soul soon to be calling her *Mummy*.

The memories of the day around kids rise up along with the bile. Smiling happy families. Laughter. Singing. Innocent little cuties with parents who love them to bits. And then me.

A hooker in elf tights, praying that my boss is in love with me.

In love with me enough to have a fucking kid with me. How fucking ridiculous.

I'm glad I'm on a breakfast stool, or my dizziness might send me tumbling.

"Tiffany!" Reuben barks, and I realise I've been blanking him. "I'm suggesting pasta for dinner, not committing a criminal offence. Show some respect will you, please?"

His tone is another punch that throws me, and I have to retreat. I need to be Creamgirl, back in my safe zone. I want my mind blanked out with the fun of sex and nothing else.

"My pussy could do with a bit of respect first, don't you think? I'm a horny bitch, if you hadn't noticed already."

My cackle laugh is forced, and I feel like a dumb bitch. I drop my phone to the side and rest my chin on my hands.

"Come on, Reuben. Show me what Santa's got, and then I'll help you cook pasta. Fair deal?"

He doesn't answer, just stares. Trying to read me.

I don't like it.

"Fair deal, yeah?" I push, and he tips his head to the side. I feel uneasy at how well his stare is digging. Probing.

"You're trying to provoke me," he says finally, and turns back to the fridge. "Remember, patience is a virtue, and I have the patience of a saint. You can eat your dinner first, and you can apologise later when you're taking my cock on the back of it."

He gets out some tomatoes, and takes some spice jars from the rack. He's really going to blank my pussy. He's going to keep me hanging, as though he needs dinner more than he needs to get his dick wet.

But I don't want him to be patient, or sensible, or kind. Not when my insides are churning and eating me up. Because if I'm this needy and desperate for him... this invested, and twisted up with stupid dreams that might never come to anything... where the fuck will I be if it all goes wrong?

Hurt.

That's where I'll be.

Abandoned and hurt. Broken.

Home is where the heart is, and I'm scared to be in Reuben's now. I'm scared of falling too deep.

Unless I know he's falling with me.

I need to see it.

My words come out of my big mouth without a thought.

"Patience, right. Will you have the patience of a saint when it comes to other men fucking me?"

He stops chopping tomatoes and turns around. There is no sweet Santa in his eyes when they meet mine this time. His stare gives me tingles.

"What?"

"You heard me." I smirk like a vixen out to snare. "Tell me, Reuben. How will you feel about other men fucking my cunt? Will you have the patience of a saint then, when you're having to wait your turn?" I lick my lips. "Maybe you should take advantage of it while you can, hey?"

I get a thrill at his glare. *Jealousy.*

"Watch your mouth," he says. "This is about pasta, not your cunt."

"It's always about my cunt." I laugh. "You've read the reviews. You know how many proposal requests are in my inbox, so if you don't want to give me a filthy time…"

I pick up my phone, but he moves so quickly that I don't so much as have time to unlock the screen. I'm down from the breakfast stool in seconds, dragged down the hall by the scruff as his hand fists my hoodie and holds tight.

"Don't you *ever* forget who the fuck I am," he says as he shoves me into the living room. "Don't ever forget how you met me, *Creamgirl.* Now STRIP!"

I flinch at the boom of his voice, heart pounding. He tugs his tie free, and takes off his shirt as I stare up at him, dumbfounded.

He's unbuckling his belt when his eyes lock back on mine, and they're filled with absolute fire.

"I SAID, FUCKING STRIP!"

I tug my hoodie off, and the oversized t-shirt underneath. I push Reuben's joggers down my thighs, my breaths shallow as I slide down the boxer shorts he's lent me. I kick them aside as he kicks off his trousers, and his cock is raging proud.

"Get the fuck here," he says, and grabs my arm.

I shriek as he shoves me forward and I tumble over the arm of the sofa. My face slams into the cushion and he slaps my ass once, twice, three times, real fucking hard, and I shriek again when my ass cheeks are spread and his cock slams into my pussy, all the way to the balls, so deep it knocks the breath out of me.

Jesus fucking Christ.

He fucks me like a demon with its ass on fire, his entire weight on my back as he slams his hips at lightning speed. I feel powerless as I whimper, because he's got me pinned and he's hitting exactly the right fucking spot. I feel his rage with every thrust, and it makes my cunt burn and tighten. He presses my face against the sofa cushion so hard that my cries are muffled, and he ramps up the force, slamming with all his might. I have no control here. My legs are trembling as the sensations rack up inside me, my muscles gripping his cock in a vice as I rise, rise, rise, then explode.

I feel it spray out of my pussy in one huge downpour and rush down my legs. I groan into the sofa at the climax, but he doesn't give me a single second before he pulls his rampant cock out of me and stabs it straight into my ass. I cry out to a different crazy tune as he spreads my cheeks and drives in deep.

I try to arch up against the invasion, but it's pointless. He crushes me back down. My pussy is still leaking in little squirts as he fucks me raw – my ass on fire. It feels like I'm being fucked by a red-hot poker, but I don't give a shit.

I *can't* give a shit.

I buck back at him, trying to clench, trying to milk his dick. I want him to come as hard as I did. I want him to fill my ass with his cum. But it doesn't work.

"You fucking asked for this," he says as he slams me. "I'm not always a fucking saint, Tiffany, and you fucking know it. Don't make a joke out of it, and don't ever make a fucking joke out of me."

I can't speak. Can't think. Can only try to bear it as he fucks my ass like a piston, my soul rising into blissful subspace.

Strong hands grip my hips as my asshole is brutalised. Reuben slams in and out with so much force that it feels like I'm turning inside out, but that's not enough for him. He drives his fingers in along with his cock, one by one.

All I can do is moan and take it.

I've been here before. Fucked like this before. Only usually I'd have a hood over my head.

"Take it, you filthy fucking slut," he says, pounding into me. "That's what you want, isn't it? To be a filthy fucking slut. If that's what you want, you can fucking take it."

I can feel his cock, hitting my guts.

I can feel little squirts, pumping from my cunt.

I try to clench amongst the madness but there's nothing there.

Nothing but heady bliss.

I'm powerless.

He pulls out of my ass with a wrench that has me cursing, and I know his slap is hard by the way it jolts me, but I don't feel it.

The cushion dips as he kneels in front of me on the sofa, wrapping my hair around his fist and pulling my face up.

I have no balance at all. I'm just a meaty whore staring up at a master with a filthy hard-on.

"Open your fucking mouth," he says, and my eyes are on his as I do it.

I open my mouth for Santa and he jams his dirty dick right to the back of my throat. He pumps my face like he pumped my ass, deep and vicious, while I quack and retch. My eyes stream trails of watery tears as I give myself up to the man I goaded.

He can take my cunt, he can take my ass, he can take my throat. He can take *me*.

I only want him to love me in return.

When I see the anger in his stare, my heart leaps, because the rage has come from the depths of him – just as the need for the validation came from the depths of me.

I give myself up completely as I choke and drool. He has full control now and he uses it, leveraging my hair so strongly that my scalp burns. His filthy dick is slick with spit, and he buries his way into my throat so far that my ears ring, my nose crushed against his stomach.

I suck in the breath of my fucking life when he finally pulls out of me, and that's when he spurts. Long, hot streams right into my face, splattering my tongue, my lips, my cheeks, and jetting one load straight into my fucking eye. I'm blinking stinging cum as he puts his face up close to mine – my breaths still ragged.

"Do you really want any other man's cock after that?" he asks me. "Tell me now, and you'd better fucking mean it."

His voice is simmering. The jealousy rife.

"No," I tell him. "I don't want any other cock, I swear. Pinky fucking promise."

He lets go of my hair.

"Good."

I'm still a slobbering mess over the arm of his sofa as he gets up and walks away.

"Dinner time!" he calls from the kitchen. "Get your sorry ass back in here."

I wipe the cum from my face with the back of my hand, my vision blurred and burning with jizz eye. Fuck, he got me good. I haul myself up from the sofa, padding my way back through to the kitchen, stark naked and a trembling mess.

I'm so nervous as I approach him.

"Want any help?" I ask as he continues chopping tomatoes, starkers like me.

"No, thank you," he says, and flashes me a fresh smile that has me gooey. Animosity forgotten. "Just sit your butt down on that stool, and get your phone out of sight."

"Sure thing, boss."

He slaps my ass when I pass him, and I poke my tongue out on my way.

His jealous outburst has worked black magic, deep in the sanctity of my heart. I'm done for as I look at his naked body as he makes dinner for us. The butterflies in my stomach are going fucking crazy, and the fear in my soul is even worse.

I was telling the truth. I don't want any other cock. I don't want any other *anything*, I only want him.

His cock, his kisses, his heart, his home… and his children.

I want a baby bump like Caroline, more than anything.

And I want Reuben to be the man who gives it to me.

CHAPTER 23
Tiffany

When the alarm goes off, I can hardly be arsed to face it. I'm too comfy in Reuben's deluxe bed with the gorgeous hulk of him lying beside me. He switches off the bleeping and I snuggle closer, hoping I can drift back into dreamland and he'll come there with me, but of course not.

It's another day at the grotto. For both of us.

But not just yet…

Reuben doesn't shake me awake and announce the morning dawn like a cockerel. He leans over and places a gentle kiss on my forehead, peppering a line down to my ear, where his breath makes me tingle.

"Morning, Tiffany."

I yawn. "Morning. Can't believe we stayed up so late."

"I can."

My body moves on instinct when it's touched. My knees part wide as Reuben coaxes them open. I'm happy as Larry to feel his horny cock on my thigh, despite the fact it had to be after two by the time we got to bed.

A selection of my clothes are now hanging in Reuben's wardrobe, having dashed like a thief in the night over to my apartment to throw some into a suitcase. I knew Josh and Ella were working a double proposal – a mega hardcore one, over in Notting Hill. No chance of seeing me and asking questions. And no chance of spotting Reuben by my side.

I love how strong my saucy Santa is as he positions himself on top of me. My arms reach up around his shoulders.

"Hey there, Santa Claus. You got a present for me?"

"Yes, indeed. Santa's sack needs some attention before the grotto."

I giggle. "My elfish pussy *always* needs attention. Grotto or not."

"No getting too *grotto* this morning. Let's keep it nice and gentle, shall we?"

"Gentle sounds good to me for once."

Reuben and I had such filthy fun after the clothes dash that I'm still battered and bruised to shit from it. My ass is gonna be purple from paddle blows, and my tits were bound so tight that the twine grooves are still hurting. The founder side of Reuben sure showed himself in its full glory, and I loved it.

I love his morning glory, too…

In fact, I love every single filthy, sweet side of him. My beautiful silver fox Santa. Santa, boss, founder, lover. Jealous, possessive, and selfless. All in one package. *With* a package that can send me sky high.

His dick glides all the way in, I'm so wet for him. He slides his thumb between my puffy pussy lips as he circles his hips, seeking out my clit. It doesn't take long for him to find his target, and he's a fucking pro – hitting double whammy on the sensation spots. Inside as well as out. But he takes it so fucking slow. Teasing so gently.

He lowers his head and flicks his tongue across my nipple. It's still so fucking sore from being clamped. The tenderness is divine as he sucks, just a touch.

"You were such a good girl last night. Incredible," he says, and I smile up at the ceiling at his praise.

My five-star reviews have always given me a massive glow of accomplishment, and I figured I'd miss that without the constant stream from my clients – but Reuben's words are worth a ton of five starrers.

"I made you take it so fucking bad," he says, shoving his cock deep and pressing on my clit. "And you played the game like an absolute dream."

I arch my back as he laps at my tits, my breaths already ragged from the way he's using my pussy.

"It wasn't a game," I say. "It was all real. Everything is real with you. There's no Creamgirl here anymore. It's just me."

He puts his face up to mine, brushing my lips with his.

"I'm glad about that, because Tiffany is the one I want, princess. She's the one I need."

The contrast in him is like yin and yang. The brutal Reuben from last night, who treated me like a slut while I cried and screamed, and the loving, tender Reuben in bed with me this morning.

I'm in love with all of his flavours. Every single one of them.

"You'll drive me mad with the teasing," I tell him as he pulls out a little way and strokes his thumb over my clit.

"Good. I want you needing me so bad, it drives you to insanity."

"We're already long past the insanity point," I say, and pull him in for a kiss.

My tongue sweeps against his so softly, it's like a brush of wet velvet. Our kiss is delicate but desperate, both at once. A fascination that captures us like moths to a flame.

"Do it, Reuben," I whisper against his lips. "Fuck my bruised cunt nice and hard."

"No," he says. "I'm going to fuck your bruised cunt so slowly you'll be begging to come."

He stays true to his word, in complete control of every flex and every plunge. He's a man of steel.

Only he wasn't so calm and calculated when we first got home last night, and he dragged me through to the living room. There was no calmness in him as he shot his load into my petulant face after I talked about taking other men's cocks.

Jealousy.

I can't help myself wanting more. I'm moaning at the thought of that fire in his eyes.

Praise and jealousy from a man like Reuben Sinclair is enough to light up the world.

"Tell me what you're thinking, princess," he says, sliding his cock in slowly enough that I moan for more. "You'd be a terrible poker player. Your face is too beautifully expressive."

I look into his gorgeous dark eyes.

"I'm thinking about how annoyingly fucking good your cock feels."

He won't break the stare.

"Don't lie to me. You're thinking about more than that."

"I'm not." I buck my hips. "It is annoyingly good, and you know it. You like driving me insane, don't you?"

"I think we're both insane. You said it yourself. It's very clear to see."

I wrap my legs around him, trying to spur him on. The slow builds are always the mightiest, but so infuriating when you're a gagging bitch wanting a hit of cum.

"What are you really thinking about?" he asks again.

I wish I could tell him. I want to.

I want to share my deepest everything with him, but I'm still too scared to be that vulnerable. I want to tell him about my hurt and devastation when my relationship with Kian fell to pieces, and how I lost my head after the miscarriage that followed. How I swore I didn't want anything serious again. No risks, no depth, nothing but dirty, filthy fucking. Carnal pleasure and a healthy bank account.

No stress.

No soul.

I look up at the man fucking me tenderly, and a part of me hates the fact that the stress is showing its face again, like roots growing back up from dead earth.

Reuben Sinclair could hurt me. Destroy me. Tear the world from under my feet.

Because I love him.

"What are you thinking, Tiffany?" he repeats, and his voice has more bite to it, even though the rhythm of his hips stays in line.

"I'm thinking about us," I say. "About how fucking insane we really are." I smile. "No, scrap that. I'm thinking about how insane *I* am. For letting myself be so crazy."

"Keep going."

He sucks at my other nipple, sending sparks down to my clit.

"Since we saw each other, it's like we've lost our heads, isn't it? And the thing is, I don't want mine back. Not yet." I groan. "I never thought I'd be alright with all my proposals slipping out of my calendar. I never figured I'd hack being so consumed with just one guy."

"Monogamy? Is that what you're referring to?"

I urge him on with my hips, his cock right on the fucking spot.

"Yeah, I guess so. Hardly a thing for a hooker, is it?"

"That depends if you want to be a hooker anymore."

He laps at my nipple as his eyes look up at mine. I must look so unflattering from this angle, but the adoration is still obvious on his face. It makes my pussy sparks worse – or better.

"Do you want to be a hooker anymore, Tiffany?"

My heart races at the question, battling my head with all its might.

I'm torn. Split. Divided.

I love my job. I love the anonymity of my clients, and being the top of the tree. I love the income. I love being a dirty bitch, without consequences. Without having to hope for anything more.

But I love Reuben.

I crave the idea of a life with him.

If he'll give me one...

"I don't know," I tell him, and run my fingers through his hair. "Do you want me to be a hooker anymore?"

"Good one-eighty."

I grin. Soppy and stupid.

"Got a bit of time to decide yet, haven't we? I haven't got any more proposals booked in yet besides the founders gig. We can get that out of the way and have a jolly Christmas. Think it through in the New Year."

He tenses up, pausing with his cock all the way inside me.

"What?" I ask, his face so close to mine. His eyes have the same fire they had when he dragged me through to the sofa.

My butterflies do a spin in my stomach.

"Go on," I say. "Be honest. Do you want me to stop being a hooker?"

I run my nails down his back. Part of me wanting him to admit it, part of me not.

"Fuck waiting until New Year until you make the decision. I want you to cancel the founders' proposal in the meantime."

My eyes widen in shock, because he can't be for real. Him tampering with my bookings and me blagging to Orla that I've got some personal shit going down is one thing... but to cancel the founders, with their reputation, and status and the huge sum of money involved. That's a whole other ballgame. A serious one.

I stiffen underneath him.

"Are you being serious?"

"Deadly."

"But that's—"

"Insane, yes. I know. It won't please them. But people get flu, Tiffany. People get unwell."

I have to laugh. "I'd have to be pretty fucking unwell to cancel a founders' gig. Hardly a gold star on my agency resume."

Reuben slams me deep. Harder.

"I don't want other men to give you gold stars, Tiff. I don't want other men to give you *anything*, especially not while I'm in the same fucking room as them."

So much for slow and sensual. He angles his cock into me so sharply that I'm wriggling, groaning like a bitch as he works me up.

"I want you to cancel the founders' proposal," he says. "I can't do it for you. Not without raising suspicions, so it would have to come from you. You'd have to be the one to feign illness and hit the cancel button."

I don't want to answer him yet, because the idea of cancelling the founders gives me serious heebies. It's not anything I ever thought I'd be doing. Most of the hardcore team of entertainers would give anything for a night of that value. For the recognition in the Agency that brings. I've relished it, time after time, like a status symbol.

What I do want right now is for Reuben to make me come, and unload into me before we leave for the grotto today. I let out a grunt and urge him on.

"Make me come, please. I need to fucking come, Reuben. Take my insanity and use it. You drive me fucking wild."

The kisses come back, deep and all consuming. We're a sweaty mess of flesh and lust as he unleashes the pent-up want that he's been stoking. I don't give a fuck when I gush and soak the sheets underneath us. I keep pushing down on his dick, spraying like a hose until he curses against my lips and comes inside me. Deep inside me. Thrusting hard with every spasm of his rock-hard cock.

My sex god Santa.

Mine.

Anyone would be lucky to have him, even for a few days. Christmas is being kind to me for once, but will my good fortune last?

It feels like for ever, our panting breaths as one as he holds me, his dick still inside me.

"That was amazing," I tell him.

He drops a kiss on my nose and eases his cock free.

"We need to make a move," he says. "Don't want to be late," and heads off to the ensuite.

I feel so awkward as we shower together. There is no soaping each other up. No languorous kisses. Santa is in a hurry, that much is obvious. It's also obvious that Santa is stewing over the fact that I didn't grant his Christmas wish.

Fuck.

"Jam? Marmalade? Butter?" he asks when we hit the kitchen. "I'm still unsure of your breakfast favourites."

"Just butter, thanks."

I watch him making my toast, sitting at the breakfast bar and kicking my heel against the leg of the stool.

Can I do what he wants of me? Really? Is it worth the risk of pissing off the Agency, and leaving a black mark on my scorecard, AND missing out on nearly one hundred grand?

It's one hell of a fucking decision for 7.30 a.m. after a few hours' sleep.

I'm supposed to be acting like an elf today, not a headcase. So, I should leave it. Think things through when I'm not high on Santa vibes and waiting for the toast to pop from the toaster.

Shame that the word impulsive might as well be my middle name. I hate hanging in no man's land.

I take my phone from my pocket, and Reuben does a double take when he reaches for the butter – catching sight of it in my hand. He knows what app I'm scrolling through. The look between us says it all.

"I'm sorry," he says. "Upstairs earlier, I got jealous, and possessive, and that isn't fair on you. It's your career, and your accomplishments at stake, not mine to impose upon. I need to keep myself in line."

"Nah, you don't," I say, and turn the screen around. I rub some fake snot on my sleeve with a sniffle. "Had to message Orla and break the news to her. Seems I am coming down with flu after all."

CHAPTER 24
Reuben

I've always loved the grotto – that's no secret – relishing the Christmas spirit of the families enjoying the run up to their festivities, but watching Tiffany as an elf, singing along with the children in the queue is raising things to a whole new level with every passing moment. It also reminds me of the true needs I've been masking for years.

It's just gone ten when a toddler enters the room with her father. She's barely able to walk yet, gripping her daddy's finger as she toddles along. She has a bright smile and a twinkle in her eyes, and so does her father. He's so obviously proud as she lets go of him and toddles on over to me. I pick her up with a *ho, ho, ho* and she giggles as she pulls at my fluffy beard.

Her humour and enthusiasm pain me today as well as bring me joy. I wish that I was her father, with her tiny hand gripping my fingers.

"This is Santa Claus," her dad tells her, then looks at me with a grin. "She's been such a treasure this year, even through the teething."

"I'm sure she has." I bounce the little tyke on my lap, with another *ho, ho, ho* and she giggles as though she's on a fair ride. I see Tiffany in her eyes. I see the joy and the amusement. The life and soul.

I want a child like this one of my own, birthed by the woman handing out candy canes in the queue outside.

Tiffany cancelling the founders' proposal was a huge statement this morning, spawned by an impulsive move of jealousy that I should never have allowed myself to make. I feel disgusted at myself for it.

Tiffany is a woman with an impressive career, who has built up her reputation over four years. She may be an elf volunteering at a mall grotto right now, with her stripy tights and bobble hat, but she is a sex goddess. A hardcorer. One of the Agency's finest.

I'm torn in two different directions. For once, I have no clear route in sight.

The tiny sweetheart on my lap holds out her arms with a *dada* once her picture is taken. Her father sweeps her up, and I hand him a goodie bag with a miniature reindeer and some penguin stickers.

"Have a wonderful Christmas," I say. "Ho, ho, ho!"

"You, too, Santa."

I can only hope, since a *wonderful Christmas* doesn't usually bless me. This year the potential of spending the holidays with a woman like Tiff has given me a light on the horizon I never imagined coming my way, but it might be a high before a terrible low.

Can Tiff give up the Agency? Her career? Truly?

Would she want to?

I know that sex workers build relationships with each other. I'm well aware that they can separate their personal lives and their professional careers, with no jealousy or suspicion whatsoever.

But I'm not an entertainer like Tiffany, and I'm not a man who will be able to bear my jealousy easily. I want monogamy, with Tiffany, in my home and by my side.

Even if I was able to bear my jealousy, our liaisons are strictly forbidden. It's not only Tiff who has deep connections with the Agency and what she has accomplished there. I've been a proud stakeholder for years, creating a safe space for both entertainers and clients while making a killing on the back of it. It's a huge part of my life. A staple in my portfolio.

Me and Tiffany are both playing with a fire that is far more powerful than a warm Christmas hearth. It's got the potential to blow our world to smithereens.

Fuck it. I have to cast the thoughts aside for the sake of sanity.

The next little boy is around eight years old. He dashes in with a *Santa!* and I'm enamoured as he lists off his amazing achievements this year, counting them out on his fingers.

I kept my bedroom tidy.

I cleaned out Lily's hamster cage every day.

I played in the football team every single weekend, AND I scored six goals.

I came second in the class on the spelling test.

I let my older brother watch TV in the middle of a movie, because I wanted to be nice.

The list goes on and on, and his mother is another smiler, giving a proud nod at every achievement he shares.

"You *have* been a good boy," I tell him. "Very good."

"Can I have a new bike, then?" he asks. "I'll ride it all the time, I promise."

I glance at his mum, and she gives the tiniest nod.

"We'll see, young man. I do have a lot of bikes I hand out to good children. Let's see what I deliver to you on Christmas Eve."

He wraps an arm around my shoulder for the photo, and skips on out with a *see you later* and a high five.

I've always dreamed of having a daughter, but I'd love a son like him, too.

I need to stop dreaming and focus on my task at hand and nothing more, but Tiffany is so close to the front of the queue that I keep catching sight of her. I can hear her laughing and joking when the door is open between visitors. It's addictive.

It's only a few short weeks until the New Year will be upon us, and the question of what happens next is hanging like a sword I don't want to have to face. I'm a strong man, but the thought of Tiffany turning away from me would buckle my legs from under me.

Still, I'd put her needs before my own. Always.

I'm exhausted when the grotto winds down for a late lunch. I must have seen about fifty children walk through the door by now, but Tiffany's joy-filled face is by far the greatest thing that appears to greet me. Evelyn and Jen have closed the queue, and Toby has shot out of the grotto for a break from photography, already glued to his phone when he left with a *catch you in a bit.*

"Hey, Santa." Tiffany shuts the door behind her. "Lynn and Jen have gone to get a sandwich and do a bit of Christmas shopping. I thought I'd hang around, take a later lunch."

She sits down on my lap like she did the very first time we locked eyes, but this time there is no simmering chemistry that hangs unfulfilled. I pull my beard down and go for her, and she twists to kiss me back, both of us frantic as I grope at her tits through her elf dress.

"There's only one thing I want for lunch," she says and grinds her big ass against my crotch.

The bustle of the mall is still loud all around us. The thin fake doors are unlocked as she twists herself to straddle me. My pillow belly meets her real one and she laughs.

"Think we'll manage?"

I kiss her neck. "I'm certain of it." I inch forward in my sleigh seat. "Can you be a quiet girl for Santa?"

"I'll try."

She scrambles to tug her elf tights down, and my fingers are straight to her hot cunt, sliding between her pussy lips. She's so wet it makes my dick throb.

"I've been thinking about this all morning," she tells me. "So many *good little girls* on Santa's lap. I've been so jealous."

I'm tempted to tell her that I've been thinking of filling her up with cum and making a *good little girl* of our own. A little sweetheart with Tiffany's grin. Her eyes. Her wavy hair. I want to share how badly I want to fuck her with a big baby belly. How badly I want to see her straining with contractions as our baby stretches her pussy open, both of us desperate to meet our child.

I've stretched Tiffany's fleshy cunt with my fist a lot of times now, but it never loses its fascination. I've asked her to push down with everything she's got, loving the way she groans as she tries to force me out of her. I've imagined how she'd look in childbirth. I've punch fucked her and made her take it so rough that she's wailed. Tipping her head back with her legs spread, gushing her orgasm as if her waters had broken.

I manage to get my cock out of my Santa pants and she lowers herself with a grin. She could be a pelvic floor champion, because her pussy grips my dick like she's a fucking virgin, squeezing to milk me dry.

That's what I want. I want Tiffany's cunt to milk me. I want to fill her up with round after round of cum, and put my baby inside her. I want to watch it grow in her swollen belly, and suck on her lactating tits to milk her. I'd love her milk in my mouth. I'd love squeezing her big tits while our baby is sleeping, and watch her nipples dribbling milk down her stomach.

I grit my teeth to stay silent in the grotto, my hands on her ass as she rises up and down.

The risk of being caught here makes me harder than ever and I know Tiffany can feel it with every buck of her hips. She speeds up, and I ease myself back in my seat as my curvy beauty bounces. Tits and belly. She braces herself on my pillow stomach and goes for it like a whore on a mission, whispering curses as she uses my cock to make her come.

It's a silent O for her. Her face is so beautiful as she closes her eyes and rides the waves, then grimaces in the silence. And thank fuck it's over too quickly to have her gushing.

It's over quickly for me, too, the thought of the door opening and one of the girls walking in spurring me on. I grip her hips as I shoot Santa's load into her hot elf cunt, imagining it spurting deep, right the way up into her fucking womb.

She's still on my lap as she catches her breath. I give her gentle kisses as she calms, wishing the grotto break was longer, so I could switch places and fuck her from behind with her face mashed into the sleigh seat cushions. But I can't do that. Not today. Jen and Evelyn will be back at any time now, and so will Toby.

Tiffany winks as she gets up from my lap and squats. She runs her hands between her legs and collects the dripping cum from her pussy, then she sucks her fingers clean as I watch her.

"That's just what I wanted for lunch," she says, then pulls her tights up. Such a travesty to see that dribbling pussy hidden from view.

"How about you, Santa? Feeling better with an empty sack?"

"If only you knew," I say, tucking my cock away.

"Knew what?"

"How much better you really make me feel, just by being here, never mind milking me dry with that amazing cunt of yours."

"Aww," she says, adjusting her elf hat, "look at you, being all soppy."

"Just being honest," I say.

"Then we should make emptying Santa's sack a habit. Eve and Jen can always take the earlier time out. I'll be conscientious and make sure the grotto is all set, ready for the queue to start up again. We always need a good elf on site with Santa, after all."

"Maybe Santa will indeed deliver you a present every day, Tiffany. If you're a good girl."

"I'm not used to being a good girl," she says. "I'm normally on the naughty list. Literally."

She starts rearranging some of the fake gifts around my feet at that, and I get a punch in the gut. A fresh reminder of what lies ahead for us.

The Naughty List will be calling Tiffany with every passing minute. Her inbox of proposals is full to bursting. I've checked, and she's been ignoring them, just as I've been ignoring the founders' thread. But it's there for both of us. We can't ignore it for ever.

My dirty elf is making sure her dress is back in position when Jen walks in. My heart thumps at the realisation of just how close we were to getting caught. A minute, tops. If we're going to play this filthy game every day, it's going to get risky. Really fucking risky.

But as Tiff winks on the way out, I know I won't be able to resist. I never will. I could never turn down my elf princess.

"You alright, Reuben?" Jen asks, and pulls a sandwich from a bag. "Grabbed you a tuna mayo baguette."

Tiff is still in the doorway, smiling at me.

"Enjoy your baguette, Reuben," she says. "If you're back now, Jen, I'll go grab myself some lunch. Might do a bit of shopping, too."

"Go for it," Jen says. "Head up to Janie's Bakes on the top floor. Plonk your tired butt down and have one of their cappuccinos and carrot cakes. Bloody delicious."

"Might just do that," Tiff says.

"Don't miss out. Trust me, you'll be a regular!"

I don't think Tiffany has been to the top floor of the mall before. It's a shame I'm not taking her myself, as I'd love to treat her to a cappuccino and carrot cake. I'd be focused on her hungry mouth as she ate it. Her groan of appreciation at the taste.

I have to eat my tuna baguette quickly, and hit the bathroom like lightning before the grotto line opens up again. It's going to be a busy afternoon.

I *ho, ho, ho* non-stop from the off, adding to the mountain of Christmas lists and cards the kids have written for me, and hearing how much they want to see Rudolph in the sky.

I've just finished hearing how a young pair of twins want matching kittens under the Christmas tree when Evelyn arrives in the grotto. She has a look of confusion on her face. Her eyebrows are creased, and she points over her shoulder towards the grotto door.

"There are some people here to see you. They say it's urgent."

"Urgent? What people?"

She nods. "One of them said his name is Bry, and the other guy... I think I've seen him before. People are talking to him. Mayor of somewhere."

I sit bolt upright in my sleigh seat and pull my stupid beard from my face, my heart fucking racing.

"What shall I say?" Evelyn asks. "The queue is massive. Shall I tell them to come back later?"

Fucking hell, this can't be happening. Please, God, fucking no. I don't have time to think, time to act, time to collect myself together. Not with Bryson and Castian outside.

"Shut the grotto," I tell Evelyn. "It's closed, as of right now."

"Shut the grotto? For real?!"

"Yes. Shut the grotto. Disperse the queue. Head off now, Toby, the day is done." I suck in a breath as everyone jumps into action, cursing myself for ignoring the chat thread. I should have seen this fucking coming.

Bry pokes his head around the grotto doorway a few seconds later. He's hardly smiling with festive cheer.

"Gooday, Santa. Thought we'd drop by for a quick hello."

Fuck!

CHAPTER 25
Tiffany

I can't hold back the grin on my face as I wander through the mall and it blows my mind to see how so many people grin back at me, especially young kids – waving at the happy elf in the bobble hat. I could get used to this. For real.

I get the charity work thing now, and why Reuben spends so much time as benefactor for other people. I'm used to serving humanity by getting people off to their wildest fantasies, which is cool, but putting effort into charity from the goodness of your own heart gives me a different kind of glow. I'm beginning to love my elf garb. I'm also loving the mall, too. This place is magnificent.

To think this whole complex belongs to Reuben is beyond impressive. The whole bloody mall is owned by the man who owns my heart. I'm buzzing, alive. *Me.* And it's all because of him.

The memory of first walking into Santa's grotto and seeing him on his sleigh is burnt into my soul – Reuben's stunning grey eyes staring at me in instant recognition. And now, here I am, having just fucked him in that same sleigh. What a crazy fucking ride.

I sit down and chill at Janie's Bakes, and Jen's recommendation was spot on. Their cappuccino and carrot cake are fucking yummy. I'll be a regular customer, that's for sure. I'll be trying everything on their menu.

I survey the surroundings, no longer intimidated by the love in people's eyes as they share snacks with their young families. I'd usually be glued to my phone, busying myself with social media, or browsing through my proposals, but I'm not interested. I replied to yet another message from Josh earlier, giving lame excuses about taking some time out. *Busy with friends.*

He's going to get on my case soon, and I know it. If it was the other way around, I'd be climbing the walls wondering what the fuck was up with him. But I suspect he knows the truth.

I've met someone. Finally. That's what he'll be thinking.

He must be itching for me to blurt out the news and share the details. Him and Ella would be over the moon to see me happy and settled with someone cool. But they wouldn't be quite so over the moon if they knew that someone cool just happened to be one of our bosses. Their congratulatory smiles would turn to horror and a serious round of *are you fucking insane?!*

The answer is yes. I am fucking insane.

But it's making me happy.

Not the *I love cock because I'm a dirty bitch* kind of happy. Or the *I have the best besties in the world* kind of happy. Or the *look how nice the view is from my Belgravia apartment* kind of happy. *Actually* happy.

Real *happy.*

In love *happy.*

That term still gives me the heebies along with butterflies, but I eat the rest of my carrot cake regardless. Delicious.

I hope Reuben's got a filth fest planned for later on, even though I'm still battered from last night. Santa makes me a very hungry girl, and it's not for carrot cake. I want another late session where the founder side of him comes to the fore, and he sends me to subspace with a smile. I'm down for some risky exhibitionism after the session in the grotto. Maybe he could take me back to the trash bin site one night and fuck my brains out far better than my client did. I'd like that.

It feels like a lifetime ago, as though Reuben has been in my life for years, not just weeks.

I get tingles remembering him standing there in the club as I went out for my session with my client…

I want to call up the proposal, just to bring the memories back, so I take out my phone for a cursory glance over things while I'm finishing up my cappuccino. May as well take a minute to check out what fresh proposals are actually coming through. Client 2906 – the guy from the trash bins – has sent me a new proposal. So have a whole plethora of my regular clients. Not one of my clients has turned down the proposals Reuben shunted without me knowing, and there are a load of others I don't recognise. I could fill my calendar up until at least March with a series of thumb clicks… but that isn't the only reason I'm on here. Not if I'm honest with myself.

I'm also checking for any correspondence or questions from Orla about my founders' postponement. Luckily, there is nothing from her. My message inbox is up to date.

Thank fucking God for that. My flu bug lie must have been sufficient enough to explain my absence.

I have no idea what the hell I'm going to end up doing with all these proposals after Christmas. Josh and Ells do fine with each other being entertainers, happy for each other to fuck clients without any issues – but it's obvious that Reuben isn't that kind of guy.

The weird thing is, I'm not sure I'd want him to be.

I finish my cappuccino and shove my phone back in my bag. Fuck knows what's going to happen in a few weeks, but I don't care right now. This is a Christmas that I'm going to properly enjoy for once. Caroline can have her glory at Josh's family table and I won't give a toss. I'll be having fun of my own.

I've never been to this part of the mall, right at the very top. I'm at the furthest part from the escalators when I see a sign for a place called *Seduction* – a lingerie and sex toy store. They have some festive looking bras and panties on the mannequins in the window, with red lace and a white boa trim. Cute. They have a pair of panties with *Santa's Baby* written on them, and a bodice in red and gold. Impressive, and that's just in the storefront. I'm sure the grotto will cope for an extra few minutes without me, since I can't resist checking out the treasures inside. Reuben might well get a few Christmas surprises for later.

It's great to see this place does plus size. There's a decent selection of Christmas bras. Hell, one of them even lights up with twinkles, so that's a winner. I get some *Santa's Baby* panties, and some red and gold stockings, and one of the flashy red bra sets with a boa trim. There's a whole selection of Christmas nightwear, too. A satin slip with *Mrs Claus* on the front, and some cutesy slippers to go along with it.

I laugh out loud when I reach the back of the store and find their toys section. They have some Santa's sack love eggs, and a Rudolph's red nosed vibrator, and a whole rack of other goodies destined for my basket.

I'm on my way to the checkout when I see their Christmas treats selection. I do a double take at one of the gifts they have on offer, because no fucking way! I pick up the snow globe in shock. A woman riding Santa in a sleigh chair. She's naked, with huge tits, while he's in his Santa outfit, his gloved hands gripping her fat ass. Their expressions are so hilarious that I'm laughing when I present it to the checkout assistant.

If only I could fucking tell her. *That was me downstairs earlier! I was riding Santa in the fucking grotto!* I'd love to see the look on her face.

I'd love to see the look on *anyone's* face, actually. I'd love to scream it from the rooftops and shout to the whole mall that I'm the dirty elf who got to ride the perfect Santa, Reuben Sinclair, in the grotto earlier. I'd shake the snow globe and laugh my head off in glee.

But I can't. I have to keep my big trap shut.

I pack my items in one of the discreet *Seduction* shopping bags, then head back down the escalator, cursing my luck that I can't at least be a gobby cow to Josh and Ella. If only it wasn't forbidden, and if only they wouldn't try to talk some bloody sense into me.

One person I *can* share it with though, is Santa himself.

I can't wait until tonight to show Reuben the snow globe. No chance. I want to shake it in his face with a cackle, and hear him laugh along with me. I can't wait until he sees the woman's big tits and ass, and Santa's red cheeks. It's bloody perfect.

The rest of the surprises can wait until later, but not this one. I dash along from the escalator to the back of the grotto, because it won't hurt if I sneak in for a second or two. I can say hi to the kids on his lap and wait for them to leave, and then I can steal my opportunity. Not even Jen or Evelyn need to know, and I'll be able to block out the view from Toby just fine. He'll be too busy on his phone anyway.

I go in through the exit door, so I don't need to go past Jen and Evelyn or the queue. I feel like a dirty sneak as I approach the grotto doorway, pulling it open to see my hunky Santa sitting in the sleigh seat with nobody on his lap. What a fucking bonus.

"Reuben!" I laugh a cackle laugh. "Got something to show you—"

I already have the snow globe in my hand when I see the two men seated opposite him, one in Toby's chair. They are professionals, both of them in sharp tailored suits – and they are definitely not there for a goodie bag. The hairs on the back of my neck stand up on instinct, and my stomach lurches in recognition, just from the scent of their cologne.

I know these men.

Even though I've never seen them before, I know them.

Know them.

As their eyes lock onto mine, my world stops dead in its tracks. One of them – the stockier one of the pair – has a particular paunch to his stomach. In my memory I can feel it slapping against my ass as he fucks me. I can recall the slap of flesh on flesh by heart.

Time slows to nothing as I look at his hands. His fingers. Knowing they have plunged inside me when I'm already crying full, and as for the other guy…

I recognise him from more than the founders' meetings. Fuck. He's from Westminster. One of the famous MPs…

Just like that, my memories consume me, my flesh on fire as the snow globe goes tumbling from my hand. It smashes on the grotto floor in a glittery puddle, and I take a step back, my mouth open wide.

"Creamgirl," the MP says. "What a surprise." He pauses. "Only it's not such a surprise, is it?"

I look at Reuben, and he's as pale as a ghost, his hand on his forehead and his eyes full of horror.

"Glad to see you've recovered from the flu," the other guy says. "Such a shame you had to cancel on us." He glares at Reuben. "Only now we know why. Did you think we were fucking imbeciles? Taking the piss out of us like we're blind to your bullshit?"

I hate myself for bursting in here, and I hate the horror on Reuben's face. *The shame.*

I want to drop to my knees and beg forgiveness, from him as well as them. I want to take the blame for the whole lot of it, to make it better, and worship them, and tell them anything they want to hear, just for the chance to make things right for the man I love.

The man who I've driven insane along with me.

Because that's what I do.

I create carnage. I fall in love, and it turns to shit, and then it spits me out again.

"I'm sorry," I say, and it sounds so pathetic it's embarrassing. "I, um, took up volunteering at the grotto because I got a thing for Reuben and I–"

Reuben holds up a hand. His eyes are full of pain.

"Stop, Tiff. It's ok."

But it's not ok. It's anything but fucking ok. It's a disaster. A tragedy. A fucking nightmare.

"Leave us," Reuben says. "The grotto is closed, Tiff."

"But I–"

"Go," he tells me, and he means it. He really does want me to leave.

That single word is a stab through the heart. I'm powerless. Open and vulnerable and such a fucking idiot. I should have known all along this would end in tears.

I manage to retreat before the tears do hit me. The people in the mall are a blurry mess as I try to dig my phone from my bag.

My fingers are shaking when I click on my contacts list.

Please.

Please answer.

Please, please, please fucking answer!

When I hear Josh's voice, the sobs come rushing, threatening to eat me alive. I keep walking, blanking out everything as I focus on breathing. I step out onto the street into the winter chill, but I don't feel it. I'm numb.

Numb and fucking terrified.

"Tiff?" Josh's voice sounds so far away. "Tiff? Are you alright? Tiff?!"

"No," I whimper, feeling like the biggest fucking idiot in the world. I hate myself.

I hate the way my stupid dreams have ripped the ground from under my feet.

"What's happened?! Do you need help? I'm coming now. Just tell me where you are, and I'll be there."

I manage to hail a passing taxi and throw myself into the back seat.

"I'm in a cab. You don't need to come," I tell my best friend.

"Ok, but *you* need to *come* right here, right now, understand me? Straight to Belgravia and up to ours. No more excuses, Tiff. Just get here."

"On my way," I manage to say, and then let the tears fall.

CHAPTER 26
Tiffany

I fall into Josh's arms as soon as he opens his front door, relieved when he squeezes me tight and lets me cry against his chest.

"I fucked up," I sob. "I fucked up so fucking bad."

He doesn't push me for words, just rocks me gently as my tears stream against his shirt, comforting me like he did when I last felt this kind of pain. When Kian gave his final goodbye, and I watched him walk away.

I don't bother trying to wipe my tears away, just let them fall, gripping on to Josh with all my might, because he is my true constant. The person who's been there for me through thick and thin. He's the person I should have trusted with my secrets the very moment they started spiralling into madness.

Yet another thing I fucked up.

I'm still dressed up like an elf, but my grin at being Santa's helper has been burnt to ashes.

Go!

That's the word I hear in my mind. All I can see is Reuben's mortified face as he sent me away.

"Come here, let's get you settled," Josh says when my sobs calm. He takes me by the hand and leads me to the sofa, and there is Ella, with a pillow held to her chest as she looks at me with nothing but love in her eyes. She's on the verge of tears herself, hurting for me, even though neither of them has any fucking idea what I'm hurting from.

I drop into my usual spot on the sofa, with Josh right beside me. He rests his hand on my knee and tells me to breathe. Calm. In and out, in and out. I listen to him, sucking in air through my nose and blowing it out through my mouth, trying to regain the use of words.

Both Ella and Josh are staring patiently at me, waiting for me to speak. I almost choke as I try.

"I fell in love with Santa. At the mall." I gesture to Ells. "When me and you went that day, and I sat on his lap."

"I remember," she says. "The client with no bookings. Were you his first? The owner of the mall?" She pauses. "Oh crap, have you fallen in love with a client, Tiff? Has Orla found out or something?"

I shake my head, a fresh sob rising from my chest.

"He's not just a client… the owner of the mall is a, um… he's a…"

It feels so hard to say it, to admit what I've done.

"He's a founder. Reuben Sinclair. He's a founder, and I went back to the grotto, and I fell in love with him. And now it's over. It's all gone to shit."

The pair of them turn as pale as Reuben was when I left him. Josh runs his fingers through his punkish hair, and looks over at Ella, the gothic beauty who knows exactly who I'm talking about.

"The mall?" he asks her.

"Yeah, we went shopping. Me, Tiff and Eb. We thought it would be fun to go in the grotto. Just a stupid game."

"A stupid game, no shit." He looks back at me. "And the prick has called it off now? Had his fill and turfed you out? I know you get these obsessive streaks, Tiff, but he's the one who crossed the line if he fucked you over."

I shake my head. "No. He didn't fuck me over. It was the opposite." My lip trembles as I speak. "He loved me."

"Loved you?" Josh raises his eyebrows. "A founder dressed up as Santa in the mall sought you out, fucked you, and told you he loved you? And then what? Loverboy kicked you to the kerb?"

"No. It wasn't like that!"

"Sure it wasn't. What a fucking tosser."

I love how protective he is. I have to smile at the way he grits his jaw like he's ready to go and pick a fight with a lion to avenge me.

Ells shifts closer to him, resting a hand on his arm.

"Santa isn't like that, Josh. He's a really nice guy."

He looks at her as though she's as insane as I am.

"You've bought into this Santa crap as well? Seriously? He's a fucking founder." His eyes lock back on mine. "Did you know he was a founder when you fucked him?"

"Yes. I knew he was a founder the moment I met him in the grotto."

"But you'd never seen his face. You've always been under a hood."

"I didn't need to see his face. I just knew. I knew the way he felt when I sat on him. I recognised him." I rub my temples, trying to explain it. "I just knew, ok? And then I saw his eyes, and he saw mine, and the rest is history, as they say. Or in my case an absolute fucking nightmare."

Ella holds the cushion tighter to her chest, and Josh shakes his head, trying to process things.

"Shit, Tiff," he says, and that about sums it up.

It is shit.

And it's way more shit than they know.

"It gets worse," I say.

"Worse? Jesus, Tiff, just take it from the top, will you? Fucking hell."

I take it from the top. The very top.

I tell them how I fell in love with Reuben right from the off, even though Josh doesn't want to hear that part, since he's heard about plenty of my infatuations before. He thinks this is a mega crazy one that's torn me apart, because I've fucked someone I should never have touched in a million years, and I've been spat out by him. That I should have seen it coming. But he's wrong.

I see his expression change as my story continues. He pulls me into him as I cry, reliving the special times Reuben and I shared. How we holed up together, and kissed all night, and *needed* each other. I manage to smile as I point to my elf tights, and tell him and Ells how being around kids even got to be fun for me, helping at the grotto. Josh looks choked up himself at that, because he knows how hard being around kids is for me, after I miscarried Kian's baby during a massive row… before he walked away and left me grieving.

Only I didn't grieve. I partied, and fucked and pretended I didn't give a shit, because I didn't want to be a mother anyway. I was a dirty bitch, not a *mummy*. I swept it under the rug and let myself run wild.

"That's where you've been the whole time, then?" Josh asks me. "That's why you postponed your proposals? You've been holed up with a founder, falling in love with him?"

Ells smiles at me, and there is a knowing in her eyes. She gets it better than Josh does. She met Santa – Reuben – herself when he booked her for a fake proposal last Christmas. He was feigning desperation to see if anyone would support him out of charity.

Ella did, and he rewarded her for it. And in turn she rewarded everyone else for his generosity – sharing the crazy amount of cash around homeless people and struggling families.

"So why did he call it off?" Josh asks me. "Why the fuck did he call time out, if you needed each other so bad?"

Time for another deep breath. I'm shaking as I prepare myself to confess.

"Because I cancelled a founders' booking. I messaged Orla and said I had flu and was too ill to attend."

"Holy shit!" Ella says.

"You did fucking what?!" Josh says.

The pair of them sit bolt upright at that. Josh's hands shoot to his cheeks, and Ella's mouth drops open.

It sounds so stupid now I've said it out loud. I cancelled a founders' booking. The most powerful men in the Agency. The hidden masters behind it all. You never cancel that kind of gig. Ever. It's beyond fucking ridiculous.

How could I have possibly expected no consequences? How could I have been so fucking dumb?

"Did Orla pull you up on it when you cancelled?" Ella asks me. "Did Reuben freak out about it? I mean, he must answer to them too, right?"

She knows the gig. Any entertainer who goes within a fifty-mile radius of a founders' proposal is obliged to uphold confidentiality to the utmost degree. Even we don't usually talk about them – me, Josh and Ells. That's how sacred it is.

"Orla didn't pull me up on it, and Reuben didn't freak out. It was Reuben who asked me to do it. To call in sick and fob them off."

My best friends look confused as fuck, and I don't blame them.

"Why are you in a state, then?" Josh asks. "If nobody freaked, what's the problem?"

I close my eyes.

"Because the other founders themselves must have suspected something was going on. Two of them turned up to see Reuben at the grotto, and I burst in on them wearing a fucking elf costume with a sexy snow globe in my hand, laughing my head off. I didn't know they were in there, but I recognised them the second I saw them, even though I'd never actually seen them. Another crazy experience like with Reuben. It was fucking crazy. And fucking horrible."

"Oh shit," Ells says. "Well. I guess they recognised you, too. You're quite recognisable, even with a bobble hat on."

"Yeah. *Oh, shit*, and now we're both *in* the shit. Both me and Reuben. Brilliant. Just fucking brilliant. No wonder he told me to go. I should have already been legging it out of there as fast as my fat ass would carry me. You know how brutal the founders can be. They might throw him to the wolves as well as me."

I well up again as Ella nods.

Ella does indeed know what the founders are like. When a douche of a lettings agent she was going to be renting an apartment through found out she was a whore and tried to dig around her references to make an *enquiry*, the founders tore him down in a flash. He was instantly removed from his job and cast out of the city, never to be seen here again.

The founders don't take prisoners.

I don't tell Josh and Ella that one of the guys was from Westminster. It would freak me out more as well as them, but it's so bloody obvious now. I bet there are others amongst the group that are high profile. The kind of high profile that demands a hood and an *at all costs* level of anonymity.

I'm such a stupid dumbass.

I wonder what's happening with Reuben. He looked so fucking petrified himself.

"They've cancelled you, then?" Josh asks, and his words hit me like a hammer in the ribcage.

I've been so caught up in losing Reuben, that I haven't even thought about that. I dash for the bag I dumped in Josh's hallway and scrabble for my phone. I'm back on the sofa when I try to call up the app, but it doesn't show for me. Incognito mode or not, it doesn't appear.

Josh calls up the app on his phone and I try my login details, but no. *Profile not recognised.*

The spread of panic races like wildfire through every cell of my body. I'm shaking. Quaking. Terrified. Ella searches for my profile page when she's logged in on her version, but there is no sign of it, and all my forum posts have disappeared.

I've been kicked out of the Agency.

I have no profile. No proposals. No income. No Creamgirl.

And no Reuben.

Oh, fuck, how I scream. I scream and rock and lose my fucking mind, back like I was in the wreckage of the Kian aftermath. All alone, with nothing left.

My mind races through the four years of my career – so many accolades, and bonuses and regulars. So many reviews. So many clients who meant more to me than I ever figured, now that they've been taken away.

User 706 – abusing me in his cow farm, with my grazed knees dragging through cow dung as he pulled me along by my hair. *Daddy* – User 762 – spanking me after finding naughty notes in my schoolbook and scrubbing me clean in the bathtub. One of Ella's favourites.

User 6978 – making me drink a whole stream of his piss without spilling a drop and rewarding me with an orgasm every time I managed it. User 1029 and his boyfriend – and some of the hottest DVP I've ever known.

Rough play, daddy play, watersports, roleplay, group sex, stretching, groping, chasing… even fucking radiator kinks and my kitty daddy.

All of it gone.

It hurts so much I have to race to Josh's bathroom and throw up my carrot cake from earlier, and then I lie on the floor in the fetal position. My soul is screaming for everything that's been lost.

But mainly it's screaming for Reuben.

He'll never be able to see me again. No fucking way.

They'll never let him. They'll cast me out of the city, and out of his life, and away from anything that could ever risk their identity.

"Calm down, Tiff," Josh says as he and Ella join me, but I can't. I don't want to move or think or feel. All I can do is try to breathe.

"Maybe I can do something to help?" Ella says. "Drop a message to Orla, or…"

Her voice trails off. She knows as well as I do it's pointless.

"Keep out of it," I tell her. "It'll only cause shit for you, too."

That's the last thing I want – to drag them into this muddy cesspit with me.

I hate myself.

I hate every stupid fucking bone in my body for ever daring to believe.

"You're staying here tonight," Josh says and hauls me to my feet. "We'll take care of you, Tiff. We'll go to your place and pack a case and set you up in the guest room."

Ella nods. "Yeah, stay here. With us."

She hasn't got the same amount of alarm in her eyes as Josh has. His stare is more piercing, because he knows just how fucked up I got over Kian and losing the baby. He knew what was going through my mind to ease the pain. How close I was to breaking for good and ending it all.

I want to say I wish I'd never walked into the grotto, but I'd be lying. Just as I'd be lying if I said I wished that I'd never met Kian. Because even through the pain, they gave me so much life.

Everything else I've done since has been superficial. Fun, but meaningless. Happy, but empty.

"Come on," Josh says. "Let's go."

I'm slinging my bag over my shoulder when my phone sounds out with a message.

My heart thumps, because it must be from Orla, making things official… with instructions on how I have to get away.

"I can't face it," I say and offer him my phone. "Can you look, please? I'm too scared."

I suck in a breath as I prepare for the worst, because I might not be staying at Josh's tonight after all. I might be staying far, far away.

"Sure, I'll look," he says.

I brace myself. What the fuck are they going to do to me? What the hell is going to happen now?

Josh's eyes are like saucers when he's checked out the message.

"It's not Orla," Josh says, and gives me back the phone. "It's Reuben."

CHAPTER 27
Reuben

My heart lurches when I see Tiffany's stunning red hair in the doorway of Belgravia's West tower. Her bobble hat has gone, but she's still in her elf outfit.

I stare out at her through the car window as I slump in my sad sack of a Santa costume, minus the cushions and fake beard. I feel exhausted, both physically and mentally, my emotional weight lying heavy in the pit of my stomach. It's been a long afternoon with Bry and Castian. I never imagined such a serious showdown would take place in the mall grotto – but the curvy, happy elf bursting in on us sealed the deal. And sealed our fate along with it.

The reality smashed in as loudly as Tiffany's snow globe when it hit the floor.

I'm about to get out of the car until I see the two other figures marching out of the tower after her, clearly in opposition. I recognise them both, Holly and Weston, or Ella and Josh. Two other entertainers on the Agency hardcore list, and Tiff's best friends. I already know the charitable soul that is Ella, and Tiffany has told me plenty about the *incredible* Josh. And from the way Josh is pointing back at the tower as he argues with her raised hand, I'm almost certain she has told them plenty about me, too.

I take a breath and force myself to stay in my seat. Entering the forbidden realm of personal engagement with Agency staff is a crime I've committed once already. The last thing I want is to drag any other people down with Tiff and me.

They don't deserve it. Neither did she.

"I'll let you know when I'm *D&S* okay?" I hear her tell Josh as they get closer. "I know you love me, and want to protect me, and want to punch him in the face or whatever, and I'd do the same if I was you."

"Then why the hell are you leaving?!" He shrugs, clearly exasperated as his girlfriend takes his arm, trying to calm him.

"Because YOU would do the same as ME if the roles were reversed. I wouldn't be able to stop you from going, either."

I stare at his expression, watching as her words sink in. She's got him. She folds her arms and he shrugs again.

I've never been a man to wade into drama, I despise it. I was always the calm boy in the school yard. But sitting here and watching Tiff battle Josh's resistance alone would make me nothing more than a coward.

All three of them look my way as I climb out of the driver's seat.

I must look like a wreck as I approach them, hardly the multimillionaire founder they expected in the Belgravia courtyard.

"Ella," I say, and tip my head. She smiles at me – no malice there, at least.

But as for Josh, his face is a picture of hatred as I meet his eyes.

"Why the fuck did you get her caught up in this shit?" he asks me. "Now look at her."

He gestures to poor Tiffany, whose cheeks are swollen from tears, eyes red from crying. My heart pangs to see her pain.

"He didn't get me caught up in this shit," she says to him. "It was me who rocked up at the grotto, Josh. It's my fault."

I shake my head at that.

"No, Tiffany, it's not your fault. It's mine." I look at Josh. "I apologise, and take full accountability for my actions. I assure you, there will be a *done and safe* from Tiffany when we've resolved things. She isn't going to come to any harm."

His eyes dig into mine, and I get why he's such an asset to the business. The guy is stunning, with his perfectly unkempt dark hair with a streak of purple. It's clear why people pay thousands for him. Just as they do with the gothic goddess, Ella.

"You're going to bring her back here, are you?" he says. "Not force her out of her home and shift her away from the city somewhere. I know how powerful you are, even in a fucking Santa suit."

"Stop it, Josh!" Tiff snaps. "If you know how powerful he is, then keep your trap shut and head back upstairs, for Ella's sake as well as yours!"

He flinches as she says Ella's name, and I see the pain of the conflict. He wants to protect his best friend, and would do so at the cost of himself, but as for his girlfriend.

"I'll be fine," Tiff says. "I'll see you later, alright? I'll D&S when I'm finished. I'll come to yours."

He glares at me once more before he heeds Ella's tug on his arm and steps away.

"Don't fuck her over any more than you already have done," he says. "Don't use your founder power to turf her out of her home. She belongs here. With us."

"I won't be using my *founder power* to abuse Tiffany, Josh. She'll be fine to send you a message whenever she wants to."

He doesn't say *alright* before he walks away. Sweet Ella gives me a wave and I raise a hand in return as she leads her boyfriend back to the tower, leaving a broken looking Tiffany standing before me, with her arms still folded across her chest.

"Get in the car," I say. "Let's go."

"Go where?"

"Wherever we need to go to talk. I was thinking my place."

Her bottom lip trembles. "Your place? Are we safe to go there?"

I smile at her, such a beautiful princess in her vulnerability. I hold out my hand.

"You're safe, Tiffany. Come along, please, before your best friend comes charging back out again. He might be bringing a machete with him next time."

She smiles. "Yeah, he's, um… protective. It's cool. Usually."

"Yes, it is."

It's a relief to have her in the passenger seat as I pull the car out of the courtyard. I drove straight here from the mall, hoping this would be where I found her.

"I'm sorry," she says. "I had no idea, Reuben. I should have noticed, or checked, and been more careful before I barged into the grotto. I should never have flaunted myself around the place as an elf. I should've stayed out of sight, and not cancelled the founders' proposal, and kept some common fucking sense about me."

"And so should I. The blame is not on your shoulders. It's all on mine."

"No, it isn't." She shakes her head. "No, no, no. I'm the one who goofed up, over a snow globe. A fucking snow globe."

"It was already goofed up, Tiff. They were at the mall for a reason."

"Probably because *I* cancelled the bastard proposal!"

"Because *I* asked you to, and I was the one who postponed

every one of your others and ignored the founders' thread. I was in the position of authority, not you."

I hate how she sucks in a breath, staring out of the window as we head through London.

"They've taken my Agency account away."

"Yes, I know. I'm sorry."

"It's my own fault."

This conversation could go around in circles, spiralling around over who is to blame for what, so I stay silent for a few minutes, focusing on getting us back to my place. This isn't the location to delve deep into the who, whats and whys. I hate how Tiffany has taken the burden like a wrecking ball. All I want to do is hold her tight, but I daren't touch her. Not after what I've done this afternoon.

It wouldn't be fair.

She's still silent sobbing when we pull up in my driveway. She rushes to the door with her head down, as though we're under surveillance. Maybe we would be, if Bry and Cas hadn't been appeased by my words.

"You can relax now," I say once the door is closed behind us. I take off my stupid Santa coat and hang it up.

"Relax? Yeah, right." She kicks off her shoes. "Hardly the time for some yoga and incense."

Even now, I adore her dark humour.

She walks through to the kitchen, plonking herself on her regular breakfast stool. It's so bizarre. When we were here this morning, we were glowing happy. Loved up and excited for the day ahead. The memory feels so far away now, like a lifetime has passed. And in a way, I suppose it has.

"Coffee? Juice?"

"Just water, please. I might throw up if I drink anything else." I get a fresh pang of horror as she wipes her tears away. "Come on, Reuben, get it over with. What do I have to do now? Move out of Belgravia? Fuck off to a cottage by the sea somewhere like I'm in a witness protection program?"

"That's a bit dramatic."

She cracks a sad grin. "Yeah, you know me. I am a bit dramatic. But still, I know you lot don't take this kind of bullshit lightly. I recognised the guy from Westminster. They must want me out and gone."

I hand over her glass of water, and she pulls her stool away from me as I take a seat. The distance feels horrible.

"I can handle it," she says. "Just put me out of my misery. Tell me what the fuck is going to happen to me. I'm done at the Agency, I know that, and I'm done with you, since they must have given you a right fucking kicking for it, but what else? What else do they want me to do?"

I wait until her eyes meet mine before I speak.

"I'm sorry about your profile being removed," I say. "I know it must have been devastating for you."

"Yeah, just a bit. I'm smashed up worse than the bastard snow globe." Her lip trembles fresh, and I get it.

I've seen how many clients she's taken on, and how well her performances have been starred. How hard she's worked, how much she's earnt, how much she's enjoyed it. I know it must cut like a knife to have your world pulled out from under you, when you've built your life around it for four years straight.

She wipes some fresh tears away. "Ah, fuck it. It's done now."

"No," I tell her. "It isn't. You can have your profile back, under close scrutiny. Orla is aware of the situation, and will be vigilant on exactly which proposals you are taking on and when." I pause. "There will be no more proposals with the founders, but you can work with your current clients, so long as you agree to a very hefty non-disclosure agreement."

Her eyes widen.

"You what? I can still be Creamgirl?"

I nod. "Yes. I assured the others that there was no malice or ill doing on your part. They know you are a valuable asset."

She tenses up, uncertain.

"Sounds a bit weird to me. What's the deal with that? They just let me waltz back in with a slap on the wrist?"

I clear my throat. "Not quite, no. It will be on the condition that you never see me again. No contact via the Agency, no contact via business, or the mall. You'll be expected to keep at least a mile's distance from this place and any other of my properties, and there will be no leniency."

I watch the simultaneous clash of her relief and horror as she braces herself on the breakfast bar.

"That's, um, cool, I guess. Thank you. For saving my career."

If only she knew how hard I'd had to fight for it. Plead for it. Take all of the blame on my shoulders.

"It's cool, is it?"

"Yeah. I really appreciate it. I thought me and Creamgirl were done. Jesus Christ." She slaps a hand on her chest. "Fucking hell, Reuben, I owe you the world. I really thought Cream was a goner. I thought I'd be spat out like a piece of shit."

"You want to go back to being Creamgirl, then?" I take out my phone and place it on the countertop between us. "I can let Orla know and she'll press the button."

Her eyes dig into mine.

"What choice do I have? I've lost you, so at least I get to keep her. Thank you. Honestly." Another lip tremble. "I'm sure you've had way more of a bollocking than I'll get. It's all come crashing down over a stupid snow globe, but it was going to happen at some point. I broke the rules, and now I have to pay for it. We both do."

She's still blaming herself. I see the wounds under her brash exterior, so raw.

"There is a choice," I say. "You can either take your position back at the Agency and never see me again, or you can resign from your role."

"Resign from my role and what? Move away?" She scoffs. "Fancy living in a beach hut with me? We can elope together."

"It's your choice, Tiff. Creamgirl with the conditions attached, or resignation."

"And what about you? You just go on with the Agency regardless? Don't worry, you can always pretend it's me under the hood, even if they don't have the ass for it."

I grit my teeth at that. Her brashness trying to play things down.

"I don't want Ella under a hood, and I don't want Harlot under a hood. I don't want any of the entertainers under a hood, actually. Not anymore. What I do want, is you." My eyes pierce hers. "If I didn't, we wouldn't be in this situation, and you wouldn't have such a choice to make right now. But the choice won't be there long, Tiffany. Orla is expecting a yes or a no within the hour."

Tiff looks confused. "You've got conditions too, I guess. You aren't allowed to see me?"

"Founders aren't allowed to engage personally with entertainers, no. That's a fundamental rule."

"Yeah, so we're fucked anyway, if you're not allowed to *engage* with me. I may as well be Creamgirl."

"May as well be, or want to be?"

"Does it make any difference?"

My stare doesn't break. "Yes, it does. Because if either of us stay at the Agency, our encounters will be forbidden. Hence, I'm asking you, do you want to continue being Creamgirl?"

Her eyes narrow.

"Wait a minute. I've got to choose between my career and you? Is that what you're saying?"

"Yes, it is."

She twists on her stool. "And what happens to you? You have to choose between the Agency and me?"

"Indeed."

She gives another scoff. "Fucking hell, Reuben. That's a done deal, then. That's got to be worth fucking millions. MILLIONS. And the associations. And everything along with it. Don't worry, I'll stay away and carry on being Creamgirl. You don't need to feel guilty about it."

My emotions want to burst out of my chest, and it's so at odds with the man I've been for years. I love power. Self-restraint. The safety of being in control. But this woman in front of me has taken so much of it away from me. She's stolen my heart and my sanity.

"This has nothing to do with guilt," I say. "Do you want to carry on being Creamgirl, or do you want to let her go?"

It feels as though we are at a poker table, hedging the bets.

"You're phrasing that weirdly on purpose," she says, and locks me with her sparkling eyes. "What you're really asking is, do I want to be Creamgirl more than I want to be with you. That's it, isn't it? That's what you're asking?"

Her words give me shivers. The sword over my head feels precarious.

I remember Jeanette leaving. I remember telling myself I would never be so exposed to heartache again. Until the curvy goddess in front of me came into my life.

"What is it you really want?" I ask her. "Not just with Creamgirl, but with life."

She stiffens up. "Like the future, future? Do I look like a married with kids kind of girl?"

There's a knife edge in her voice. Defensive.

"You look like you could be. Because that's what I want, Tiff. I want to close the door on the past and live for my own self for once. Not out of power or success or charity, but because of me. I want to be married again, to a *married with kids* kind of woman." I take a breath before the admission. "And I want that woman to be you."

She raises her eyebrows. Gobsmacked.

"Are you for real?!"

"I've never been more for real in my life."

"You're serious? You want me to be a married with kids kind of girl, with you?"

"That is exactly what I'm saying, yes. I've been very careful with risk taking until you burst into the grotto, but since then, things have changed. *I've* changed. Remember those fated words? I *need* you?" My insides swirl. "I wasn't lying, Tiff."

"Whoa, fuck. Just whoa."

She looks like she's about to fall off her chair, as though the idea is absurd.

"But I also appreciate how much passion you have for Creamgirl and the Agency. I understand how passionate you are about your career, and I'll respect that."

My goddess blows out a breath and it's as if a huge weight has been lifted, not just from her shoulders, but mine, too. I feel it as she smiles at me.

"It's not much of a question then, is it?" She reaches for my phone on the countertop and shoves it towards me. "Bye bye, Creamgirl, I had fun while it lasted."

My world starts tilting on its axis.

"That's a yes? You want to resign?"

"Yeah, of course I do, but do you? For real? You'll give up millions and a shit ton of prestige and backhanders and associates because of a curvy whore you only really met a few weeks ago?"

I smile at her as I pick up my phone.

"I already have."

"You have what?! Stepped down from the Agency?"

I nod. "Yes. I have stepped down from the Agency."

The look of pure disbelief on her face is a picture I'll remember for ever.

"That's fucking crazy, Reuben! It's mental! What the fuck?!"

With that she leaps from the stool and throws herself at me. Her arms wrap around my neck, her tits pressed tight to my chest as I hold my elf girl tight.

"I didn't tell you, because I wanted the decision to be yours," I say. "I wanted to know you felt the same way."

Tiffany kisses me like I'm a hero, holding my face as though I'm a saviour from the Lord above.

"Creamgirl can fuck right off now for all I care," she says. "Not only do I want to be Santa's baby. I want to *have* Santa's baby. Buckle up, Daddy, it's going to be one hell of a ride."

I fire off a simple *no* to Orla before my phone is abandoned at the table. I've no time left for the Agency, or the politics, or the intricacies of Tiffany's official verdict. I'm far too concerned with making a baby with my baby.

I finally shut my past behind me, and soak in the wonder of Tiffany. *Just* Tiffany. No Creamgirl left in sight.

"One last thing…" I reach into my suit jacket pocket and pull out what's left of the snow globe, just Santa, on his sleigh seat, with the naked chubby girl bouncing on his lap. "It really could be us," I say, "our worlds we knew have been shattered, yet here we are, still together."

"Wow," Tiff says as she takes it from me. "I guess we have ourselves a perfect tree topper."

I chuckle. "Good idea. We need a tree first, though."

"Come on, Reuben," she says, grabbing my hand. "Let's get upstairs and make my big belly a bit bigger, as soon as we fucking can. The tree can wait."

CHAPTER 28
Tiffany

I can't wait to get up to Reuben's bedroom. It's like a consummation. Something that feels almost sacred.

I want to make love to him.

Truly make love to the man I love.

I grip his hand in mine as I lead us upstairs. It's going to be a wild ride from this day forward, in the best of ways – I'm going to make sure of it.

I never thought I'd be in a position where Kian would pale into insignificance, but the gorgeous Reuben Sinclair has risen my soul to a whole new level. *This* is a man who knows what love is. I see it in his eyes, I know it from his smile, and I feel it in his touch as he pulls me close when we cross the threshold.

Fuck, how my mushy heart is racing as he brushes a thumb across my cheek.

"I didn't know what dreams I'd been missing, until I found you."

I still can't believe he's resigned from the Agency, abandoning such a treasure trove for a girl like me. He sees more in me than Kian ever did, and it's become so obvious now. The guy I thought was my soulmate didn't know my soul at all. Not like Reuben does.

"I guess this is monogamy, then?" I smile up at my former boss. "Wild, isn't it? How things pan out."

"Extraordinary. Just like you." He brushes my hair from my shoulder and plants a gentle kiss on my neck. "I need you, Tiff. I need our future."

"So do I." I look up into his eyes. "I lied about not being a mummy with kids girl, by the way. I just gave up on the idea long ago."

"For the sake of Creamgirl?"

I shake my head. "Nah. Creamgirl was the thing that kept me going. Throwing myself into my happy place of sex without strings just kept the pain at bay."

"What pain were you running from?"

I'm so hot and horny for my new love that it seems a bizarre time to be baring the hurt of my past, but it feels so natural. For once, I feel utterly secure. *Done and safe* has a whole new meaning. Not just in relation to Kian, but in relation to the rest of my early life. My own family didn't really give a toss. Mum was always arguing with my stepdad, who hated me from day one. My older brother never bothered with me, just called me a weird bitch whenever we crossed paths and pushed me aside.

Then there was Josh who became my family. My first taste of something unconditional.

Until I met Kian and figured I'd found the one.

"I had one serious partner a few years ago," I tell Reuben. "It was turbulent, but I loved him. I thought that was my one shot. Figured I'd lost it."

"I understand that. Taking off my wedding ring felt as though fate was leaving me in the dirt." He kisses my temple. "Did you have your future all mapped out in your mind? I know I did when I got down on one knee to Jeanette."

"Yep. To every last detail. I even knew what colour walls I wanted in our dream home living room." I shimmy out of my elf dress and tights, and he unclips my bra. "I knew what car I wanted. I knew what style of wedding dress I would wear. I knew what we were going to call our kids."

For once, the memory doesn't feel so bad.

"What were you going to call your children?"

"Raven and Rose. I wanted two girls."

"Do you still want two girls?"

I unbutton his shirt, needing his flesh against mine.

"I want whatever you can give me."

"Then you'll be needing a lot of names," he chuckles. "I'll take as many as you can bear to birth."

I get flashbacks of him in the grotto, being such a wonderful hero for the children. He'll be the greatest daddy there could be.

I dare to imagine a life with him in this beautiful house, with kids of our own. The patter of tiny feet running to greet Reuben as he comes home from the mall. Family weekends by the seaside, building sandcastles with buckets and spades.

I want a much bigger family than the one I dreamt of with Kian.

"No more contraceptives for me," I say. "I'd better toss the pills in the bin."

"You really want to begin straight away?"

I nod. "Yep." Then I blurt out the truth. "I'd have had a kid that was six years old already if fate hadn't been a piece of shit to me, but I guess the universe has its reasons, and my road was meant to be with you."

"You'd have had a baby? With Kian?"

"I was pregnant, yeah. I had a miscarriage, just before Kian finally fucked off and left me."

My heart quickens as I share my past, but I don't cry. I don't need to. Not anymore. Reuben is easing the pain, just by being himself. He doesn't flinch or pull away at the revelation. He does the opposite. He pulls me closer and presses his mouth to my ear.

"That's a horrible thing to have to go through."

"It's just one of those shitters. We were rocky. It was the straw that broke the camel's back and all that, and he walked away."

"He walked away when you needed him most?"

I try to brush it off. "It was always gonna happen at some point. We were off more than we were on by then, I was just too dumb to see it. It was just one of those things, you know?"

He takes my shoulders and looks me right in the eyes.

"No, I don't know. It will never be just *one of those things* when there is such hurt involved. He left you when you needed him most, and that's never acceptable when you love and respect someone." I adore the way Reuben stares into my raw open heart. "Trust me, Tiffany, I will never do that to you. Not in a thousand years. If we have twenty children, or if we have none. If it comes to us like a joyous breeze, or if we struggle along the way, so be it. I'll never walk away and leave you hurting. Not like he did."

My walls crumble, and for once, I'm happy to be defenceless. In life and love, not just in sex. Reuben has given me the power to be powerless. He defended me, and chose me today above any other option. I've cost him millions, yet still, he put my needs first. I was his priority. I'm the woman he chose above everything else.

"I'll never walk away and leave you hurting," he says again. "I'll never walk away, full stop."

"Same goes," I reply, and kiss him with an urgency that burns ferocious. A need to be taken and loved by this man. The man of my dreams.

"I want your baby," I say. "I want to make you a daddy, and watch you being a daddy."

"That would be the best gift there could ever be."

He drops his pants, kicks them aside, and we tumble naked together onto his bed, hands roving, frantic. I can't get enough of him. Every inch of him fascinates me, and that's mutual. He sweeps his hands up and down my stomach, adoring my curves. They will be so much bigger when I'm carrying his baby inside me. I imagine my swollen baby bump. The way it will feel to be heavy in the third trimester, waiting to meet our newborn child.

My fears that it will never happen for me have disappeared.

I have faith.

I have love.

I believe in my dreams again. I believe in *us*.

Reuben is a master with his fingers, gliding them between my pussy lips to tease my clit.

"It's going to be an honour getting you pregnant. Forget ovulation calendars, I'll be unloading into your sweet pussy every chance I get."

"Promises, promises."

"Santa always delivers."

We kiss with fervour. His tongue is hot and wet, fighting with mine.

"Promise me one thing, then," I say, panting for breath as his fingers tease my thrumming clit.

"Anything, sweetheart."

"Promise you won't lose your filthiness. Not ever. I may have ditched Creamgirl, but I'll never ditch my own sexuality. I'll still be a kinky slut, mama bear or not."

"I can safely assure you of that." He nips my bottom lip. "I may have walked away from the Agency, but I haven't walked away from filthy pleasures. I just want them all from you."

It's a bizarre sensation as I realise Reuben's cock may be the only one I ever take for the rest of my life. He isn't going to share easily, and I sure as fuck wouldn't want to share him. Even the idea of him being with someone else makes me feel sick, I'm that invested.

I spread my legs wider. "Good, because I've got plenty of filth to give, and it's all yours."

I angle my hips to take the thrill of his touch, but the skilled master leaves me hanging. He plays me like a cello, sucking, flicking, tasting, fingering – and I squirm for him with a smile on my face. Headiness growing as he slides three fingers in and licks a hot trail from my clit to my nipples.

He clamps his mouth around my tit and sucks hard, catching my clit with his thumb at the same time and it's enough to set me off on my first orgasm, rolling through me in glorious waves of pleasure as his fingers pump my wet cunt.

I moan for his dick, wanting him inside me, filling me up, but the master won't be rushed. His eyes are simmering dark as he caresses my belly.

"Give it to me, Reuben," I say, "fuck your daddy cum into me."

His grin is priceless.

"You're going to get it, *baby*, but always remember what I say. Patience is a virtue."

I grope my wet tits. "Fuck patience. Patience isn't on my list of talents. Taking cum is."

"I'm sure your patience will improve steadily. You'll need a lot of it when we've got children to take care of."

Two can play at this game. I'll just have to make him desperate for me.

"You're right, I'll need a whole shit ton of patience. So, now's the time to enjoy the lack of it, while I can." I haul myself up from the bed, giggling as I throw a pillow at him and dash away.

"What the hell? Tiffany! Get back here, and stop testing mine."

I hear his feet stomping after me as my tits nearly give me black eyes as I run down the stairs.

"Time for some champagne. Let's celebrate!" I flash him a grin over my shoulder. "Once you've knocked me up, I'll be in abstinence mode for ages. No drinking for me while I'm carrying your baby."

He reaches me in the kitchen, and I squeal as he shunts me over the breakfast bar. The marble top is so cold against my tis, his strong hands pinning me tight by my wrists. I rub my ass against his crotch like a dirty girl, adoring the pole of his cock. He's dripping, ready to burst. I can feel it.

"Knocked you up?" he says, "I'm not sure I like the sound of that. Bit crude, don't you think?"

"Knock me up, yeah. Or put me up the duff or shove a bun in my oven. I don't care, just fuck your cum into me, Reubs." I wiggle my ass again.

"Reubs? You're asking for it," he says.

"Yeah, I am. So, give it to me. Champagne as well as punishment, please," I giggle.

He lets go of my wrists, places one hand on the base of my back and I brace myself, shrieking as he gives me a serious walloping – two hard slaps on each butt cheek before he walks to the fridge. I love the burn. I also love the way he pops the cork straight up into the air before he pours our glasses.

"To us," he says, as we toast.

"To us and our future babies."

He looks at my naked body so intently. I don't feel the need to pose or push my tits out, just stay as me – Tiffany – without the performance of Cream.

"I pictured you with a straining baby belly when you were hooded on all fours, you know? One time, when you had to crouch and ride a punch fuck, that was me, imagining you giving birth, especially when you were crying out. I wished your tits were milky. I wanted to drink from you."

"Wow, that's hot," I say and I swear my clit could come from just one touch, I'm so horny.

I look down at my nipples. I wonder how they would feel to leak milk. How amazing it would feel for Reuben to latch on and drink me dry between baby feeds to keep the milk flowing.

"Have you ever tried drinking breast milk?" I ask.

"Yes. But I've never been in love with the woman whose tits I was drinking from."

I sip some champagne, admiring my lover in yet another filthy shade.

"I bet you look great with a milky beard."

He rubs at his beard. "Can't wait to find out," he says.

"What else did you imagine while you were punching my cunt?"

He necks his champagne and I do the same.

"It's a vivid memory," he says as he refills our glasses. "Punching cunt takes some skill and mastery. Despite how brutal the assault might seem, one must always consider the recipient's connection to the moment. The rhythm, the heat, the orgasm fuel. Taking you up, into that high, slowly increasing the speed of the assault as your puffed-up cunt relaxes, and..."

I neck my champagne. "And?"

"It was a vision, Tiffany. An absolute vision, my fist engulfed by you. Because that's what it looked like in the frenzied blur as you shrieked and shuddered. It looked like you were birthing my fist so beautifully."

"I remember you doing that to me. It hurt like fuck, but it felt so good. You didn't get me lubed up first either."

His cock is veined and loaded as he takes a sip of his drink.

"I loved seeing my knuckles popping in and out of you."

"How about now? Give me the treat of watching while you do it."

"I think I'll give you some lube this time." He knocks back the rest of his champagne. "Get your ass up on the counter."

"I'll need some help, Santa."

He puts his glass down and helps hitch me up onto the worktop, and I drop myself backwards, my legs hanging over the edge until he raises one over his shoulder, scissoring me. His hard, veined dick plunges straight inside, and he tilts his hips to press my sweet spot.

"You're going to take so much of my cum, baby," he says. "I'll be filling you up every fucking chance I get."

"You'll get a lot of chances now then, won't you?" I smile up at him. "Since I haven't got a calendar full of other men's cocks anymore."

"Thank fuck for that, because it would have driven me crazy." He slams inside me. "To know other men were fucking you would have driven me insane."

"Me, too. Because I wouldn't have wanted any of them, Reuben. All I want is you. Dirty. Loving. Brutal. Kind. All of it. I'm *your* entertainer now."

"You're my partner, not my entertainer, and the woman who's going to bear my fucking child."

Holy shit, he fucks me like a beast. My tits bounce against my chin as he slams me, and I feel like jelly against the hard marble countertop. He grits his teeth as he comes, and then jams both of my legs up to my chest, making sure none of it dribbles.

"This is standard practice now, Tiff. My cum stays in your cunt."

I nod. "That's where it belongs." Then I smirk. "Until it's done its job anyway. Then my ass and mouth can benefit as well."

He leans in closer, and fists his hand before my eyes. It's so big as he bares his knuckles.

"We'll make an exception for now, though."

I take a breath as he lines it up against my used pussy, knowing full well he isn't going to be gentle. I remember the pain from last time, crying out under my hood like a banshee. This time I'm going to see his stunningly filthy face as he does it.

"Are you ready?" he asks.

I laugh. "No. But that's the point, isn't it? You want to see me straining and struggling while you stretch my whore cunt. So give it to me."

"No," he says.

"No?"

"No. I don't want to stretch your whore cunt, Tiffany. You are no longer a *whore*, remember? I want to stretch your *beautiful* cunt."

With that, he lowers my feet to the countertop and spreads my legs, one hand on my belly as he shows me his fist.

I moan for him as he glides his knuckles up and down my puffy pussy lips.

And I moan some more when he applies pressure with a little turn of the wrist at the same time and my pussy glows hot with need.

"Do it," I say, "push it in."

I almost regret my words when his fist pushes against me. His knuckles hurt, and my pussy fights him.

"Relax," he says, but I shake my head.

"Nah. Make me take it. Show me what pain my pussy is going to feel when I'm pushing your baby out. Whatever you do will never match it."

He braces himself against the counter and pushes harder. I keep my eyes on his, soaking in the wonder. I love this man. I want everything of his inside me.

"You're fucking clenching," he says.

"Course I'm fucking clenching."

"Let me in, Tiff."

"No."

"If you don't relax, it'll tear you."

"So will giving birth to your child."

"I don't want to hurt you."

"Why the hell not?" I roll my eyes. "I want you to hurt me," I tell him. "I want to see that vivid vision you witnessed. And I want to love giving it to you. Now, sweet Reubs, fist my beautiful cunt and make me scream."

He doesn't reply, just stares me in the eye, presses one hand on my belly. Fuck how I cry out when he applies the pressure and my pussy finally breaks.

"In," he says and I yelp again as he gives a shove and my cunt wraps around his wrist.

His fist feels like it's in my stomach, and it hurts so bad I let out a stream of whimpers.

He wraps his free hand around the back of my neck and pulls me up for a better view, and I see he's up past his wrist. Yeah, he's fucking deep.

"Now watch," he tells me, and pulls his fist out of my burning cunt.

It's dripping with cum and laced with red. Yeah, I'm bleeding.

"Do it again," I say, and cry out as he punch fucks me in one thump. His knuckles grate as my pussy battles to take him.

"Push," he says, and I do as I'm told. I try to birth his hand from my pussy, pushing down with everything I've got, but he doesn't move, just lets me strain.

The pain feels so dirty, it's beautiful.

"Come on, Tiff, push," he says, and we go in for another round. Slowly, he lets me birth his fist, hovering in the spot where his knuckles are at their fullest, right at the entrance of my pussy.

More cum and blood. More sweat and tears.

And more love for Reuben as he coaxes me into trying harder. Taking more.

His tone is gentle, despite the fact he's being a broody monster. I imagine he'll be using the same tone when I'm giving birth for real, and it will be beautiful.

I pull him forward when I'm exhausted, still taking his fist as I press my mouth to his. I kiss him like he's my owner, my saviour... and my baby daddy. My partner. My friend. My everything.

What a beautiful combination.

He treats me like a princess when he works his thumb against my clit, to bring the pleasure as well as the pain.

"Come for me with my fist in deep," he says. "Come and tell me how much you want to be filled up by me."

I let the words come out in a ramble of truth.

"I want to be full, Reuben. I want your cum soaking my insides, and I want to watch my belly grow with your babies, until it's so big I can hardly move. I want hot, swollen tits, leaking with milk. I want you to latch onto my nipples as well as our little one. Please, never stop fucking me, and never stop filling me up. My pussy belongs to you now. Always."

"And my dick belongs to you. So does my cum."

He gives me another round of it before we're through, punching as I watch, amazed at the vivid vision he described. There's a blur of frenzied thrusts and I'm riding high, coming like a bastard, gushing around his fist.

"Wow," I say as he pulls free and I flood the countertop.

"You seem to be saying that a lot lately," my grinning Santa says.

"Because you wow me, Reubs." I shrug.

"And you need to quit with the Reubs, *Tiff*."

"Why? It suits you, Daddy Reubs."

He goes to the fridge, takes out another bottle of champagne.

"I like the look of that," I tell him.

"And my dick likes the look of your wrecked cunt." He picks up our empty glasses. "Get your sweet ass upstairs."

I used to hate missionary. I mean – boring. But not now. Not with my saviour fucking me gently and dropping kisses on my lips, an incredible contrast to our filthy fun.

This is exactly what I've always wanted.

To be loved for me, in every aspect, and to love someone back.

And to actually *make love*.

"Fill me up, Santa," I say when he picks up the pace.

"It will be my pleasure, baby," he says, lifting my legs high as he unloads.

It's late when I finally send Josh a message to let him know I'm *done and safe*, but this time I add another word to it.

D&S, forever. xx

Because I am.

EPILOGUE

Reuben

I've just waved off an adorable little boy with a goodie bag when Jen bursts into the grotto with a phone in her hand.

"REUBEN! You've got to take this. Mrs Santa is on the line."

Her expression says it all as she hands it over. Fucking hell, I knew I shouldn't have been here today, but Tiff insisted. Seven days from the due date was fine she assured me.

I'm such a fucking idiot.

"Reubs!" Her voice is practically a wail in my ear. "She's early. Get here now, please. QUICK!"

"On my way. Don't let her out before I get there!"

"I might not have much choice!"

I hear her scream out a FUCKKKKKKK, and I'm out of my seat, racing like a madman.

I let Jen handle the logistics as I make a dash for it. *Grotto closed.* The pillows get tossed aside along with the beard, but I've got no time to get changed before I get in the Jag to race over to Alexandria Natal Suite. A Santa suit will have to cut it.

The tyres screech as I pull out of the car park. No matter how many times Tiff and I have talked this through, imagining the details, it's made no difference. I'm absolutely fucking shitting myself.

My gorgeous baby girl is having my baby girl. And the last thing I want to do is fucking miss it.

I put her on speakerphone as I drive.

"Are you ok? How are you feeling?"

"LIKE SHIT!" she yells, Tiff style. "Fucking hell, Reubs, it hurts like an absolute BASTARD! I thought we'd prepared for this but Jesus Christ, it's nothing like getting punch fucked. My whole body is screaming, not just my cunt."

I hear the voices of the maternity ward nurses in the background and have to choke back a laugh. What a character. She's going to be someone to remember – no doubt an infamous Mrs Sinclair when baby number two comes along.

We have the pleasure of meeting baby number one first, though.

I beep my horn at a complete asshole who slows down too quickly and misses the green light. Every second counts.

"Is Ella with you?" I ask my wife.

"Yeah, I'm here," Ella's voice sounds out. "Josh is, too."

"Hey, *Reubs*," Josh laughs. "Don't worry, we've got her safe. The little one isn't done by a long way from the looks of it, so you'll still get to enjoy the show."

"Thanks, guys. I appreciate it."

I don't give a shit which spot I'm parked in when I bail out of the Jag and race over to the private ward. I don't bother with the elevator, just bound up the steps two at a time as people stare.

Because shit. Yes. I'm still dressed up as bloody Santa.

"Mrs Sinclair?" I ask the nurse at reception, and she leads me on through.

It still always brings a smile to my face when I hear Tiff's name like that. I got down on one knee the second we saw the plus sign on the pregnancy test, but the ring had already been in my pocket for weeks.

"We have her all set up and ready to go. She's doing very well. Didn't want an epidural, only gas and air."

My heart jumps into my throat when the nurse opens the door for me, and I see my red-haired goddess on the bed with her legs up and wide. She's red faced, grimacing as another contraction hits her.

"REUBEN!" she cries and I rush to her side, taking her outstretched hand in mine.

"It's ok, Tiff, I'm here now. I'm here."

"We'll be outside if you need us," Ella says.

"Enjoy, *Reubs*," Josh smirks as he pats me on the back on the way out.

I'm glad Tiffany was hanging out with them today on the run up to the due date. Josh may have looked upon me as a piece of shit when we first crossed paths, but he's certainly come around to me. He was over the moon when Tiff's pregnancy test showed positive back in March.

"This is your fault," my wife says to me. "If it hadn't been for the Christmas tree escapades earlier, she'd have probably stayed put a few more days."

Tiff's dirty gaze locks on mine, even through her pain. Our Christmas tree escapades were exquisite this morning – me sucking on Tiff's wet leaking nipples as I slammed her cunt deep. Her swollen belly has driven me crazy. I've had a constant hard-on since the moment my big beauty got even bigger, her stomach stretching with our child.

Tiff's nipples are leaking now as she rides the contractions. I love the way the milk dribbles down her.

If I wasn't so invested in medical professionals, I'd want the midwife to fuck off out of here and leave us alone. I'd want to put my hand inside my wife's bleeding pussy and feel my little girl's head making an entrance for myself.

"Here we go, ten centimetres dilated," the midwife says during the next contraction, and I shift position to get a better view. "Time to push! Push, Tiffany! Push!"

Punch fisting has nothing on this. I'm utterly transfixed as my baby's head begins to bulge from my wife's pussy. It's so big. So beautiful. So fucking primal in its brilliance.

Tiff's screams are feral as she enters the final stages. The forums weren't lying when they said the baby's head would be the size of a grapefruit. Tiff grips my hand like a vice as I urge her on, crying out between waves and claiming she can't take any more.

I can't, Reuben, I can't. I'd want to call TIME FUCKING OUT if this was a proposal!

But she's underestimating herself. Tiffany Sinclair was a hardcorer for a reason, in spirit as well as body. She can take it all.

Her pain is forgotten when our little girl finally bursts free, and cries fill the air. My eyes fill up as the midwife places her on Tiffany's chest.

"Our little Rose," Tiff says with a grin that lights my world.

I stare in shock at my daughter – my child. I have two goddesses in my world to live for now, and seeing our sweet Rose only reinforces what I already knew.

I want as many children as Tiff will bare for me.

It's me who cuts the cord, bringing our daughter into our world for good. Tiff and I are left to share a moment together at that. We kiss as our little baby settles on her mummy's chest, and I tell my wife how proud I am of her. How grateful I am. Seeing the tiny wonder of our creation surpasses any achievement I've ever known.

"Same goes," she says back. "And you get another thanks on top. Your fist training didn't seem to have made all that much difference when I was screeching my head off, but I bet you it did. If she'd have come out without a decent warmup, you'd probably be able to fuck my pussy and ass as one single hole."

"Hmm, I'll bear that in mind for next time." I smirk. "Having your ass and pussy as one dirty hole sounds quite tempting."

"You're a dirty bastard, you know that?"

"Yes, I do. It's one of the reasons you married me, if I recall."

Rose gives a whimper, and both of our attention turns to her in a heartbeat. We're going to have to learn to keep our dirty mouths clean when she's in earshot.

"I think she wants her daddy," Tiff says, and gently lifts her over to me.

I take my little one in tender arms, greeting her with all my heart.

"Hello, my darling. You're a beautiful girl, just like your mother. You're the greatest Christmas gift there could be."

"You and Rose are both winners on that front," Tiff says, and rests her head against my arm. "You got your Santa's baby, Reuben, and she got the greatest daddy in the world."

THE END

HAVE YOU CHECKED OUT THE NAUGHTY LIST YET?

Did you enjoy Santa's Baby?

If so, have you checked out my novels The Naughty List and The Naughtier List yet?

If not – get on running over to Amazon now.

Holly and Weston are waiting for you... and so are a whole, filthy collection of proposals.

They are as hardcore as the hardcorers undertaking them.

Don't miss out!

ACKNOWLEDGMENTS

Thank you, as always, to my fantabulous editor, John Hudspith. Couldn't do this without you. Seriously. Even you going on holiday puts a strain on my ability to keep my plot in line!

Thank you to the incredible Letitia Hasser at RBA Designs for such a great cover, yet again – you are always out of this world.

Sam – thank you for a whole host of graphics, and your interior formatting talents. You are super appreciated!

Nicole – wow, thank you for all of your amazing feedback and help, too. You've been a Santa's Elf I couldn't have done without!

My PA, Emily – who is also my stepson's fiancée, and does a super cool job of that, too – cracking work. Here's to our first release with you on the team! To Misha as well, for being another awesome cog in the Jade West wheel. And my stepson. Double win.

This acknowledgement is also to my first boyfriend, Malcolm, who passed away on December 11th 2006, aged 24 in a motorcycle accident.

It's December 11th 2024 as I'm writing this, 18 years since he left us.

Malcolm was one of the most important people I've ever had in my life. We were partners, friends, and friends with benefits on loop for almost a decade. He was responsible for a huge amount of the woman I am today – especially when it comes to Jade West.

Without him, I wouldn't be a goth, still adoring black velvet. I wouldn't have been a chatline operator, since it was after his death that my life took an entirely different direction.

I wouldn't have a lot of the interests I have in my genre. Make of that what you will…

I wouldn't know nearly as much about The Matrix or have had philosophical discussions around the Alien movies.

I wouldn't be a writer.

And, most importantly, I wouldn't be me.

As always, to my family, friends, and author buddies. Thank you.

And to everyone in the book community. Seriously, your support and enthusiasm mean the world.

ABOUT JADE WEST

First and foremost, I'm as filthy as my books suggest. There – got that one out of the way.

I am a total fantasist, living in the English countryside, with a great family and some amazing friends.

I'm epileptic, which has been quite a journey – still ongoing. Learning to live with disability when you're used to being independent is... hard. My support network is incredible, but I despise seizures and I miss my car. Badly. What I mean is, I miss freedom. Still, I have it easier than a lot of epileptics. I'm in no position to wail too loudly.

So, what else... I haven't grown out of being a goth since I was seventeen. Black velvet is my friend, along with glitter, long hair extensions, and Carl Jung.

I don't like tea or coffee, but I wish I did.

I love power ballads. A lot. I obsessively ruminate over lyrics, swimming in memories of the past as well as conjuring up projections for the future. So much for 'live in the now', because I don't do a great deal of it.

Oh, and I love books. Writing them, reading them, losing myself in imaginary realities. Can't get enough.

I'm best known for my novels Sugar Daddies, Bait, Call Me Daddy, and The Naughty List.

Please do check them out if you enjoyed this one – ESPECIALLY The Naughty List. It's pretty relevant.

JOIN JADE ON SOCIAL MEDIA

www.facebook.com/jadewestauthor

www.facebook.com/groups/dirtyreaders

www.instagram.com/jadewestauthor

Tiktok - @jadewestauthor

Sign up to my newsletter at www.jadewest-author.co.uk/newsletter.html

www.jadewestauthor.co.uk

Made in the USA
Las Vegas, NV
28 December 2024

15497936R00184